Julia Medearis

Julia Medearis

by David Torigoe

iUniverse, Inc.
New York   Bloomington

Julia Medearis

For my mother and father, whom I love with all my heart.

iUniverse books may be ordered through booksellers or by contacting:

iUniverse
1663 Liberty Drive
Bloomington, IN 47403
www.iuniverse.com
1-800-Authors (1-800-288-4677)

ISBN: 978-1-4401-4007-5 (pbk)
ISBN: 978-1-4401-4006-8 (ebk)

Library of Congress Control Number: 2009926802

Printed in the United States of America

iUniverse rev. date: 4/27/2009

Wer immer strebend sich bemüht, den können wir erlösen.
(*We are allowed to save / Those who strive with all their might*)

— Angels singing in *Faust*

The wreath of leaves.

When Julia first came to Michael Hardy's house her heart was empty and she felt no love for anything.

Inside the stone entry to the yard Michael watched a small girl shudder and shake herself awake. Round the stone house and through the yard ran a ring of whistling leaves, skittering, flowing one way and then another, flying in one direction then in another and finding themselves time and again caught inside the walled enclosure of the yard.

The girl had risen and took a few tottering, painful steps into the turmoil of the leaves, which now lay down settled in the yard as if to obey a master. Three feet high and frosted with caked mud, she held herself steady at the wall, holding a jar of jam or jelly, and peered backwards into the windows of the house.

A single light shone out from within the house, reflected onto a few front, lower windows. The upper windows of the mansard roof flit with light from the moon, not from within. This night was the first frost of the autumn and she felt this chill in the bones of her feet and hands. Already the trees were bare of their coats, skeletons stripped of their purple cover. She stood so quietly and patiently an owl hooted from the tree beside her.

The gate with its paint flaked off in wide patches gave the visitor an impression of derelict stateliness, seeming to proclaim this was a family and estate in decline, the gate plain except for a weathered, armorial escutcheon no longer readable. From a distance the house seemed seedy, derelict. But from within the gate the Hardy house had a pleasant, very amiable and homely appearance. Built outwardly of weathered brick, eight narrow dormer windows were set into the black slate roof which rose upwards fifty feet above the ground, sloped at a steep incline as if it had been designed for a country with heavy snow. Its appearance was somehow classical and austere, out of place in this tidy Northern California town.

When the girl raised her hand, before her face, no matter the direction she was turned, the hand acted as if it would be pulled towards the house, even if it twisted her around — something impelled her towards the house. For hours she'd lie still and observe the two inhabitants, in the infrequent times when either appeared outdoors. In back stood an abandoned shed, made of glass, as if a fairy hut with a greenish hue that soothed her tangled heart. In warmer days she liked to bury herself under the uncombed hair of grass nearby, atop a knoll further beyond the glass shed, nearer to the wild ghauts. Caterpillars and ladybugs, benign creatures, lived in this patch, the hair of grass, and trails of black ants. One day she watched a pupa break open with energy from within and a butterfly hesitantly unfurled its wings like so many legs stretching after confinement in a box. Armored bugs but not frightening would curl up at her touch and seeing herself in this bug, she did not touch the bugs again for fear they would be frightened and in sympathy for their response to the strangeness of her touch. As the shadows coalesced around her each evening, her resolution firmed against something unseen, she muttered quietly and unbelievingly, "The fish laughed with us. The sun was warm and we danced with it." She raised her fists.

Warm grasses and a knoll beyond a glass shed with metal tools and friendly implements of plant growth. Red bulb fruits in pots. Green leaves with caterpillar-like furs, a low stone fence, rippled reflections of white and shining clouds. Cows chewing gums, goats and gamboling, tinkling bells and the sounds of a pig's laughter. Otters speaking with polite forms of greeting. These appeared in the girl's dreams in daytime when she fell asleep on the grounds of the house.

Michael Hardy noted the absence of the girl for several weeks and absently monitored her presence from time to time when she reappeared, when he found himself sitting on a toy chest built into the sill of an upstairs window. So long as a single light in a lower study remained lit he wandered the upper floors in darkness and the girl, observing this, probably thought the upper floors were unoccupied. In this way he sat upstairs unobserved by her. Often the girl appeared only when he himself had remained motionless for an hour while he debated something aimless in his own mind.

One evening he sat on the sill by the window in blue cotton pajamas decorated with a rocket-spaceship pattern with his chin propped on a fist. The black-haired girl limped in shadowy darkness along the street edge until a gully cut across a gravel walk, so as if to avoid a more dangerous route, to be caught in the single pool of light, she furtively skirt around the halo of the lamp into the street, taking a few minutes to traverse ten yards, and head down half hobbled across the street. A dog followed, itself seeming to limp, either from injury or else out of sympathy, Michael did not know for certain.

The headlights of a car rapidly appeared, which the girl scampered to avoid with a hurried and pained struggle, but the dog disappeared under the body of the car with a soft, excruciating, crunching sound. Then it lay shuddering alone on the street. The girl had been thrown forward, struggled to remain upright with her head and neck rigid then dropped into a heap on the asphalt. Michael raced downstairs to shake his grandfather's arm, who had fallen asleep in a wing chair with an open book in his lap. The grandfather hurried outside in a bathrobe and fuzzy slippers.

He knelt in the street and turned the girl over. She appeared unbloodied though her shoulder was thrown out of the socket and began to stir fitfully in an internal distress, shaking silently when her eyes opened and received his gaze directly, oddly as if she did not recognize whether he was a human being or not. Perhaps, Michael thought, if she believed he was human she would have screamed and run for the sewer. He expected her to bolt out of his grandfather's arms; instead she lay passively as they looked at each other with curious regard. The grandfather searched for bleeding but found none — he held her firmly in his own arms and eased the shoulder back into the socket. However he could plainly see how her leg had been broken long earlier, swelled and turned blue above the joint. He carried her out of the street and propped her up in a semi-sitting position on the curb, with her leg thrust out awkwardly. She glanced around aimlessly, shuddering uncontrollably as if cold, then topped off the curb unable to sit upright.

When Michael wandered down to the curb it seemed that sensation slowly returned to her body and to her mind. She shook in alarm, or startle, at his presence and scuttled along the ground nearer to the grandfather and also to her dog, which lay in the street where it had collapsed. At seeing the dog, she forgot about Michael and he was able to stand beside her as their small group gathered near the dog.

The girl grit her teeth, grimacing at sight of the dog with its shattered leg. Not entirely with sympathy, more like a sense of grim, shared pain. Its ribs rose and fell laboriously. A thin stream of blood dripped out of the corner of its mouth, through black, rubbery lips, with a softly serrated edge like the coxcomb of a rooster. While it lay on its side, the whites of its eyes jumped as Michael moved, scared and vulnerable. The girl touched the dog lightly on an ear and on its leg, where the cut ran deeply past the fur, rawly but cleanly. A flap of fur had peeled itself neatly from the red striped, striated muscle beneath and, gingerly, the grandfather pressed the fur back into place. "Get my sewing kit," he asked and Michael sped away, hopping on one foot where the cold of the street seemed to stick his feet to the pavement. Seeing no other cloth useful, the grandfather used the sleeve of his bathrobe, after deciding no other cloth could be cut as a tourniquet, he reluctantly ripped off the sleeve beginning at an old tear, and daubed at the wound on the dog's leg until the bleeding ceased. Then held the cloth down firmly upon the staunched blood. The dog too, like its companion, looked at the grandfather curiously as if by this kindness he was performing an unexpected act.

When Michael returned with a sewing kit in hand, wearing shoes, the grandfather stitched the wound on the dog's leg shut with broad strong motions, tore off another section of the sleeve until the robe was armless and tied the bandage to the dog's upper foreleg and after a few moments reflection, it stood with the grandfather's helpful hand on its belly and hobbled to the curb. When they turned back to the girl they discovered she'd disappeared. Turning quickly back they saw the dog had run out too, hobbling through the arc of the street lamp and disappeared down into the tangled depths of the ghaut beside the street.

The next night Michael continued to monitor the movements of the girl and her dog. The dog Maggie continued to limp, with three good legs, and one cut leg with its now dirty bandage held awkwardly at an angle.

Prodded by curiosity Michael decided to set a baited trap. From the attic he brought out several pairs of old shoes and laid them in a trail from the ghaut in front of the house to a section of fence near the edge of the walkway leading to the door. The girl reappeared, avoiding the street completely, suspiciously and warily following the trail of shoes. She looked at the first shoe, a floppy moccasin, inspected it and judged it better than what she wore, after sticking a finger through a hole in her old pair and left the old shoe neatly by the path side, as if another more unfortunate girl than herself might come upon it and find her abandoned shoe useful. Though mismatched, shaking her feet to be sure her new acquisition wouldn't fall off, she continued on the way up the path. In a few yards she came upon a second, larger pile. She found the moccasin's twin, wrestled it on but sat on the ground to inspect the others in the jumble, pressing some against the bottom of her foot, and glancing up frequently, sniffing the air. She kept the moccasins and arranged the pile of unneeded shoes neatly, for the other shoeless girl who might follow. At this point the limpy dog emerged from the ghaut.

It must have been a difficult walk since the underbrush was heavily tangled and thorny, Michael knew, since he was the town's expert in navigating through the brush. He would often camp by the stream waters and explore through the wild country, the "west" he called it, with an interest unmatched by any of the other neighborhood children. While she sat preoccupied by the shoes, sorting through the pile, Michael made his way silently outdoors. He said to her, "Hey," and the wind carried his voice to her on the sidewalk in front of the house. She froze at hearing a voice so he was compelled to say, *hey*, again. "Why do you run away from everybody," he added. She shook her head, then ran, pausing only to look back at a safe distance.

"Let us fix your dog's leg. My grandfather can take the dog to an animal hospital." Michael pointed away in the general direction of the town's vet but the girl wasn't paying attention. He saw she had found a ragged coat with pockets and had transferred the customary socks on her hands, to her feet. They turned to leave, limped away, but ten yards later she slowed and surreptitiously turned to see if he remained at hand. She kicked a rock that stood nearby, then because it rolled near but not over the gully mouth, she followed and gave it another kick to propel it over the edge of the little cliff. And she smiled with satisfaction, turning to face the boy in his own yard. Her teeth were blackened with dried blood and the smile had a touch of the macabre that chilled Michael in his pajamas.

Upstairs and quickly Michael told his grandfather of the girl, her habits and location in the yard, how she exchanged shoes and that the dog ate rats. The grandfather said little else, pursed his lips in thought and became preoccupied with a worried expression wandering like a shadow over the external features of his face so when a particularly heavy thought passed through his mind his eyes blinked involuntarily.

Groaning a bit, the grandfather fit his feet into the slippers and ventured outdoors at night for the second time, clad again in his bathrobe, missing the sleeve. Unaccustomed to the outdoors, even to be outside his own study, from time to time he stumbled and grumbled at the wetness of ground and general features of nature. "Stop gusting, wind," he ordered, muttering. He searched out methodically and found the girl by flashlight, when the gleam of her widened eyes flashed back to him out of the dark. Huddled under a blanket of leaves near the fish pond. He knelt and waddled up awkwardly on his knees, slowly, quietly and calmly so she was not afraid at his appearance through the orange paperly blossoms of a wild rhododendron which flourished untended on this portion of the yard. Though she tensed and readied herself to run, one arm poised upwards and the other bent behind her at the elbow in a comic and exaggerated posture of flight, to Michael's surprise, watching from behind a redwood trellis laced with a similar, wilted spray of rhododendrons, she did not flee, but paused tensely and listened to this grandfather who asked in a voice raspy from his exertions, "Where do you live?"

The girl pointed to a stand of poplars, beyond the pond to an angle. He could see, with a gesture of the light, that she had dug out a shallow grave-like hole beside her in the dirt beneath the stand of clustered trees. Her digging implement lay near, a discarded melmac plate, muddied in a crescent shape on one edge.

"Why don't you go back to your family?"

She did not answer.

"Are you afraid to go back?"

She waited a few moments before moving her head in a gesture he didn't understand.

"How long have you been gone?"

She held up her hands perhaps in a gesture of counting, as if she meant to show a number but was uncertain of the number on her hands. Both the grandfather and Michael saw but made no comment on seeing how two joints on her right hand were severed at the first knuckle.

"Ten days? You've been hiding here ten days?" Michael and his grandfather would later learn that the ten fingers gesture represented the highest number she could express, and that she had lived here in the woods much longer than a single fortnight, months already.

"What's your name?"

She didn't answer.

"Are you hungry?" The girl dipped her hand into a pocket and opened it to show, as if a sign of legitimacy she owned a half-eaten dinner roll. He recognized the bread as leftovers from their dinner the previous week and left buried in the garbage cans by the street. Looking more closely now, he recognized her red pants as once belonging to Michael. When she held up both hands to show her count, earlier, the pants sagged, and he could see she wore another, even more ragged pair beneath the red. She had tugged up her pants again, and throughout the rest of the conversation held up the pants with a spare hand.

"I think you should take a bath."

She nodded in a wistful expressive motion, as if she had wished this for herself.

The grandfather's voice became more commanding, "Go into the house and take a bath in the tub by the kitchen. Then eat any food you find in the kitchen. Do you know where that is?"

She nodded her head, unbelievingly, stunned, weakly.

"Or else you'll find a sleeping bag in the linen closet.

You can use that and sleep here by the poplars if you prefer."

She was not certain, Michael could tell, what he meant by the poplars, and understood his intentions only by a broad sweep of his arm at the grove of shady trees. Yet when he expected her to move, she remained as if rooted in the earth. He motioned that Michael retreat and they both turned to return to the house, gesturing that the girl follow, which she did, slowly and warily.

She would later explain to them about the tremendous surge of courage and elation that filled her, like a god's touch, to enable her to step into the house. "Otherwise I would have stayed under those leaves by the pond my whole other life that never happened." The grandfather ran the hot water in the tub for her and left her in the room with towels and the dog.

In the morning Michael was woken by the grandfather with a liver-spotted hand shaking him awake at the shoulder, "That little girl is gone. Help me look for her." He groggily rose and, in rocket pajamas still, roved through the house and yard seeing nothing. Only later in the late afternoon, with binoculars and by creeping from window to window on the upper floors of the house, did Michael see a small head poke out, as if from a cartoon, upright in a pile of leaves in a recessed portion of the yard in back, and disappear again leaving behind a tuft of leaves suspended, settling slowly after the head disappeared from sight. She remained hidden within the embankment, leaves, twigs, strands of moss woven into a protective nest on the edge of a grove of white birch in back of the house. Every few minutes as he watched, her black haired head peeped over the leaves in a different direction and plopped down again, as if for intruders or what not. On the whole, Michael admitted to himself the site she had chosen in back was well-sited since they had infrequent visitors. Once her dog reappeared, carrying the limp body of a rat in its mouth, and nimbly leapt into the leaves as if to share its discovery. Michael rummaged in the larder and found a can of dog food belonging to a long lost, long dead Hardy dog, and left the spooned-out contents of the can on a plate on the back porch. Before going to bed he checked, and saw the plate had been emptied and only then thought, "I shouldn't have left dog food. Maybe the girl ate the food or shared it with her dog."

After his discovery, Michael ran to the grandfather to show him the hiding place of the girl but found that the house was empty — the grandfather had walked alone into town to ask a few questions. In the meantime Michael quickly surveyed the grounds of the house and yard with birding binoculars.

The grandfather had come out to the back.

"Julia," he said, as if not to her but sadly to himself, "Julia." The leaf pile remained forbidding, still and unmoving. The grandfather said nothing more, but made an absent-minded patting motion with his hand in the air as if summoning a genie or charming a snake and the girl rose on unsteady, quivering legs out of the leaves and wobbling, stepped once or twice forward.

In the process of approaching, Julia began to bend low with each new step, until beside the grandfather within arm's reach she had shrunk, bent over as if a single narrowing of an eye, an expression on his face, were enough to smash her into the ground, so that as if sensing this he did not raise his hand, feeling that any movement of his hand would be construed as a feared attempt to strike. Instead, he bent forward, imperceptibly, slightly and spoke quietly for a few moments. Though the girl tensed while speaking, with clenched fists, the grandfather and girl conversed for a few minutes. When he turned and walked into the house, the girl followed hesitantly and furtively, in a bent over fashion, as if she were carrying a crushing weight and were not allowed to raise even an eye at a world that had beaten her out of humanness. Her pace was crooked, partly due to her comical staggering, hunched posture, but also from a crick, or limp, in the leg.

Before he passed indoors, the grandfather turned and gently spoke to her, without glancing directly at her, "You can come into the house every day if you like, whenever you like," and swept his hand inwards with an unmistakable gesture of welcome, which Michael couldn't be certain that the girl perceived, since her head remained bowed to the ground.

Michael bit his lip. While his mind could analyze the actions of his grandfather, even beat him in chess, proving he believed he could vie with rules and causation in his grandfather's mind, other parts of the grandfather eluded his understanding. He could not fathom parts of his grandfather's actions, for example, why did he bother so gently with the girl? He felt, in a tremor beneath his bare feet, the faint timbre of water and knew that his grandfather was running a bath in the laundry room. "Come down here," came the order though if Michael actually heard it or not, he didn't know. He had become so accustomed to the habits of the man they did not talk much anymore. Michael tiptoed downstairs to find the grandfather at a steamer trunk, and seeing Michael said, "Look through here or another old chest for something for her to wear. Leave out some soap and towels."

Michael walked into the bathroom and saw something that frightened him. He shut the door. He explained what he saw to the grandfather, who knocked on the door and with the softest possible voice spoke to the girl for several minutes. When his grandfather emerged, he showed his grandson a frightening face that Michael had not seen before. His face had tightened, as if stretched over his skull and his eyes were deeply recessed, his lips absolutely without color, tightly pressed together. "Stay out" came the simple command, in such a voice that Michael backed without looking until his arm touched the doorknob on the opposite side of the room.

Michael's pediatrician, the pepper bearded Dr. Bernard Rush had been summoned, and the grandfather with an unaccustomed rigidity and anxiety had taken the doctor by arm to see the girl. In turn, much later, a police officer arrived, a second woman officer, a police detective from Vallejo and still later more official people throughout the day.

A new lodger.

By the late afternoon, the house had emptied except for its usual sour-tempered inhabitants and dinner was a somber affair, no one speaking, both reading from books in their own laps while picking at the food on their plates. At the large table, as usual, the grandfather and Michael occupied the adjacent corners within touching distance of the other and the remainder of the table, built to accommodate a party of twenty of more could not be seen in the dimness. While a third place had been set at the table for the girl, she had not appeared when called. The grandfather had bundled up dinner in the kitchen for her to eat later, perhaps when she felt more comfortable in the house. He left a portion in a bowl, covered with a linen napkin for the dog. Still no light elsewhere in the house. In the library as Michael made himself inconspicuous near his grandfather and tried to read, he began to worry at the change that seem to infect the man. If disturbed, the grandfather would have sighed and shaken his head, but tonight he only stared into the floor or into his own clasped hands. And the whole evening passed this way.

Michael woke earlier than usual and with quiet house to explore he methodically rummaged through top floor attic to basement. Nothing seemed disturbed until he opened the triangular storage door under a stairwell, and saw in that cubbyhole, hidden behind the swinging door, beneath a stifling barricade of blankets and frozen still was the shrunken figure of the girl, with shocked eyes unable to look at him, motionless and shaken by the movement of the door. Her hair had been shorn close to the skull a few days earlier by a visiting nurse and deloused. Michael saw she was much thinner than he thought, skeletal at her neck, where purple bruises unmistakably made by fingers in a grip on the throat, without the bundled coats she'd worn, though a few blankets were wound around her in the cubbyhole, as if she were poked out an anthill. Her appearance wasn't less ragged for having been scrubbed clean, Michael saw her affrighted air wasn't due to the dirt but belonged to her in person and couldn't be scrubbed off. She lacked expression, besides a blank expression of shocked fear, he thought, welts beneath her eyes, a patch of hair missing entire on one side of her skull. Unable to sit upright, even in the cubbyhole she leaned to one side, and rocked side to side in a perpetual wobble as if trying to retain her own balance.

Strangest, to Michael's eyes, the expression on the captive's face as he realized she remained in deep sleep. Her eyes bored open and fixed on a motionless point in front of herself, and her hands were tensed, frozen upright in her sleep though jerking reflexively out now and then as if fighting an attacker.

Before he could observe any further, he found himself lifted off the ground by the scruff of pajamas, the door closed behind him, and he was carried away into another room. When set down, the grandfather bent very close to his face, "You will not disturb or bother her. She is fragile and needs to be left alone. You must even not look at her. Do you understand?"

"How can a person be fragile. Fragile means something that can break, like a dish."

"She has suffered a huge amount. Can you understand that?" The grandfather looked at Michael curiously, closely.

"Why doesn't she go to the hospital. Why doesn't she talk?"

"Michael, the girl needs a little time before she can mix with other people. Since she seems more comfortable here for the moment, she can slowly adjust to human company again." The grandfather's expression took a new appearance of worry, not for the girl anymore but his grandson. Michael shook his head in disbelief at what his grandfather was saying, he could not imagine a hurt that would take even weeks to heal. The grandfather saw this impossibility of belief in the boy's face, an incapacity to empathize with the girl and the corners of his mouth turned downwards as if in sorrow for Michael. And Michael himself, feeling that his answers or his misunderstanding were a shortcoming of some sort, blushed and retorted, "When is that girl going to leave here then?"

"That's not for me to say." Now the grandfather stood at his tallest, in an imperious fashion and Michael's head shook slightly, filling with blood, in the dizzy sensations he felt whenever scolded. But an obstinacy in this matter seized him, "Why should I get in trouble for thinking this? I don't know why I'm in trouble. Just because I don't think that people are like a dish. If that girl is hurt then she should go to the hospital. If she's afraid then she should just get brave."

"Michael. The most complicated, the most interesting, the most difficult single thing in the world is inside the mind of any single person. That sort of thing, what a person is, it eludes understanding."

"Not for you. You understand people." Michael's confidence in his grandfather's powers of analysis was unalloyed, pure.

"You don't understand. Any person eludes understanding."

"No," insisted Michael, urgently, he believed anything could be understood.

"Then we disagree on this," said the grandfather in tones that effectively ended their conversation. This had been their longest conversation for several months and both tired quietly of its continuance so that their words trailed off into an inconclusive silence, as quietly as a wisp of steam.

Michael complained that the equilibrium of the house had been disrupted for the next few days as one visitor or another came indoors to confer with the grandfather and to examine the girl who emerged from under the stairwell, pained and reluctant. Seven years old and precocious, Michael felt that his grandfather, until this time, had given him unqualified approval and sympathy and he didn't understand why he was not praised for his scoffing and inflexible attitude. He behaved perfectly courteously to her, respectfully distant, but not ignoring her, even to the point that in time he and the girl could inhabit the same room, though always at opposite walls if unexpectedly brought into proximity. In the evenings, she cautiously learned to creep along the edges of the walls, to capture her bundle of dinner in the kitchen, and to let the dog wolf down its own dinner from a dish on the floor. When they unexpectedly met in a hallway or kitchen, she regarded him with the wary, alert eyes of a prey species, the wide-eyed look of a gazelle, and he felt uncomfortably as if he had been expected to attack, felt uncomfortable as if regarded with the apprehension — as if with look or gesture he could stab or harm her. He tired of the sensitive alertness required of him while she remained in the house. He wanted things to return to how they were, without intrusions, without the need to stay emotionally alert for the presence of the unwanted third person in the house.

At dinner, as they were accustomed at the corner of the table, Michael piped up with a bitter tone, "Her nose is turned up at the end. She looks like a pig. Her eyes are close together."

"None of us should be too proud. None of us have much to be proud about."

Michael began to protest and blurt aloud saying, "But what about you. You have lots to be proud of!"

"I'm proud of nothing Michael. What have I done in my lifetime that has the slightest meaning?"

"You're famous and you're rich, and everybody wants to talk to you if you let them."

"Michael, do you know what *meaning* is?"

"I think I do."

"What *meaning* is depends on each individual person. What you find meaningful probably will change from one year to another. But in my life, I don't think I've done much that is meaningful. I feel as much to be ashamed of as to be proud, and those two seem to cancel each other out. If anything seems meaningful to me, it's only begun since you came to this house, and now too since this girl, Julia, came here also. Can you understand?"

"No!" Michael had divined indirectly, from the tone of the infrequent visitors, letters, newspaper articles, of the esteem in which his grandfather was regarded by those people outside the house — professorships, learning, authority. Michael liked the esteem in which his grandfather seemed to be held because indirectly he himself felt well-regarded also by those same people.

Out of the pan and into the fire.

Michael left his aunt and the bottle glass window.

Michael did not seem to inspire his grandfather with confidence that their conversations had much effect and Michael kept to his proud and haughty attitudes, but from time to time in the next months, in quiet moments, he did give Michael food for thought and meditative musing. Michael first saw his grandfather through an unusual window made with the circular bottoms of recycled bottle-glass, belonging to his aunt to whom he was assigned after the death or disappearance of his parents — which at that time had been unexplained to him. The window had been hand constructed by gluing in the round bottoms of many bottles into the glass so that it was not a practicable window, barely translucent, and thick as a kitchen cutting board. In the otherwise unremarkable house it was the single feature that attracted Michael's attention or interest. Left alone by the aunt, he spent much of the day studying the window, counting the number of bottles, dividing the number in his head, multiplying the number, and imagining the size of a window with some random number of bottles chosen in whimsy.

The crunch of footsteps sounded outside the door, and his grandfather entered, followed by a man and woman trailing behind the grandfather almost deferentially. The tall man did not resemble the ogre or troll that ate children, as his aunt had warned him to be. Only aloof and commanding, thought Michael, immediately taken by the intensity of air that seemed to accompany the man. He'd been warned not to even look at the man but he couldn't help himself. Being told he was a cannibal, that he ate people, Michael felt disappointed, thinking that a cannibal should have had a more distinctive, fearsome appearance. Not until the grandfather turned his gaze, examining and questioning, onto Michael, did Michael experience a jolt of the grandfather's power — something searching and questing.

She'd said, "His temperament is the same as your corrupting father's. He's unsociable no matter what people say, and his thoughts are queer. If you look at him or listen to him you'll be hypnotized, just as your deluded simple mother had been deluded by his own deluded son."

"Aunty..."

"Their high thoughts destroyed your mother's peace of mind. She never was the same after she left with your father, and she was doomed. I said so to her but she was spellbound by those cannibals. They'll eat you and they'll cook you in a roasting pan."

Now seeing the cannibal stand without impatience in the entry, not curious or even giving a glance to the interior, Michael thought, "You are dead wrong Aunty." And she had been wrong. Michael had not for even one iota of a second regretted that he'd become the ward of this man, whom had transformed his life and commanded him with a forbidding, and kind, and thoughtful way. In his whole life in this house, Michael had never given a single thought to defying his grandfather, despite the terrible reputation he had gained at his aunt's house, the school near the aunt's house, the school near the grandfather's house, and among the children in both neighborhoods he had lived among. Michael had toted his small bag of belongings into the trunk of the car driven by one of the other people in his grandfather's party and never looked backwards as they drove back out of his aunt's house, and driven for a long time, until they came to this stone house with the empty though not forbidding rooms.

He'd read in the Napa library of the checkered history of his father's family, the Hardy clan, and felt that the accounts of his family were written by ancestors of his aunt's family, because an emotional tone, an antipathy seemed to accompany even newspaper articles whenever a Hardy was mentioned in a story.

In the attic papers, as many of the Hardys left voluminous correspondence and journals, he'd read of accounts of crossing the Atlantic, of crossing the prairies of America, of wandering over seas and tundra and jungles, yet settling on this edge of the continent. Many accounts told of a pattern that seemed to run in these men and women: they were restless, they were discontent, they did not hesitate to speak out and seemed to invite confrontation. Even in Napa, they argued for independence, freedom from their taxes or meddling by government, their disagreements with the local church, and easily offended their neighbors by lack of attendance at the local church. Their comings and goings and visitors, and mail, and the influx of strangers caused consternation and even fear among the older inhabitants of the town.

One article bemoaned the strange habits of a family that could order two grand pianos in one year, delivered to different houses along the road. If a stranger disembarked from a train, carrying a large cello case, they were directed to the Hardy houses. If a package with foreign stamps arrived in the Napa post office, without glancing at the address, the postmistress would slot it for the Hardy clan. If anyone in the town had a gripe, it would directed at the Hardy family.

But at the turn of the century, much of the Hardy activity seemed to dwindle, and several houses emptied. Several families had returned to their old countries as the first war in Europe threatened their old homes in the Dordogne or in Flanders. And too the remnants seemed to depart during the thirties, reading with alarm of the changes in Germany that seemed to threaten their old homes again and rather than immigrate into America, these few, last Hardys emigrated out of the U.S. and returned to Europe, as if to counter these changes of intolerance, but they were not seen again in Napa, and few, if any letters with foreign stamps came to the Napa post office. When land became more valuable and fewer people could afford the manorial home that required expensive upkeep, they were demolished, and only a very few homes remained with occupants. The street was renamed in the fifties when a development craze overtook the town and a major rezoning ordinance was passed, and this colorful period in Napa history passed unremembered, except in the archives in the last Hardy house attic or the reading room in the Napa public library.

By and large Michael had been left to his own devices. The grandfather and he had commerce only in the books they had read in common, or in the food that one or both prepared in the afternoons. Michael took long solitary walks in the woods, and camped in the woods. He would not be missed except for dinner, and if he explained his absences, the dinner would proceed without him.

Yet when he could better speak he did speak fearlessly with this enigmatic and thoughtful man. Usually these conversations took a form of question and answer that the grandfather seemed to enjoy with an easygoing patience.

"If this earth is round, without corners or a side, how can it stay up in the sky?" "Why don't Australians fall off the earth?" "What side is up or down in the universe?" "Why is blood red?" "Where does smoke go?" "How does gravity work?" "Does a refrigerator put cold into the food or does it take out the hot?" "Is a zebra white, with black stripes, or is it black with white stripes? And so on, the grandfather had never, in Michael's memory, dismissed a question and often, to Michael's delight, had taken a question seriously, giving Michael's question his full attention as if he were grown up. Even when Michael had desperately not wanted to take a bath, and discovered that asking a good question would defer the bath, even as the grandfather knew the reasons for his questions, even under these conditions the grandfather never dismissed a question. On those occasions Michael would inconspicuously stuff the bath towel into a bookshelf hoping it would not trigger a memory of his responsibilities, while he loitered outside the door of the study hoping for inspiration to strike and that he could present an suitable question. On occasion the whole bath would be neglected and the evening, even past bedtimes would be occupied with the exploration of an answer to the question. And, sometimes, to Michael's puzzlement, awe and disbelief, the grandfather instead of saying, "Let's find out," would say, "I don't know, and I don't think anyone knows. Why don't you think about it, and then you can tell the world about it."

The first time this happened, when he stumped his grandfather with a particularly good question, and cried, "Ha!!" the grandfather shrugged as if this were not a defeat of any kind, and admonished the little boy, "Admitting ignorance isn't always a bad or a wrong answer. Sometimes that is exactly the right answer, and any other answer would be wrong? Do you believe that?"

Bernard Rush.

The most frequent visitor to the house, the local doctor in town and local chess champion, Bernard Rush, inquired frequently about the health of the new inhabitant of the house and at the grandfather's gentle request to Julia, examined her wounds. He saw, after one of these visits, "When her leg heals from the second break, she'll be in good physical health. The most lasting physical injury were the blows to her abdomen and pelvis. I doubt she'll be able to bear children when she's older. Her innards are twisted up and bruised, and I saw blotches of internal bleeding. I saw the x-rays and MRIs, and can't believe she survived the punishment."

"Yes," the grandfather motioned with a gesture of his hands, a gesture of helplessness.

Rush had lost a daughter and wife early in his married life to an influenza pandemic in Trenton, New Jersey, several decades ago, and felt partial to Julia's case. "I'll keep an eye on her time to time if you like."

"Thank you. She seems to respond to you in ways she doesn't to others."

Michael, half-illumed on the side near to the windows, ran his hand along the sills, paused in his midnight peregrinations with head turned to an unnatural angle, motionless to detect better if he could the origin of a tremor felt in his fingers. He pressed two fingers downward as if taking a pulse of the hardwood sill and slipped away from moonlight, through the library door, down the stairs, with fingers alighting on the banister, as if to detect again the pulse or quiver in the wood of the house. Turning head one way or another before committing his body to motion, he stopped in front of the cubbyhole beneath the stairs. And glancing around, fearing reprisal from his grandfather, carefully slipped the two pulse-taking fingers between the door and swung it open.

After adjustment to the darkness within, he saw a mound of blankets, winter coats, shawls from forgotten relatives, piled haphazardly on top of a bundle of the girl, whose foot stuck out revealing a thin pale bone. Michael had found the source of the tapping. This foot twitched, in Julia's sleep, this little foot, banging away on the floor like a dog's tail. He closed the doorway without a quiver itself and returned to his own bed, thoughtful but not knowing why he felt ashamed.

When the girl walked through the house, she pressed herself against a wall and her hands trailed lightly along the walls. The dog wandered behind her, head-down like a guilty conscience, it seemed to have lost its bristly, antagonistic protectiveness inside the house and never showed the sharp teeth of the ratter it once used to be. Perhaps as if sensing that it would remain safe here within the walls if allowed to stay within the walls, but embarrassed at being seen, or as if in being seen it would be chucked outdoors, the dog trotted meekly behind the girl, both as if afraid to cause offense or afraid of discovery.

The girl and the grandfather disappeared one day in a medical van, of which Michael caught only a glimpse as he awoke and hurried downstairs. Though a gurney had been wheeled into the house, after a discussion in which the grandfather served as a translator of sorts the girl limped outdoors under her own swaying gait and the gurney followed unused. Hours later they returned with the girl's leg encased in a blue plaster cast, decorated with decals by the hospital nurses. Around her waist and extending along a leg ran a metal brace. The grandfather carried an impossibly small two wheeled cart, no longer than his forearm, which when he set on the floor and assembled, Michael saw, was a wheelchair meant to help the little girl scoot along when walking would be too difficult. She never used the wheelchair and preferred to half-crawl and struggle along in the brace and cast.

At mealtimes she gradually became accustomed, though not comfortably, to sit at the table with himself and the grandfather, feeling awkwardness at being observed with her struggles with mobility — she often struggled to the table alone and sat, waiting for the others to join her later with the accouterments of the meal. After, with a face plainly full of some strong, inward emotion that she couldn't voice, she slowly and painfully again with her excruciatingly slow movements crawled back into the triangular space beneath the stairs. Her face as she turned to swing the lateen door shut was one of grimness and often a blankness that astonished Michael. He saw an expression empty of a readable thought or emotion in an eerie way. Her eyes would often sweep over him as if blankly noting his presence, though not any longer acknowledging him as a threat in the house — the eyes did not see him, did not react as was normal with the normal give or take of commerce between social people. In the next weeks he realized he had never heard her voice. She had not yet spoken aloud even once.

On that first day when Michael was instructed to find clothes for her in the steamer trunk, among the surplus trunks in the attic, he found several children's pants but even these were too large. The grandfather cut several inches at the cuff and returned to cut the pants shorter at the knee, and even then returned again to cut the legs above the knee, and these were long pants for the little girl. She'd seemed normally tall when creeping through the woods but once when unexpectedly finding themselves briefly face to face in a doorway, before she'd scuttled backwards along the hall wall, he saw she barely came up to his waist and that she was ridiculously short.

She used two hands to open a doorknob as one was not large enough to give her purchase on turning the knob. She once wore a shirt that belonged to the grandfather but when buttoned into the shirt the cloth trailed onto the floor as if a robe.

Because she did not venture into company except for the solitary presence of the grandfather and their experiments at luring her to their companionable table in the study after dinner failed, the grandfather found a footstool and a small wooden box that served as table and chair in the kitchen, which he thought was the warmest place in the house and most comforting for her and the dog. Michael laughed aloud at seeing the impromptu table setting in a corner of the kitchen, reserved and tidy in its own corner. "It's a little doll house kitchen!"

Time passed, though, and the girl became more comfortable in the house. Having crept in from one of her mysterious afternoon rambles with dog and pockets full of sandwiches, crackers, fruits, nuts, carrots, and a can of condensed milk, Julia gave a short grunt at trying the knob and having it twirl in her grasp without a purchase. And the door opened from within, she in shadow from the aching tall form of the grandfather whose attention, thankfully, was not focused on her but on the recalcitrant knob. "Sometimes," he said in a quiet voice calculated not to upset the girl, "the door seems to lock or unlock by itself and when it's locked the whole knob seems to spin around all by itself without opening." He disappeared inwards and fished around in a drawer while Julia remained on porch, as a penitent or a half-forgotten saleswoman, when the grandfather returned, giving to her a long antique, old-fashioned key, "In these modern days these old door locks are almost ceremonial and won't keep out anyone who wants to break in but if the door locks again, you can always try this key. Now you can't ever be locked out." Julia received the key, as large as her own hand, and nodded solemnly as if having been dispensed a great privilege. The grandfather found a shoelace in a drawer nearby, thread the key through the shoelace, tied the lace into a loop and placed key and shoelace around her neck so that the ensemble rested at her waist.

"I'm hungry. Aren't you?"

Julia nodded her head in agreement, shyly, without glancing upwards, and they companionably assembled sandwiches and ate their lunch at the table, grandfather at kitchen table, and beside him at the doll's table near the door sat Julia in her own chair. Both were content at the progress in the past hour as their friendship seemed to grow in small bursts each day.

As the medical van once appeared to take the grandfather and girl away mysteriously into town as her leg cast appeared, one day the same van reappeared so later that day the cast was removed.

The dishwasher.

After dinner at an early evening hour the grandfather absently brought an armful of dishes from the table and stopped short halfway through the kitchen door seeing the strange sight of Julia kneeling on top of the kitchen counter, bent over the sink at its edge, as if she knelt at a river bank or a village well, industriously washing a pan with sponge and soap in the sink with awkward, studious circular motions of her hand.

"What's this!" cried the grandfather but in such a way not to alarm the worker. "You'll fall…You'll," he didn't want to say she'd hurt herself, "You might drop the pan!"

He grasped the pan in her hands, meaning to wrestle it out of her grip but Julia's eyes widened and she made a moaning, despairing, short sharp wail with closed mouth, from somewhere inside her, so that instinctually the grandfather's hand arrested itself midair.

"You shouldn't do this. Cleaning up is my job, or Michael's. You can't even reach the sink." He watched and saw her eyes plead mutely with him. He turned but not to leave the kitchen. Under the sink he extricated a sturdy footstool, on which he motioned that she stand. Finding a thick, dry dishrag, he motioned that she use the cloth for drying the dishes. His hand grasped her arm, in a warm and reassuring grip, "If you hurt yourself in any way, I would feel just terrible. Would you remember that?" Julia nodded her head in a solemn and promising way, with the faint beginnings of a smile, the first sort of smile she wore in the house.

A second day had passed and Julia sat in her chair by the door watching the grandfather and Michael finish their dinner, and with the last of his meal chewed Julia jumped up and firmly took the plate out of his grasp, which Michael held onto playfully and they tussled with the plate. Julia gave a short grunt of protest, seized the plate and ran with it into the kitchen, where they could hear sounds of running water. In this way Julia took to dishwashing tasks in the house, hardly waiting for meals to finish before bustling away with tableware and silverware.

After the next dinner when Julia had decided to become the steady dishwasher of the household, she took Michael's plate, entered the kitchen through the swinging door and nearly dropped her dishes at seeing a new addition to the kitchen. Built against the wall, catty corner to the counter, was a duplicate counter almost miniature and doll-like with a small copper sink and reduced size fixtures, built at her height, so perfect did it look in all details. She set her cargo on this lower counter and gasped, again audibly, despite her own hand slapped over open mouth when the small scale faucets at a twist loosed a stream of whistling water that twisted and gurgled down the copper basin sink. Topping off the ensemble was a squeeze bottle of soap and friendly pile of newly washed dishrags arranged on pins set into the wall and a small rug to stand on. She seemed as if she would cry but in a cry of happiness then the need to work overcame her thankfulness and she scraped, washed, dried dishes and put back on the tall counter the unused containers and saw that the contents of the kitchen had been subtly arranged — that the spices, condiments, and cooking materials usually in the lower drawers had been carried to the high shelves which remained out of reach. And the glass-fronted cabinets below the counter now held the remainder of the family dishes and silverware, so that after the washing she could easily place in their proper place the dinner dishes.

Michael watched Julia emerge from the kitchen, looking grim, and opened his own mouth in surprise at seeing Julia place her black-haired head against the grandfather's leg, where he sat at the table and wrap her arms around his leg, except her arms wouldn't reach far and came nowhere near to meeting. She rested her head for a moment then feeling she was performing a great imposition, sheepishly let go her grip, looking at the floor, wandering back out of the dining room with another armful of dinner remnants.

Michael stifled a laugh and quietly giggled to his grandfather, "She's a weird girl!" The grandfather smiled at this and motioned that he be quiet.

In the next few months Julia's mania for washing grew to an obsession, as she not only washed dishes, but took to washing everything inanimate in the household. She washed floors, windows, sills, walls, and learned to wash clothes in an old-fashioned machine, learned to scrub the claw-foot bath tub, learned to manage the old-fashioned mangle to smooth dry sheets. Sometimes Michael and even the grandfather himself could barely suppress grins or laughter while sitting in the library as Julia wandered in through one door, sponge in hand and eyes darting over the furniture then wandering out again through another, so intent in her hunt for objects to clean that she appeared to take no notice of their own presence.

Maggie, too, suffered under the strain of this washing mania and during this period Julia had only to throw her glance to her and the poor dog's expression wilted and she sunk low to the floor, so often had she been scrubbed and laundered and combed, hot weather or cold and her fur was brushed, so she became more of a presentable, thoroughly tidy dog.

Typhoid fever.

Michael pressed his hands onto stomach and made a retching motion with his mouth.

"You're not going to avoid sweeping the walks with that stratagem."

"But I really do feel sick. I feel terrible."

Something in his voice rid the grandfather of the skeptical tone in his voice and expression.

"Maybe I ate something bad," offered Michael. His face shook as if he'd endured a spasm somewhere within himself. The grandfather put the palm of his hand onto Michael's forehead and felt the pulsing warmth and clamminess of fever.

"I know you must be honestly sick," he said, "because tomorrow isn't a school day."

Michael nodded his head in agreement and explained where he thought the sickness originated. Earlier in the week, living as a wilderness explorer overnight in one of the backyard ghauts, he drank water from one of the trickling streams. Since drinking this water, he felt a fever and a wrenching sensation in his gut. According to Bernard Rush's quick office diagnosis, without seeing the results of sera tests, to the grandfather out of Michael's hearing, "I think typhoid fever, a more virulent strain." Several of the seasonal fruit pickers and families had contracted the same disease from drinking similar water in the field and a little girl from one of the labor camps had been moved into the intensive care ward with her vital signs dipping very low. Each of these children eventually were shuttled to a hospital in Palo Alto, and their progress became front page news in the local paper, at first because the town attracted little novelty worthy of news and later because their conditions worsened. Eventually the little girl died.

Michael was hospitalized in a similar hospital bed and a host of epidemiologists moved into Napa, testing water in the ghauts, trapping bugs and insects. But this didn't help Michael whose condition worsened. Later in the week he became incoherent and could not recognize the grandfather's face or respond to spoken words and then Michael slipped into a coma.

By this time his grandfather had undergone a transformation so had Michael's aunt seen him all her predictions of vindictive spite would have been satisfied. He seemed at last the ogre and child-eater of myth, which Michael once expected to encounter in the house with bottle-window. His hair disheveled, the expression on his face didn't elicit concern or sympathy from the nurses. They avoided his gaze and feared him more than Michael's condition. It seemed at times that he had taken on many of the symptoms that Michael had — at times he acted feverish and incoherent himself, he coughed, trembled and vomited.

At one point, in the middle of the night when Michael's body had tensed and knotted in pain so that the cords in his neck stood out as if they were cables on a web of netting, the grandfather burst out in a cry that echoed down the hallways of the ward so that patients woke and listened but hearing no more each turned back into himself, each thinking that the cry had been their own and made no more comment.

In years past he had been a judge on the 9th U.S. Circuit Court of Appeals based in San Francisco. Called the bench "philosopher" even in his younger years because of the logical detachment in which he approached legal details and obscured the human aspects of the case to see, past and forward, the origins and repercussions of the case in a way that the fellow jurists appreciated and admired. He had dealt penalties to criminals, mercy to sufferers, and rendered compensation in response to many injustices as best he could. And treated all with an even equanimity as if he could judge the atrocities of humans preying upon one another with a remove or distance, as if he lived on another planet and inhabited the body within judicial robes only as a day job and was not entirely human himself. But he lost his treasured detachment during this time, far removed from the eyes of the court, during the six weeks of Michael's illness.

When his symptoms worsened, Bernard Rush brought Julia into the city in the evening dark when it was thought to be less upsetting to her and walked with her through the corridors to Michael's room. The doctors believed it would be his last night alive. Julia looked at Michael in his hospital bed through the barrier of glass, with an impassive expression, as if her concern were swallowed up in a pit in her own heart and wishing to spare her any more Rush brought her back out momentarily to sit in a waiting room until he could bring her home again. She fell into a restless sleep on the cushions of a sofa.

Left alone with his grandson, the grandfather gripped the door knob with his hand tightly so his grip began to tremble from its own force. His face reddened, and spoke out as if possessed with a third spirit in the room with a barely contained fury, not with his old, calm voice but an inhuman and furiously angry voice, "If you kill my grandson, I will retaliate. I will unleash every evil I can imagine. I will wreck every human life within my reach. You'll hear a cry from voices that will make you tear out your own eyes. I promise this."

He stood and looked for anything, anyone, to suffer this vengeance, and stopped at the door in the space leading to the corner of the room where Julia lay barely visible under the cushions and Bernard's old coat, whispering, "I begin with that girl. Her blood will drip through the floors if you kill this boy." Julia slept unknowingly, curled up with her nose pressed into the juncture of cushions on the sofa. He pressed his fingers against the glass, almost to the point that the glass of this door seemed to bend and buckle under this weight. However after a few moments looking at Julia's sleeping body, he seemed to calm somewhat, noticing absently how she seemed less troubled in her sleep than when he used to anxiously watch her in the early morning hours when she had first arrived, different in kind from the earlier episodes when her sleep was not so untroubled. When composed more calmly he left Michael and sat beside Julia on the sofa. He ran a hand through the strands of his unwashed hair. His eyes were red-rimmed and speckled with blood from tiny burst vessels. His lips bled from the bite of his own clenched teeth.

Ironically, while Julia slept on the other side of the glass partition, Michael seemed to respond to the grandfather's energy and activity in the room, energy that didn't belong to himself or to the fever. His eyes had opened at the quietly spoken words of his grandfather, which had jolted him awake. He watched and listened without turning his head, body motionless, even devoid of power except for his moving eyes and attentiveness. His sheets damp from sweat and the bleeding of fever. His face looked as if he had dipped his head into a sea, wet and drenched, his eyes blinking from the salt sting. The grandfather turned at hearing a catch in Michael's throat, and watched as Michael spit out a spasm of vomit that choked frozen and hot in his throat, into the sheets beside the pillow. Michael lay back, his shoulders motionless again but watching his grandfather with a boring, examining glance that lasted long.

The grandfather could not return Michael's glance but his hand pressed the button on the wall beside the bed to summon help. And Michael continued his watchful, thoughtful glance at the grandfather even as the bustle around his bed increased with the busy occupants of the hospital.

Michael awoke with the grey of near-morning pressing on his eyelids. His eyelids opened first then his pupils dilated slowly in response to the grayness and to consciousness. He bolted upright, bent at the waist with eyes opened in a panic. A seizure jolted through his body and he fell back into the bed with a squeak.

This motion caused his eyes to close and he groaned so that he could hear but not see the grandfather's voice summoned out of its own sleep, a murmur of inquiring, that Michael answered with a croaky voice, "I thought I was late for school." With eyes remaining closed, Michael's lips worked open and closed like a fish gasping in a pail. The grandfather smiled at seeing this gesture as if a sign of impending wellness. Michael, still, remained anxious until sitting upright he saw the tip of Julia's black-haired head at the lower portion of window, patiently waiting for someone to lift her up so she could see through the window. When she peeped around the door sill, inquiring with blank eyes to his health, he couldn't meet her eyes himself but sighed with relief himself that she too seemed well and hale.

Michael's wellness, Bernard Rush reasoned, increased in proportion to his complaints about the embarrassment at having to use the bedpan and the small portions given to him at meals. Almost hourly Michael spoke with one complaint after another. To Bernard he said, "I decided not to be sick anymore." In his gut sprung full-formed a detestation of sickness in all forms and a decision that he would henceforth study ways to cure illness to spare other boy explorers from similar suffering. "I don't like the smell of this hospital. Can you open a window?"

To the nurses, Michael's response was nothing short of a miracle. His eyes were dark and large and round but clear and focused. He lay passively on the bed, exhausted and unable to move without shooting jolts of pain, but his temperature had dropped. Some regulatory system in his body had triumphed over the pathogens. Somehow he had lived when other children, receiving the same treatment had died. The doctors said, "It was nothing special that we did," explaining to the grandfather who wanted to know if the farm worker's children had received less thorough care. "Diseases come and go like this, sometimes, striking out for completely unknown reasons. Then they disappear in the same way." No one in particular could take credit for his recovery.

The grandfather responded somewhat in kind and recovered some of his former composure. He sat back in the hospital room chair in the remaining days of Michael's stay and told Michael stories, stories about court cases in the past, stories about his early life, stories about the troubled Hardy family history.

"You come from the Albingenses and the Waldenses clans, Protestants from the south of France. In the thirteenth century, Catholics declared a crusade against us, and waged a war against our family — which fought back against the excesses of the papacy. My father told me many stories, and I told your father, but I don't think he said so to you. So I'm saying it now, doing my duty."

"People didn't like our family. Sometimes people don't like it now."

"Have you noticed that? Your father said the same thing. He was expelled from several schools. You're so much alike. I think I was the same. Perhaps less so."

"What about the markings on the house gate. Are they related to the Waldo family?"

"My father, your great-grandfather carved that crest into the gate when three of his sons died in wars, just before he died himself. My brothers. He kept me indoors and built up that library. He vowed that the worst I would suffer would be paper cuts from all the books and papers he said would pass between my hands."

"What do the markings mean?"

"He said it was the constellation each of us is born under, a constellation of his own creation. He said it wasn't part of the regular zodiac. He called it the constellation *Rain*."

Michael said nothing so the grandfather continued, "The constellation *Rain* supposedly lies between cusps of the regular zodiac. He didn't believe in astrology but he needed an explanation and this seemed to satisfy him. He said that early in our family history, being protestants, we caused strife and conflict with our own beliefs, so that the conflicts inflicted pain on ourselves and upon other people — but not any more than we inflict on ourselves singly. He believed that the people who suffered most were those people closest to ourselves. Not anyone who deserves it, simply those people we cared for in our own families. This came true for your grandmother, whom I cared for very much but who could not say that she lived a happy life. And she died when she was still a young woman. Your mother seemed happy but she didn't live long and died painfully when you were born. Though that was none of your own fault. That was your great-grandfather's belief at work. We seem to invite others into our lives and they would suffer. Yet somehow we ourselves come out, externally, unscathed, though unhappy and unsettled ourselves."

"I think astrology is fake."

"I'd agree with you. I said so myself to your great-grandfather when I was a little boy watching him carve the design into the gatepost with a chisel. I think your own father did too. That's probably normal for a Hardy. Disbelief, I mean, being protestants. You can believe it or not. I'm just trying to explain the markings on the gate."

Michael looked upwards to the ceiling and spoke to the ceiling, "Stars or tides or planets can't change my own will to do something. If I want to do it then I will."

"Ahh," said the grandfather, only nodding his head, understanding but not agreeing. A nurse entered and as if by silent agreement they began to talk about something innocuous and less important to themselves since they shared a disposition among themselves to exclude strangers from their own private thoughts.

When the grandfather returned home with Michael in tow, after more than a month's absence, he noted in passing how assiduously Julia cared for the house and yards in their absence — houseplants were watered and more healthy than before, cabinets and countertops scrubbed and clean, windows clear and the landscaping in particular, all that she could manage, had been well-tended. He stood first in Michael's room, overlooking the eastern part of the town, overlooking the river woods where Michael had spent his last ordinary day in camping, and his throat choked on some strange emotion to which he wasn't accustomed and his shoulders shook. He choked on some emotion that he believed he was not earlier capable of feeling, as if possessed with the felt life of another person entirely which in passing released a huge, slow tide of sadness that rushed over him and through him and began to crush the earlier blanked emotions previously known by him — seeing Michael's meager possessions, their smallness and meaning to the boy – a toy drum and piano, scribbled notes and scale models of planes and clipper ships. He struggled to contain how much he loved the little boy, trembling hand on sill, so after a brief struggle to contain the feelings hidden inside himself, he walked downstairs stiffly to make breakfast for the household as he was accustomed.

Julia had risen before his arrival, had squeezed oranges for juice, and buttered toast, brought steaming on the plate, so precisely had she timed his arrival downstairs, waiting quietly herself for his footsteps above her on the stairs. She climbed into her accustomed chair, atop an atlas, which fit exactly the dimensions of the seat and kept her above the tabletop. Mechanically he cut a grapefruit in half, put half on a plate for himself and on its own plate slid the remainder to Julia. He avoided looking at her and kept his expression to the center of his grapefruit, where the peel or pith like so many spokes in a wheel met in the center. He fiddled with his spoon.

She smiled at him, not perturbed at his solemnity, with her shy smile looking upwards at him with a soft red gap in her mouth where her front teeth should have been. Through the corner of his eye he glimpsed the smile and this tore at something inside him, that made his breakfast seem very bitter though normally the grapefruit would taste sweet to him. He ate the grapefruit with a wincing expression on his face, section by section and sat motionless looking into his hands when Julia took his plate and spoon into the kitchen to wash up.

In the eight years that he remained alive he would be affectionate and utterly considerate to Julia, though if it seemed to her that his countenance to her had changed, even to be more kind and considerate, so her heart seemed to blossom in secret at his continued kindnesses and courtesy and become ever more confident within her life in the house, so she judged that this change was due to the pain she saw he had endured in his concern for Michael's life during the sickness. She felt, not saddened for the change in his behavior — the exchange of a former gentleness towards her for an odd, newer remoteness — but on the contrary, she cared for him and respected him ever more greatly that he should have been so affected by Michael's illness — as if his subdued behavior towards her was due solely out of increased concern for Michael.

Michael twisted his head at the window upstairs from its cradle in his arms to see the little girl lodger hurry across the yard as quickly as she could, with her comic, limping gait, head lowered to the ground and arms swinging in her haste and stopped to pause in the shadows of the peach trees, chest heaving and tongue lolling. In a moment along the same path appeared the grandfather hefting a basket piled high with wet clothes from the washing machine, oblivious to Julia's hiding. He set the basket on the path beside a clothesline and reached back with a two handed push in the small of his own back as he arched himself backwards then straightened. He stuck clothespins and wet clothes onto the line simultaneously so that at a slow pace the line acquired a flapping, showy set of teeth. When finished, the four strings of the clotheslines sagged with the weight of the fluttering cloths and throughout the whole period Julia remained motionless and hidden in the trees. To himself but aloud he muttered, "That girl is a lunatic."

When lightened and empty, the grandfather carried the basket back down the trail he had climbed and disappeared from Michael's view at the window. The girl waited a few moments then crept back down the trail in pursuit but barefoot she stepped carefully to avoid the snails that appeared after the previous day's rain or a spongy peach, here or there, that had fallen onto the ground.

The next day at the same window, Michael watched as the scene seemed to repeat itself except that Julia appeared with the basket of clothes herself— but with her practical sense pulled the basket in a wagon. She tugged with a two handed grip near the lip of the path's height and under the clothesline bent over with hands on her knees and panting from her exertions. The grandfather waited for her to recover breath and when Julia stretched out her hand, he gave to her a cloth bag full of clothespins. While he secured each piece of clothes to the line, Julia dispensed the clothespins, one by one, until as before all lines billowed and furled in the breeze. The grandfather returned down the hill and Julia followed pulling her empty wagon.

They took such pains with the laundry because the grandfather changed Michael's sheets every day, partly perhaps because of Michael's brief comment how much he liked the smell of the sun-dried linen, and falling back into the newly made bed each morning, rolled over and buried his head into the pillow or into the sheets, sniffing and nodding. He said he tried "to smell up all the freshness." The grandfather asked, "Why are you turned around?" And Michael answered, "I'm using up all the leaf smell on this end of the sheet too."

Part of the day's regimen became his daily lunch. Julia had taken upon herself the dual responsibility to carry up his daily bowl of soup and sandwich, concentrated, determined to not spill a drop and also to watch that Michael drank up every drop. If he indicated he was finished and pushed back the bowl onto the tray, Julia would examine the bowl and if any soup remained she would mutely push back the bowl, pointing to the remainder that he must finish. And Michael obeyed her reproving and stern expression. She brought up books chosen from the weekly bookmobile that made a special stop outside the house, chosen by the grandfather after their weekly consultation on what Michael would like to read.

When one day the grandfather entered and saw the two at loggerheads over the bowl of soup, Michael refusing to eat any more and Julia refusing to take away the bowl until he finished, the grandfather shook his head and said, "Julia, don't worry about that spoonful of soup. Michael is well enough to fetch his own food." Julia gave Michael one last glance of reproof and placed the bowl onto the tray, shaking her head at his folly. Thus to everyone's relief the typhoid fever was pronounced cured and Michael could roam free without a jailer.

The illness had not passed without effect. In time while Michael still ran about with abandon, perhaps with more intensity and enjoyment and he mocked Julia with a greater enthusiasm, he had become more circumspect about dangers that previously he treated cavalierly. Julia too seemed freer and more open to speaking and arguing with Michael, and rather than scold both for their conversations, heated though they be, the grandfather strangely enough seemed to encourage them and interceded only when the tempers rose and the noise disturbed his equanimity.

The grandfather had been making sandwiches for Julia and himself and saw her in the kitchen doorway at the entrance to the house when she turned her head in response to a whistle from out-of-doors. And in the moment she turned, the whole doorway filled with the explosion of water and Julia reeled slightly, holding onto the door jambs in her surprise. She turned in to look at the grandfather whose mouth had dropped open. Because he feared she would react in the old way by retreating inside herself. But he had been moved to laughter and mirth when he saw that as the water dripped through her hair, and darkened the neck and shoulders of the coat, knowing from Michael's cackle that he'd thrown a water balloon, Julia's expression of surprise slowly turned into an incredulous smile and she gave a few short barks to the grandfather that he confused at first – then understood as the first attempt at laughter that he'd ever heard from her. More like the sound of a clearing throat, Julia stopped her laughter and turned to look at her out-of-sight attacker, and her face filled not with hurt and not with pain but with a new and fresh and a determined look, perhaps simply of a child's happy raging, of plotting revenge. Her eyebrows rose and eyes narrowed and she leapt off the porch so that Julia's new though awkward dog-like, barking laugh began to recede into the distance. Then the grandfather, holding up two sandwiches, took one bite out of each, and thoughtfully chewed on his double lunch while he stared at the wooden slats of the floor.

The grandfather studied her eyes, though she averted her face and gaze as if out of a beam of strong sunlight, "What bothers you at school? Do you have a friend in the classroom?" Julia moved her forehead, not in affirmation of his question but seemed torn one way or another, that to speak was difficult but also that not to speak to the grandfather would be an equal or even greater evil. So as the saying goes a thirsty horse, equidistant between two pools of water can't move to either pool, so her eyes remained downcast though her lips seemed to quiver and she seemed tensed and ready to burst.

He had visited the school and unknownst to Julia peeped into the classroom, seeing her sitting among the younger children but not seeming any older than they — she not larger or taller than the Napa children three or four years younger. She ill-at-ease and nervous in her chair in the back corner.

"Well then. Don't worry Julia, we'll find something

that you like and so you'll feel safe and happy. Okay by you?"

She turned up her face with neck bent as a wrist on an arm, strangely, so that the expression on her face caused the grandfather to step back one small step. Because in her eyes, he saw, behind her eyes seemed a blue stoniness, an aridity or a weird and boundless pitiless, an emptiness that discomfited. In that moment a thought occurred to him, "She is a coeval, she is even older than I am. She is not a human child at all. And, who have I let into my house?"

Whether she saw this in his eyes or not, he never knew. He lost a sense of time, felt dizziness as if he'd risen too quickly from a sitting position and wobbled on his feet. Julia put out a tiny hand, no bigger it seemed to him than a small leaf yet that hand seemed more powerful than any child's should be. And he recoiled from that hand that touched him, and at that touch his own fears melted and he saw the bird-like child again.

From his chair near them in the room, Michael stirred out of his book and smiled at them impishly.

"Yes?" said the grandfather, smiling in a relieved and disjointed way.

Michael turned over the cover of the book and peered again at the title as if disbelieving something about the contents, "Gulliver just peed on the queen of Lilliput, because her apartment was on fire." He looked part perplexed, part delighted and guilty as if reading a book he shouldn't be allowed.

"Well, foolish people call that book a classic of children's literature mainly because they haven't read it themselves. Wait until you get to the end, if you want to finish it, and then we'll have a good talk about it."

Michael's attention turned back to Lilliput. The grandfather placed his hands on Julia's bony, sad shoulders, "Let's eat something," and they walked quietly together, side by side, to investigate the pickings for a sandwich.

In their nightly sessions in the library the grandfather also noted a change in Michael's reading. When before the illness he would desultorily leaf through one book, then another in a restless wandering among the shelves, having in the confinement nothing to do but read, a different concentration and readiness to learn seemed to have overtaken Michael so nightly he wandered less than he was accustomed and they talked less because Michael read more — more deeply absorbed in the book than before and more concentrated and focused in the book contents.

To Michael, after the illness, the books had acquired an unexpected power to still or temper a quavering that overtook his consciousness and thinking mind and provided a calm hand to the instability introduced by the pain of the illness.

Michael tried to explain this to the grandfather in one of his pauses as he raised his head at the end of a chapter one evening, "Once when I was sick I saw things turned inside out."

"What do you mean?"

"When I looked at anything in the room or through the window, the nurse or at the machinery, it seemed transparent and in everything I saw gears and winches and pulleys and everything seemed explainable though

I wouldn't know how to explain things yet. You read a passage to me in the hospital in the whale book, how Pip the cabin boy had drownded…"

"Drowned."

"Drowned, and at the bottom of the ocean he saw a vision and he saw I think you said it was God's foot on the treadle of the loom and the whole world above him in a vision like a dream."

"Something like that. Do you want to reread the passage again."

"No. But I felt something similar. That's when I woke up and I understood."

The grandfather said nothing while Michael turned his head right and left and pressed his tongue and front teeth together in an open mouthed expression of thought and they were quiet for a few minutes. The fire cricked and crackled and when a log snapped to sink deeper into the orange pit of hearth the grandfather spoke again, "I've wanted to ask the son of an old student of mine to come by the house every day as a tutor. I already talked to him about it last year and he said he could do it about this time of the year."

"I don't know why we need another stranger in our house."

"We already live in too much solitude as it is. I'm very glad that Julia has come to live with us. Besides as a tutor Jonathan will only be here a few hours during the weekday."

"I already go to school in the daytime."

"Only for a few hours more in the daytime. He might work out as a special tutor for Julia because she needs to catch up on her schoolwork. I'm not certain how well she'll do in the public school. If it works out with him then perhaps she can become home schooled but also I think you'd like Jonathan. I only met him once but he says he's very confused about everything, though he had studied and learned all he was supposed to, and with a Ph.D. now he said he doesn't understand anything more than when he was little."

"What does he do? Why is he confused?"

"He went to law school and his father was one of my own law clerks, but when he became a lawyer he became unhappy."

"What does he do now? What other school can he go to? He can go to driving school and become a driving teacher."

"He doesn't do anything, that's why I spoke to him. He said he mopes. He's a professional moper." Michael shrugged his shoulders, "I can learn what I want by myself. If you want someone to help Julia then that's fine. But I bet I can drive him crazy."

"We'll see."

Homo necans.

Michael's defense of the woodshed.

Michael was nine years old when snow fell on Napa in record depths. Two years had passed since Julia arrived and by the next year they would be separated. In later years when reminiscing, the winter full of snow was one of the few memories they could recall in common. When the snow fell, no one, even his grandfather whom most in the town felt must be older than Moses, could recall such a flummox and storm. Michael's attention wandered as the grandfather told of past storms, good and ill, west and east, but his ears perked open when he heard, "A storm worse than this one occurred when I was your age. The children in my neighborhood fought snowball battles in the street." Michael heard this but having not seen snow before was curious and uncertain about what could be done with the powder. It looked harmless enough. But in fact the snuffy powder was to send him careening off into another course of life entirely different had the storm not occurred at all.

One afternoon the grandfather stood at the library window and watched as Julia trotted into view with her peculiar limping gait, exaggerated by the knee deepness of snow and before disappearing from sight, as her dog sat to scratch itself behind the ear, so Julia paused and with mittened hands scratched her ear similarly, though with hand bundled so she couldn't get a good scratch and kept at the attempts until the itch was satisfied and she turned the corner.

Owning a newly discovered ear muff and an abandoned scarf from the steamer trunks in attic which wound around her head and body like a furry anaconda, Julia figured she was set for the cold and welcomed the frost with a defiant shrug of her shoulders as she stood at the ghaut mouth watching the changes overcome her territory, with arms raised high and apart in welcome. Though the scarf wound around her head, she found that the sides of her head were insulated but her face was not, and when pressed felt distant and near-froze. Criticisms about her pig-like nose by Michael who only the week earlier called her "snout face" until his grandfather picked him up by the collar and took him to the library for a discussion, made her grasp the tip of the nose and try to pull it outwards. But her fingers were too cold, her nose was too cold, and in the end her self-feelings were too distant to be bothered about any further. By turning the ear muff ninety degrees she found she could warm her nose and still keep her ears muffled, and satisfied with this arrangement, surged forward into the ghaut and fingery trees. Maggie bounced after.

Roads remained impassable for a day or two, until snow plows could be brought from a northerly county. Mittens and parkas sold out of the O'Dell general store. Without more, substantial snowfall in the following few days, the calamity seemed managed and some routine returned to Napa, roads opened, and horrors to the children the school resumed.

On the playground during a bitter frosty recess, during the frenzied activity, girls made snow creatures, snow imps, sculpted snow dogs and plowed snow angels. Several fights broke out and when the recess monitor, Mrs. Beeson, intervened she was pelted by a barrage of icy pellets and retreated to the teacher lounge. Several private fights resumed, heightened and more vigorous lacking supervision. One bloody nose. Later in the hour, Michael had been struck on the ear with a snowball hurled with such a violent impact that he dropped a set of colored pens and fell face first into the fluff. And in rising again and shaking his head to clear the fog and rid himself of the snow, he saw that the other children, his own friends included, laughed at him. Unsure how to react, his face appeared quizzical, puzzled, then he put back his head and laughed with them, all were happy. However, when his attacker had waddled across the yard to play in another corner, Michael had a snowball ready and tossed an accurate throw at such an opportune, unexpected moment that the boy was thrown completely off his stride and by forward momentum dove headfirst into a snow bank and disappeared completely from sight, plastic boots and all.

The playground turned silent appreciating the thoroughness and precision of Michael's revenge and when the boy crawled back out of his burrow, he marshaled two of his friends and they chased Michael back into the school house, not even with a smile on their faces. When recess ended, therefore, Michael was already indoors and didn't hear about the newly-hatched conspiracy. The boy had extorted a promise from everyone in the whole fourth grade to make snowballs, and keep them hidden nearby in a secret cache.

When the class shuffled back indoors and rid themselves of mittens, coats, boots, and ear muffs, Michael could tell that something was up by the giggling and furtive looks at him which he appeared to ignore but watched curiously as a tension clearly had filled the room. Mrs. Beeson, too, sensed this and partly because the unraveling of muffs and unlacing of boots had taken such a long time, she dismissed the class early with a wave of her pudgy hand, with a flourish as her fingers rose up with a wing-like gesture or flutter. So when the class shuffled outdoors he was met at the school gate with a fusillade of snowballs, hurled at him from all directions, even by the girls. Everybody laughed and would have got back onto the school bus without fuss, incident forgotten, but the boy, Matthew Gorda and his friends ignored their accustomed bus and followed Michael on his walk home, pelting him with snowballs already prepared for this purpose.

Michael endured the hits on his head and back, until the amber gate of the house appeared at the end of the street but the boys caught hold of his arms at this point and tackled him to the ground. They stuffed him headfirst into the bank of snow beside the road, stuffed his mouth and nose with snow until he choked and in unison picked him up and threw him into a brick wall beside the road. But they misjudged the depth and Michael's head struck the brick wall under the whiteness and at the sight of the bright red stream dripping starkly out of the snow their eyes widened and they backed down the street, turned and ran as quickly as their sliding and jerks of balance would allow. When the grandfather walked out to check the mail, he saw Michael's shoes sticking out of the snow beside the post and the trickle of red.

While lying in the mush, unconscious, Michael's mind filled with odd and strange unbidden thoughts, fleeting thoughts that were at first foreign to him but that in time would become so closely entwined in his mind that he couldn't imagine a life without them. When the grandfather grunted and slid Michael out of the snow, Michael awoke and his first expression was one of a smile, mixed with thoughts and plans for revenge. The grandfather's eyes widened at seeing the expression in his grandson's eyes, then felt a bit saddened, seeing a look he'd seen in other members of his family but which he hoped to avoid in Michael.

In Michael's mind, for the first time, he'd been placed outside a society, excluded from a group, discriminated against by a majority and while he mused on this, rolling it around in his mind, so to speak, like a gumball in his mouth, he decided after the newness of the feeling wore off that he liked this feeling and something gargantuan and awful woke up from a deep recess somewhere inside him. He had discovered the peculiar trait of the Hardys, the reason for their bloody history and the odd symbol on the house gate. He sensed a kind of strength in this solitude, which he hadn't felt possessed of, in the least, even a half hour earlier. And when he became accustomed to this feeling of ostracism, he felt smugly pleased and encouraged by these odds, of twenty-two, including the girls, to one. As he formulated and processed these new thoughts, realizations, strategies, he felt a persistent tugging on his shoes. He found himself pulled out of the snow pack by the grandfather.

In response to the expression on the face looming above him Michael answered in a new, querulous tone, with a new edge to it, "You should have left me there a while longer. I was thinking."

"Do your thinking like I do — in my bathrobe and slippers — and I sit in a chair and doodle with a pencil with a cheery fire in the grate."

"I don't like to doodle."

"Then just use the bathrobe and slippers."

"Maybe I think better in the snow. I was trying it out."

"Try out the slipper at home. Now. And wipe your nose." He daubed at the cut on Michael's head but saw its shallow incision and merely clamped a bare, chilled hand onto the wound, to staunch the wound but also with a gesture, almost a helpless gesture, at seeing the changes that had so suddenly overcome the features and disposition of his only grandson.

The next day, all the children of the upper grades

collected themselves around a paper taped to the door of the classroom:

This means war.
M. Hardy
P.S. You're all going to get it.

When finished reading the declaration, those in back jumping with hands on the shoulders of the child in front, the school bell rang and they looked around. Michael had ducked out of the class early by asking to go to the bathroom, never returning, and in racing outside they saw his retreating form at the end of the street, headed home. With happy shouts and joys and cries of ecstasies at the prospect of a hunt, the children took off behind him, following the trail of footsteps in the middle of the road. Many of them left without coats or mittens or hats or galoshes and they would later rue this lack.

They busily jumped over the brick embankment leading up to the gate and skittered around the gate into the yard of the Hardy house which none had seen before. The mob stopped short by a trench dug in front of the house, whose excavated ice formed a high thin wall behind the trench, frozen solid, and which ran side to side for thirty meters right and left. The mob split, and the children running right came round the house entirely, where they found the ten or so children, who in running left now lay in dazed heaps, one atop another, woozy from snowball impacts, holding their heads and rolling back and forth on the ground, or else lying on their backs, weeping noiselessly into their hands flat over their faces.

Michael had built a second trench to funnel his attackers into a narrow ditch which ended in front of the tool shed. When the children ran into this dead end, they tried to turn but being in single file, he appeared behind them with a plastic pail of snowballs and threw his snowballs with such accuracy that when one kid fell down smacked right between the eyes, the child immediately behind could do nothing but rush directly at Michael to be struck down and in this way were felled one by one. The last, most hapless girl put up her hands in front of her face, and was struck in the stomach, and when she put her hands over her stomach, to be smacked by a snowball in the face, and this continued until she fell down crying and Michael threw the pail on top of her.

Those children at the back of the trench scrambled desperately at the snow walls and in a few minutes they'd clawed away the ice on both sides but Michael had begun knocking each of them down repeatedly and they all eventually collapsed into the snow. Those moving or gurgling noisily were smacked down again. Michael behaved ruthlessly, without pity. He stood above several of the prone boys, already dizzied and confused and pleading for mercy, those three who chased him yesterday and cut his head, but he ignored their pleas, and threw the last of his snowballs with special force at their heads as if dispensing each with a *coup de grace*. He disappeared around the corner of the house until each of the left-turning children lay quietly face down in the snow, some pretending to be dead, playing possum, to avoid any more of Michael's retribution.

The surviving children fanned out behind the house in eager search of him, filled with the elation of participating in a mob but he led them deeper away from the house into the river woods where they separated and became isolated. All evening long they were ambushed and smacked by snowballs from above, behind, with a shout of surprise, inevitably from an unexpected angle or direction. Several times during the day Michael raised his arm to fire away at an elusive, stealthy figure following him who remained barely out of his throwing range, irritating him with its elusiveness alone among the children, until he realized that it was Julia, in her snow disguise and ear muff over nose, that escaped him. Under short pants she had wrapped beige bandages around her legs from toes to waist. These bandages kept her legs warm and made her mobile, letting her jump a hedge or slide between trees in a thicket, impassable to the others. She had tied green leeks around her head as if this would help her blend into the forest — perhaps it would have in the spring but not in winter as she tried to blend greenness into the bare shrubbery. He realized she knew the woods and ghauts even better than he and kept out of the mouth of trees that led to ravines and would not be trapped so Michael could throw snowballs at her too. By now the balls stored in his caches had turned to large pellets of ice, almost deadly to the ragged survivors of the mob that had beset him earlier in the day. He ran quickly on solid ground while his attackers sank ankle deep into icy sludge, deceptively overlaid with blankets of twigs. The other children fell into these low flanks of water because the ground was dotted with small caves and fissures. Julia alone scurried past the obstacles, only from time to time appearing close to him, with a squinty expression as if her eyesight failed her time to time but she skittered away again before he could throw a missile at her also.

At times he'd be cornered by a pack when he ventured nearer to the house but learned to race to a corner of the mass of his attackers, so he would only face a few children at a time. While others in the middle or back of the pack fanned out right or left, he'd again jump to a corner, and in this way survived mostly unscathed or so he thought. Perhaps the children suffered the consequences of living in a town too small to field a baseball league. Their throws were ill-coordinated and ill-timed, ill-aimed and inaccurate. "These fools," crowed Michael, "if they slowed and didn't panic and threw in volleys I'd be massacred. They'd pound me into the ground to China." But they did none of these things.

In contrast, Michael found he possessed a trait of coolness under pressure. When others screamed in excitement or fear and threw while at the same time poised to dodge or flee and thus threw with poor aim, Michael stood stolidly, stock still, without fearing to be hit himself and immobile in this way, threw with practiced accuracy at only one target at a time, then another target, sequentially and logically, most dangerous target first, then onwards to the most helpless. He threw as hard as he could but without sacrificing accuracy so others began to fear his aim and in consequence made their own aim erratic and increasing his own confidence in a spiraling cycle so that by the afternoon's end, Michael's confidence stood at his lifetime's high and the other children's attitudes reached a low — as low as the temperature.

When the mothers of Napa appeared on doorsteps, calling their children home for dinner, with high pitched yodels, stragglers reappeared on the streets, cold, crying, wiping bloody noses and limping from their wounds, half from the impact of Michael's ice balls and half from tearing through the haunted woods with trees that had snagged and tore their clothes — their fingers and toes made brittle by the frozen water of the crevices and fissures that they had fallen into.

Perhaps if the Hardy house had a telephone someone in the class would have called Michael and arranged a truce of some kind but lacking a hot-line between belligerents, hostilities continued apace. Matthew Gorda exhorted his classmates to a shrill escalating hunger for revenge. One boy said to another, "I know it's mean to gang up but I don't like him somehow. I can't say why. It's in my stomach."

Michael spent much of a sleepless night shuttling from window to window upstairs, peering guardedly onto the grounds of the house for intruders through rime on glass panes. He glimpsed only scruffy Julia, wearing one of her home-assembled, outlandish costumes, though no doubt warm enough for the snow. A ragged red hood, cut from a sweatshirt had been tied around her head, and around the hood were tied a fresh series of green leeks as if sprouting out of her ears like a vegetable palisade. Maggie too assisted her in the prowl, creeping in and out of the ghauts.

As the fit of sleeplessness wound on through the night, he wandered into his grandfather's library and pulled several books. He read an encyclopedia article about generalship and following the trail of references, read in more detail about the lives and campaigns of Belisarius, Alexander, Epaminondas, Genghis Khan and the Golden Horde. He read of military campaigns in Roman Spain by Sertorius, against daunting odds, and the exciting two day long victory over Napoleon at the villages near Waterloo by Arthur Wellesley who became Duke of Wellington.

Simultaneously Matthew Gorda and his friends themselves spent the night and morning mostly in whispered conversations amongst themselves from windows and battery powered radios. Before first light, they crept in ragged formation up to the Hardy house from behind through the river woods, up from the seemingly endless and unmapable series of ghauts and ravines, where the previous day they had retreated and been vanquished. This morning they were dressed for warmth and protection from snowballs, bundled in thick coats, hats, and carried shields cut at great energy from plywood — some carried garbage can lids but these were later abandoned being too heavy and the metal too cold even for the mittened hands. Some carried their ammunition in ready canvas bags. All were grim and confident, emboldened by their numbers and resolution. They settled in clumps behind the house and waited for Michael to rouse himself.

However outnumbered he had been, Michael did not underestimate his opponents and he had in his reading quickly deduced a pattern in the victories of those generals in the books — that the victors had struck quickly, unexpectedly rapidly and from unexpected directions, and he had been emboldened that many of the most astounding victories came from those numerically disadvantaged. Thus as he lay in his foxhole, dug behind the fence and behind the children and house, he napped with a smile on his face and with packets of cheese and crackers in both gloved hands dreaming of Roman triumphs and laurels and rousing cheers of soldiery. He awoke and sipped cocoa out of a thermos, ate his provisions, vegetarian like the legionaries in Gaul and gradually rose, stretched himself and fitted his upper body with a white sheet, with holes cut out like a simple Halloween ghost costume and thus attired looked out onto the landscape. He noted contentedly as the other boys huddled miserably behind clumps of shrubbery, brick oven, any place of concealment, rubbing their own arms and legs and whispering to each other for encouragement.

Michael settled down again, judging that the time was still not ripe, saw the hoarfrost about his nest was undisturbed and curled back into the foxhole, regretting the lack of light so he could not finish the paperback chapter on Epaminondas that he had stuck in his pocket a few hours earlier. He woke with a start at hearing the other boys grumbling about the cold and suspecting they were ready to return home, tensed as they themselves rose out of their concealment, shaking their sleeping limbs to recover sensation.

When they shuffled numbly, sleepily beside his hole, he leapt up dressed all in white, a tourbillion and blizzard, bewildering and frightening to the children and attacked the besiegers one by one in a grim and concentrated silence, hurling snowballs kept convenient in an apron pocket. And the fourth graders thinking someone amongst themselves was playing at first ignored the ruckus amongst themselves, then stared open mouthed at the white apparition flinging white missiles at their own heads, and as the day before the fled back into the woods. So, in this way, divided and demoralized, the woods rang with frightened shouts and pleas for rescue that mostly went unanswered as each child ran panicked in his own pell-mell direction. In this way Michael once more carried the day.

At leisure he began throwing snowballs like a mortar, arcing them high into the sky so that at a hundred yards the snowballs crunched into the ground as if satellites from the sky, panicking the children even more, who scrambled to avoid these unseen projectiles, becoming even more demoralized and discouraged.

Finally assembled in Matthew's garage, those remainders who had not gone home to recuperate were livid with rage at the perfidiousness of his ambush, the nerve, that he dare attack them from behind. Something snapped in their minds. Instead of a fun weekend game, a bile of defeat lay sour and bitter in their throats, no one more than Matthew who spit out streams of invective against Michael, stirring up the others yet once again, "I'll beat open his head with a rock!" But his invisible tormentor did not answer.

In the evening Michael undressed and in the mirror found his lips and fingers blue from the frost, his arms and chest bruised purple from the stray shots of snowballs that found their way onto his parka. Some of the snowballs had been filled with rocks, and those left raised welts on his ribcage. His grandfather looked up in surprise at hearing the bathtub filled, at this odd and unexpected noise in the house, without precedent. Michael was taking a bath without prodding. While submerged he plotted his after-dinner strategy.

The grandfather heard odd echoes through the fields this day, children's voices calling to one another and spectral shapes running through the moonscape of deserted trees and desert-like mesas bare for ice and frost.

The Napans knew that Michael, as all boys, would take out the garbage to the curb sometime this night or tomorrow and they had prepared sheets, the Halloween ghost sheets as Michael had earlier in the day. And it was no usual sight in the town to see twenty odd children marching down the central street in sheets, pulling wagons piled with snow, carrying rucksacks, shields, padded with blankets, in orderly rows towards the edge of town to the site of battle. By now they used several of Michael's other devices. Prepared for a long campaign they carried thermoses and sandwiches. One enterprising soldier waddled past the O'Dell store within a sleeping bag having cut holes in the base for his feet and tying off the top with a rope at his neck and two armholes cut out of the sides of the bag. The pattern on the sleeping bag showed a series of furry brown bears curled up in a dreamy, happy sleep.

This time they lay outside the Hardy house, near the curb where the garbage would be set and out of range of the windows. Michael asked his grandfather for a specially early dinner, filled his mouth and swallowed the food whole without chewing. While hungry from the day's exertions he needed the nutrition. Then jumping from the table, pushed open the door and slammed it shut behind him. At the table the grandfather looked first at Michael's empty place, then at Julia who sat, face barely above the table top, chewing her own food thoroughly, deliberately, without looking up to meet his glance. The grandfather thought to himself, "I don't understand children at all."

The town's children had reorganized themselves so that even those who did not want to fight directly were pressed into service, assigned to snow wagons which followed behind the fights with a ready supply of spare ammunition or pulled homemade sleds made from milk crates and wooden planks. The Napan army gathered and squatted on their haunches or sat in portable picnic chairs, in their sheets, waiting with more anticipation than before for their revenge. Their numbers had swelled and children from the other grades had joined their ranks. After inspecting the area in their own vicinity for hidden bunkers, prodding the snow banks nearby with their boot toes or with broomsticks, they settled down for a peaceful wait.

From behind them, this time on a hill thirty yards behind them on the slopes of an upper road, Michael watched through his Zeiss bird watching binoculars and with paper and pencil marked each boy's position as they settled into their shallow trenches and foxholes. They passed shovels between themselves and when finished silence reigned again on the street.

And once again Michael proved more patient than they for only when they once again rose thinking that he would not venture out for the night and stirred out of their holes, he silently ran at them swatting their heads in the holes with hard thrown snowballs from behind so the most common sound on the street was a "whoomph" as the air would be knocked out of them. At times he stopped to consult his map wishing to be as thorough and evenhanded in his eagerness for the attack. They rose in an indignant mob and chased Michael onto the grounds of his house and had him cornered by the tool shed. There they made good use of their numbers at last and by sheer quantity of snowballs, resupplied by the wagons, beat him backwards to the woodshed. The air was filled with projectiles so heavily that it seemed that the storm had arisen again and the yard seemed beset with a blizzard and whiteout.

Michael knew his stock of snowballs had diminished and that he had to make a tactical retreat. He threw out a volley of two-handed throws and bent his head low running straight for a clump of pines. Having reached this safely, without having been tackled down to the ground, he realized that Matthew Gorda, having stood here recently found his last cache and exhausted it so now Michael was empty-handed and if he bent to pack new snowballs by hand, one by one, the other kids could rush him and knock him senseless. He ran like mad for the other side the house hoping to reach the ghauts. But his retreat was blocked by a solid line of children, emboldened by the lessening of his ferocious accuracy. Michael backed into the shed, and for the first time had been caught indoors, now the battle raged hand to hand and not with snowballs either. With a plastic rake, Michael parried blows from other garden tools, rakes, shovels, hoes. Some kids picked up logs of wood and rushed in a rage against Michael, now pressed into a corner. He desperately warded off most of the blows until a log smashed into his face, broke his nose with a splash of bright blood and knocked him through the shed wall, into the yard behind, down a hill, and he rolled downhill until he rested upside down against the stone wall at the street side.

With cries of dismay, with cries of "He's dead!" "We killed him!" and, "We have to escape to Mexico!" the children ran out of the yard and disappeared faster than would have thought possible into their own bedrooms and most did not emerge even when the next day of school began.

On Monday, expecting Michael to appear dressed for school, the grandfather suspiciously caught him leaving the house through a back door and drew in a sharp breath, horrified at Michael's face. His eyes were blackened, his nose crooked, though bandaged roughly and he carried his arms away from his body stiffly, scarecrow-like.

"Michael. Come back here."

Michael groaned, partly at being caught in his escape and partly at the effort in stopping himself and turning. He limped back into the hall.

"Your horse play has to stop. You look half-dead. What have you been doing?"

Michael smiled, ghoulishly, with his teeth rimmed red with blood, "Some of the other kids have it worse." His smile broadened even more with a burst of pride.

This day the school stood unfathomably empty and the teachers were mystified why this should be, until later in the morning when rumors of an epic snow battle waged over the previous two days reached them with sketchy details. The most prominent rumor being that kids from the larger town of Vallejo, with four times the population, had beaten the Napan kids to a pulp. But by the afternoon, they learned that Michael Hardy, by himself, had fought, humiliated and incapacitated the whole fourth grade, even a majority of the other children in the school, though at high cost to himself.

In her classroom in one of her infrequent visits to the school, Julia sat alone in her chair looking onto the desktop as if all were normal and as if not noticing anything amiss. At recess, having been ignored and seeing the school empty she returned to the house and busied herself in the kitchen.

Mimi McCarthy, a fourth-grader, had caught a ball of ice full in the face and chipped a tooth. Horrified at her appearance in the mirror, she cried in the bathroom until her mother called the police and made a report about Michael's attack on Mimi. So by the afternoon the grandfather opened the door to find the county sheriff, looking sheepish, explaining the activities of the previous weekend and trying to express his uncertainty at the novelty of this situation, "If word about this gets out, we'd have reporters from San Francisco at our doors. We'd be the laughingstock of America."

"I see," nodded the grandfather in a judge-like pose of deliberation.

"If Michael stays home from school for at least a week, unofficially, until we can sort things out, maybe we can escape this silly activity without reporters."

"Michael will stay home this week. We'll work this out," promised the grandfather and in this brief conversation, Napa chose to ignore the snow battle and Michael did not go to jail as the McCarthy family insisted. On the other hand, Michael never returned to the Napa public school system and soon he would like Julia be in need of a tutor.

Until this time Michael had been the most ordinary of kids, undistinguished in any way. But the first snowball attack, seeing the expressions of glee upon the faces of his opponents, had demarcated some part of him, set something apart that earlier had been fused whole and indistinguishable from any other part. Opposite the process how parts of an infant's skull are separate plates as a child and slowly fuse into the entire adult skull, some part of Michael began to fissure, split and he felt somehow set apart in a way he had not before. This being the first instance in which he was set apart as an outsider by a group to which he formerly belonged and the little noticed words of his grandfather about the family history now made more sense to him. These sensations of loneliness and ostracism felt vivid and painful, partly for their newness. So united were the Napans against him that their solidarity did not crack after the snows melted in the late spring. Not a single child supported him, spoke to him, all remained bitter and resolute in their shunning of the inhabitants of the Hardy house.

Jonathan Gunn

Julia and Michael get home schooling.

Following their earlier conversation about a tutor, Michael's absence from the school turned out to precipitate the hiring of Jonathan Gunn, the skeptic and agnostic who happily took over teaching duties in the house. While the grandfather patiently had taught Julia the basics of reading and writing, she had been easily frustrated and discouraged, especially in comparison to the speed and rapidity with which Michael mastered his lessons. As it turned out, Jonathan eagerly assumed the tasks of tutoring the very different pupils, and despite

Michael's vows to make life difficult for the tutor Jonathan found Michael not the difficult pupil, but Julia. She appeared disinclined to learn, to pay attention — only the threat of public school drove her attention from the window to desultory glances through a textbook. The first appearance of Jonathan in the study startled and frightened Julia so she hid under the rolling ladder against a wall of books.

"Julia, we can see you even if you don't look at us. Let me introduce Jonathan to you. He'll help Michael and you with lessons." But Julia stayed under the ladder with her eyes tightly closed. Eventually, after a few weeks of urging, Julia cautiously took to sitting at a library table, Michael at one end, attempting a few tries at the books.

"Let's try a more unorthodox approach with Julia," suggested the grandfather to Jonathan, "especially since home schooling gives us a bit more freedom in choosing curricula."

"What do you suggest?"

"That's up to you. Something unusual. Think it over."

During the first week of his new employment, Jonathan stayed on one evening for dinner with the household, nodding at Michael and the grandfather in turn, and only after beginning to eat did he notice the small black head level with the tabletop at the far end of the table. The head did not present a face to him. A small hand sought food on the plate and brought down the food to the invisible face beneath the table to be eaten.

The men at the table drank wine but the grandfather gave an inch of wine in a glass to the black-haired head and diluted the rest with a tumbler of water from a carafe. So the girl drank her wine diluted to the consistency of grape juice.

"Julia," motioned the grandfather, "won't you say hello to Jonathan." But after this introduction the face remained unseen and unheard, perhaps even bowed further at mention of her name. Jonathan chewed his own food thoughtfully. Only later as the meal finished in a pall of silence, did Julia once raise her head for an instant, and Jonathan could not help but release a short gasp of surprise, an intake of involuntary breath, at some kind of oddness in her quick glance, and the full effect of her strange expression, the smallness of her nose, the fullness of her eyelashes, and watery dark appealing deepness of her eyes, both the appearance of the eyes and a depth that those eyes invited, teased, and shut away. Julia merely looked up to smile at the grandfather but Jonathan felt a weird force in that glimpse of pained happiness.

The next evening, seeing the stranger again, Julia examined the man fully for a minute, with a watchdog expression, hurried out from behind her guardian, placed her forks and spoons and napkin on top of her plate and moved the ensemble to an empty place beside the grandfather. She climbed into her seat, and sat, remaining silent, unmoving, and looked upon her newly rearranged place setting motionless again.

Michael broke the silence by saying, "Don't try to take any of her food or she'll poke you with a fork. And don't try to take any dishes back to the kitchen. She'll bite you." He held up an arm as if this was proof of her perfidies.

Jonathan smiled, "I won't be here every meal." Then to Julia's unmoving head, "How old are you?"

Julia looked to the plate as if a deaf mute and made no answer. Months passed this way, and even if meeting in passageways Julia avoided his glance, backed out of rooms cautiously if one entered in the presence of another, and remained as mutely enigmatic as on that first day at the table.

Once Michael asked, "When will she go to school. Won't she go to college? Will she ever talk to people?"

"Oh, she'll come around by and by," excused the grandfather with a wave of his hand, an expression of unconcerned dismissal. "We have lots of time — she'll make up for lost time."

Jonathan was glad to leave Julia to completing projects that occupied lots of time independently, because managing Michael often shook his patience. One day he lifted an exam to ask, "What's this?"

"My answers."

Jonathan studied the paper, brought the sheet to a table and studied the numbers intently.

"It's customary if you use the octal system to designate this with a small lowercase "o." I don't want to convert all these numbers so in the future, Michael, would you please use the decimal system."

"The decimal system is so dull and I don't see why everybody has to count the same."

"Historical accident. The Babylonians — it doesn't matter. Western civilization uses the decimal system so for purposes of convenience we will use the decimal system too."

"Let's call this room a decimal-free zone."

Jonathan tapped the table top with the capped end of his pen, "With this tap I reconvert the room back into a decimal zone."

"You're no fun at all."

"You're absolutely right. But with math so fascinating all by itself, in itself, who needs to be entertained by a personality."

Michael smiled at this in full agreement so his answers from then onwards were decimal.

Despite the passage of time and her seeming, increasing level of comfort in the house, Julia continued to change her sleeping site. Though a room was nominally allotted to her, she had quickly forgotten which was hers and simply moved her belongings from one quiet place in the house to another — bags of onions, potatoes, a mass of blankets, coats, sweaters, recovered from the cellar bin of clothes like a nest of a collecting bird would follow beneath the stairs, in a closet, behind a settee or sofa, or amongst a pile of boxed and abandoned books.

One evening Michael once came upon her standing at the kitchen door, looking guardedly into the yard at back, as if for intruders, dressed fatly with clothes, a scarf wound around her head like a turban.

"Are you going to the Arctic?"

She ignored him and quietly retreated somewhere into the interior of the house and climbed into a hidden, untidy nest behind a sofa. He followed and saw her fold up blankets up to her chin so only her nose and mouth were visible, and the room turned to silence. He tiptoed out and the next night, when he checked, she had moved her belongings again.

Most often, he sensed, she slept in the root cellar which like the attic had long served as the depository for all the miscellany of a century's belongings. Jams and mason jars still unused, bulbs and bags of hanging garlic or peppers, hardware in labeled boxes, clothes, and photo albums. Despite the age and neglect, Michael could see that the room had been regularly dusted, cleaned, mopped, and the windows opened frequently so that it seemed a place unexpectedly cheerful and comfortable.

"Stay out of the root cellar," warned the grandfather when Michael relayed this information to him, "leave her some privacy." And by and large, mostly because of indifference, Michael did forget about Julia's eccentricities for weeks, even months at a time.

Pattering feet often tapped down the stairs and halls of the house, not furtive as if a ghost moaned through the walls but a cheerful patter, subdued and purposeful. The grandfather in particular seemed to enjoy this sound and often lowered his book as if to better hear the pattering, tapping like puffs, even to the muffled walls of the library.

Michael once felt a pang of mild jealousy, one day, seeing Julia appear at one end of the library trotting through to the other wearing an outlandish cap, made of a red handkerchief knotted at each corner, two knots in front and two in back. The grandfather looked up, "Are you a Russian washer woman?"

Julia stopped, instantly attentive at the notion of helpfulness, "Do you have warshing? I'll warsh it then." And the grandfather laughed. Michael shook his head and returned to the book.

In the morning Julia trotted to the kitchen and to her great surprise found a buttered bun on her plate, at her place at the table. Though the bun appeared each morning, in the same place, she nonetheless uttered the same short cry of pleasure and surprise that made the grandfather smile anew. And while chewing the bun, held with two hands and sipping the orange juice, the glass also held securely with two hands, considered with solemn deliberation the inevitable question asked of her at the same time each morning, "What would you like for lunch." And each day, pleasurably for both, ensued a discussion of all lunch possibilities. Fresh cow's milk, goat's milk, homemade cheeses, and jams, sandwiches made of home-cooked bread, as described by Julia, or soups born of myriad vegetables yet ungrown. Each morning passed pleasurably for both this way.

About this time came the scuffle of the mail carrier's steps on the flagstones outdoors, and waiting for the scuffles to recede, Julia fetched the mail and lay it upon a corner of the counter then helped to wash the breakfast dishes.

By the end of the next week Jonathan suggested that Julia illustrate a book by diorama. "This is how it works," he showed how by cutting a hole in the narrow end of a shoebox, "You fill in the shoebox with paper cutouts that you bend and paste to the bottom so they stand up." Julia set herself to work, first returning to ask, "What book do I tell the story of?"

"Any book that you like. Any book at all."

"I like the *Just So* stories." Jonathan helped her find jungle scenes in various books and encyclopedias and over the next few days, working into the evenings, Julia mastered the art of the scissors and completed her first assignment.

At breakfast the next day the grandfather asked, "What's in the box?"

She held up the box so he could see into the aperture.

"Why, it's a real jungle. How did you do that?" he asked in an astonishment that filled Julia's heart with an elation that grew until it burst out of her ears.

"I had to use scissors. They were hard."

The grandfather looked fixedly at her hands, ignoring the missing tips on her damaged fingers, "You're left-handed, by god, we should have got left handed scissors for you…" And so he did.

While Julia learned to construct dioramas, Michael had taken to homemade dissections, having caught several insects, worms and fish and, cruelly to Julia's mind, pinned open each specimen trying to learn the physiology and function of the internal organs, disappointed to learn how the clear and distinct drawings in anatomy books rarely corresponded to the greenish mess in the abdominal cavities of a fish, for example. He then set a snare for birds, but caught nothing, and wanting larger specimens resorted to buying cow hearts at a market in town and the brains of other animals.

At the week's end, after a long bout of concentrated labor, Julia presented her second diorama in shoebox to Jonathan, with small script written on the lid in an uncertain hand as title, "The three piggs." Inside Julia had pasted cuttings from magazines onto the far end of the box, opposite the eyehole, showing a pig in sty next to a picture of brick house. Most leftwards in the box as seen by the viewer, illustrations of food cut out from an old issue of *Gourmet* magazine and on the paper stand were the captions, "Mary the first pige. Killed by wolf. Pork chop." The second paper stand contained a piece of advertising — a slab of packaged bacon — with the accompanying label, "Emily second pigg." And rightwards in the box, set behind the other paper stands Julia had glued a pine cone to the bottom of the box, with a pair of anxious looking paper eyes pasted onto the cone, with caption, "Jennifer third pigge. Not eaten she hidd." Jonathan gave Julia an A+ for the assignment, at the same time feeling a twinge of uncertainty whether she and her shoebox should see the school psychologist but the grandfather said, *no*, the school psychologist would not be necessary.

On Thanksgiving, the grandfather announced, "Julia memorized a thanksgiving grace."

"What's a grace."

"It's a benediction."

"What's a benediction."

"What does the Latin translate into."

"Good....speech."

"So can you guess what Julia memorized."

"No."

"Then a benediction is exactly what Julia is about to say."

Michael nodded, exasperated, impatient.

Julia looking on the exchange with deliberation and

some bewilderment, refocused herself for the task at hand, face full of concentration at the plate, and spoke haltingly in her lispy voice, "God is great," she paused, recollected, let herself be washed over with a wave of apprehension and fear, changed the expression on her face, looked to the ceiling, continued, "God is good and we thank him for this food." She finished the last part in a rush. She had run out of breath and panted quietly at her place at the table.

"Ha," said Michael. "Food doesn't rhyme with good. We don't eat *fud*."

Julia bent her head lower and made herself nearly invisible at the table, feeling she had failed at her task. She said *fud* and not *food*. Despite the panting, she now held her breath and remained motionless for the duration of the meal. The only evidence of her emotion being that something invisible trickled down her face, which as usual she caught and held out of sight in the open palm of her hand.

The grandfather gave Michael a grade one stern expression, which made Michael back down, discomfited still merely by the glance.

"I'm sorry," he stammered to Julia, in answer to the glare from the grandfather. Yet the glare continued so Michael too must continue, "I'm sorry Julia. Your speech was very nice."

The gloom at the table lay heavy in the room like a fog, broken only in a few minutes when Julia's hand snuck out for a roll. She began to eat quietly, while Michael and the grandfather continued their duel of silent chastisement and atonement.

Many weeks later, the grandfather gently broached the subject of her education, and gave her the alternatives of returning to the public school, or continuing lessons with Jonathan. While happy to make dioramas, she only attended tutoring sessions in the library when asked directly.

Her lower lip began to tremble and she closed her eyes.

"Shall we try to learn with Jonathan? Public school?"

"But he helps Michael. And Michael is smart. And I'm dumb."

The grandfather looked at her askance, "How can you say that?"

"In the school, I got *effs*. And *effs* are bad."

"That school wasn't good for you. They didn't understand you. But we understand you here, don't we?"

She nodded.

"You won't do the same things as Michael. He is older than you. You do what you feel comfortable doing and Michael will do his own curriculum, whatever he feels comfortable with. Isn't that a fair arrangement?" After a prolonged debate with Jonathan and grandfather, from then onwards, Julia trudged daily to the library and began noontime lessons.

Julia's third diorama.

Another successful jungle scene.

When the viewer held up the shoebox and peered through the cut-out hole, one needed a moment for the eyes to adjust to the darkness within, then to see a profusion of jagged green paper shapes within, real grasses carefully glued to the foreground, mosses to the edge, in the background green paper cut out in the shapes of green-leaved trees and shrubs, brown wire twisted and glued with leaves as entangled vines, overhead a canopy of many carefully shaped leaves. Real twigs representing gargantuan tree trunks. Cellophane with blue inked lines shaped as a rivulet running side to side, pocked with stones. In the foreground directly staring at the viewer, Maggie the dog, intrepid explorer with black crayoned eyes full of courage, caution, and at the rightward edge, half-hidden behind a tree trunk, a black-haired girl furtively peeking out into the world beyond the box.

Jonathan would later teach Julia about valence using raspberries and white miniature marshmallows on toothpicks. To this day her conception of hydrogen was linked to sweetness and O_2 to the sour. She called molecules "the molyballs." But the sciences, the ruthless logic of *modus ponens*, eluded her or else she shook herself free from the ruthlessness and inevitability of the one-answer problems. She preferred to be a wild Jungle-girl, elusive in her kingdom of greenery who knew nothing of the molyball, who wore onions in woven neck wreaths like leis and leeks in her uncombed hair.

Jonathan did find success with her in several fields — botany being one when she was set to practical tasks, and also strangely enough he discovered her fascination with the healing process of the animal bodies — the molyball process of immunology, grafting in tree limbs, and starfish regeneration of limbs.

The grandfather craned his neck downward to see Julia trotting beside him as he carried a pair of shears to the tool shed, "What's up short stuff?" he said. He joked about her being short, especially in comparison to his lanky height but remained privately alarmed how she did not seem to grow taller since she first arrived at the house, though she was noticeably more healthy.

"Nothing. I mean, nothing special is happening today."

"You must want something in the world today. Look how nice it is," and he motioned with an expansive wave of his hand to the blooming beds of aphasia, mums, asters growing haphazardly but in lucky profusion. "It's such a good day you could make a diorama and capture the day in your paper."

"I could try," she offered, hesitantly, "I don't have paper of the same color as that blue. Sometimes I could try cellophane over a hole in the box lid. Then white paper in the diorama appears blue. One day I want to make a diorama like that. But it would be experimental."

"Something else you want besides blue cellophane?" he teased but she continued to shake her head doggedly.

He walked now more slowly, with his companion continuing to shake her head in absent-minded habit, and they paused once or twice so she could wheeze and catch her breath. The grandfather added, "I like to walk outside after the rain. The sky and the ground smells clean. The colors on every plant seem greener and they seem more bright." And to Julia, "What do you like?"

"Rain in the winter — it can feel cold and hurtful. The winter rain is wet. You can shiver."

"Now you wear raincoats and stay inside with your socks steaming, next to the fire in the grate."

"That is true. Now cold rains aren't so bad as they were. Then I do like more things now that I am older. I like to eat food with warm hands. I like to lie down in a sunny place and feel the sun on my face like warm water in a bath. I like to be in a safe place without dangers. That's all I want."

"Oh, I forgot," added the man, "I also like a good piece of rope that's folded up neatly. I like piles of warm laundry that have been sun-dried and are crisp to the touch."

"That's a good one to like. I wish I said that too," agreed Julia, putting her small hand unobtrusively in his.

He led her by the hand through the poplar grove, pointing out his favorite trees, those trees he does not like particularly, those trees that might grow into odd shapes, those trees in decline, to his favorite bench hewn long ago of a single piece of stone, but softened by a woven straw cushion. This bench was set on a grassy knoll, amongst tufts of yellowed grass, where they could sit together and look at mallard ducks flying by on their seasonal travels, who briefly touched down in the pond for a rest and bite to eat. Over a level field behind pond grew a carpet of bluebells, that hid Maggie's running form but not her barking. Julia seemed especially happy by this juxtaposition, seeing the field and Maggie's happy barking as if this were a sight beheld for the first time after a year of blindness, "This is *pretty*," she admitted with a touch of reluctance and she repeated the word as if savoring the tang of the word on her tongue. "Oh," she thought, "If I could live here for good," but she didn't mention her thoughts aloud.

Emboldened by the tacit acceptance of her word, *pretty*, she pointed excitedly to the knoll, "A cow could live there and you could have fresh milk," and her face turned up to glance shyly into his and the grandfather turned his face downwards, he to see not a greed or desire for a thing, but excitement as Julia seemed gladdened by the mere thought of a contented cow in pasture. He felt a pang, in some envelope in his heart, that beat strangely and movingly. As if Julia were clapping her hands in contentment at hearing about the good fortune of the yard for its possessing a cow.

Thinking ahead, and enlivened by a happy thought Julia ran away from the bench, down the knoll, and in a few minutes brought back a cold bottle of the grandfather's homemade beer. She pressed the bottle against her forehead to test the coldness and gave it to him with a happy smile. He thanked her and opened the bottle with its wire top, first giving Julia a sip, laughing at her grimace.

"You are so considerate," said the grandfather, "Thank you very much for the beer and for your thoughts about the cow!" Julia smiled, beamed, really, her whole face changed as the unnatural expression of a smile cracked up her usual solemn face. The grandfather thought to himself, Sometimes you seem like a regular little kid...

"You like cows?" he asked, with a mock seriousness.

"Cows have nice brown eyes that look sad. They don't try to bite you like a sheep does."

"How did you know that? Have you seen a sheep?"

"I read it in a story book. A dog walked through a sheep field and then a cow field. And the sheep tried to bite him, but the cows gave him a cup of milk."

"Cows do seem gentle and kind."

"Yes!" she exclaimed and looked upwards again, with craning neck as if in surprise that he would voice such unexpected sentiments, with mild surprise as if no one should be expected to entertain some similar thoughts as her own.

"Some people are cows," he added, "and some are sheep. What about him," he motioned to Michael who briefly opened the back door to fling some shoes out of doors.

"No. He is in the sheep field. But he might be in the cow field some time."

Coming at them at a lope, Michael appeared and motioned to Julia, asking, "Don't you have a key? The back door is stuck. Can I borrow the key?" And grasping the key around her neck, Julia looked back at him and then at the grandfather with an expression of consternation, part with fear that she had to relinquish her possession.

"You don't need the key. Go in at the front door if you insist," said the grandfather. And discretely, Julia returned the key inside her coat for safety.

After her painfully borne lessons, Julia hurried head down in haste, out of the room, books in hand, and after setting the books on the kitchen table for later scrutiny, she raced out of doors, Maggie limping behind, to revel in her natural environment — the yard, the ponds, the gardens and woods.

The grandfather came upon Julia fishing in the brook, sitting on a large boulder shaped seat-like at the stream edge, sandwich in one hand, tree branch fishing pole in the other, staring with great concentration on the piece of cork and line bobbing in the eddies and curls of water.

She had brought a glass of her water-diluted wine and the grandfather helped himself to a sip, wincing at the weak taste, almost sour with its watery flavor.

"What do you want to catch?"

Julia turned her head up, as if in the clouds she could see the answer. Then, "A fish?"

"What kind of fish?"

"Maybe a whale, one that strains out shrimp with its teeth."

"I guess you're studying whales now."

"And tunas."

"Do you have a hook and bait?"

She nodded her head negatively and seeing his mild perplexity, added, "I didn't want to hurt the fish if he ate the bait."

They sat in companionable silence for a few moments while Julia finished her sandwich, then deftly, shuttling pole to other hand, reached into her pocket and brought out, wrapped in wax paper, a large pickle. She offered the pickle, with both a shaking of her package and a nod of her head, motioning that he should help himself. But the grandfather nodded, *no*, and much of the afternoon passed this way with bobbling cork and the shared quietude, and time to time the crunch of the pickle in Julia's determined concentration.

"Maggie!" The dog raised its whiskered head, wet around the mouth. "Look at this! It's raining but my feet are dry! Look!" The sky gray, rain ceased, sun low, inert. Julia twirled in a circle, raising her hands, wearing a pair of gummed boots and a yellow oilskin coat. "Do you want to try the shoes too?" She held in one hand a soft yam, liberated from the kitchen, and she bit from the yam.

Julia shook her foot loose from a boot and busily

tried to fit Maggie's good leg into the boot, but Maggie struggled not to be shod. "Okay then, be wet."

Testing the seaworthiness of the boots, Julia sought out a deep puddle, and marched into the puddle and out, marveling at the working of the boot — then stepped in a freshet. True to her hopes the socks were not wet in the boots and she smiled to herself at her own good fortune.

The Mud Puppy.

Despite the grandfather's efforts, the Hardys had never known the date, even the year of Julia's birth, though estimated four or five years younger than Michael. One day while reading the newspaper, the grandfather set the paper down on a library table with a rustle, saying, "Do you know what day it is today?"

Julia rose and next to the calendar on the wall began counting with her fingers, losing her place, crossing her eyes and beginning again.

"No, not that way. I mean today is the day we'll celebrate as your birthday. Isn't today a good day?"

As a sign of her acceptance or doubt, they knew

not whether it was one or the other, Julia waved both her head side to side and shrugged her shoulders, as her way of noncommittally and cautiously agreeing to his notion. At receiving a nod from the grandfather, Michael groaned and trudged to the door where, opened, Julia saw a miniature sized bicycle, rakishly aslant as it rested on training wheels. Sprouting from the handlebars at each end were blue plastic streamers and attached was a horn with clay colored bulb.

She blinked her eyes at this, turned to Michael as if expecting him to claim possession, and seemed hurt at his refusal, "You don't know what this is anyway."

Some spirit of protest animated her as she stepped up and with a light touch, said in a muted voice, "This is a bicycle." And as if seeing the bicycle up close glazed over her eyes in a shock, the grandfather said, "Go on, take it out for a spin."

The tires were wide and knobby, a boy's model as she never seemed inclined to like girl's colors or items. The model name, called the "Mud Puppy," was emblazoned in paint on the main strut. Julia and Maggie both sniffed at the tire which had a new bicycle smell to it.

She rode in circles, endlessly, as if racing on a nightmarish bicycle course designed by M.C. Escher. When called in for dinner she rode once, twice, past the open door of the kitchen before their voices acquired a tinge of exasperation as if they want to eat and were willing to begin without her, and even hearing this exasperation Julia felt torn between dinner and the freedom of the road, weighing the possibility of hunger versus another mile around the yard.

The grandfather finally brought out a pot of stew to the table, and waved the lid to better strew the smells to the bicycle and this decided the issue for Julia who had never yet been late for a meal let alone considered the possibility of missing a meal entire. She left the bicycle on the back porch, upright on its training wheel fully in the middle of the doorway, and did not even walk all the way to the table without stopping to look back at it. She glanced up time to time to reassure herself that the bicycle remained safe and unstolen. When finished she stuttered first to the doorway and to the Mud Puppy when she remembered, belatedly, her duties as dishwasher.

"Go on," said the grandfather, "It won't kill Michael to wash dishes tonight."

As an indicator of her newly acquired love of the road, Julia actually devoted a moment or two, debating in her heart the fierce question of divided wishes, but her responsibilities in the household had never been taken lightly, adding resolutely, "I am the dishwarsher." Though slowed by the need to turn and run back into the kitchen to better keep a watchful eye on the bicycle, she finished washing and returned to the bicycle in time for an evening jaunt.

Many months passed pleasantly for Julia. As forager and gatherer she had prospered materially, collecting the detritus of interest to herself, though not to others, stored with great care in various cubbyholes on the grounds of the house and within the house itself. She often felt a need to refresh her memory by seeking out her caches and examining each item in turn. As a measure of her new found confidence she began haltingly to offer resistance to Michael's teasing and pranks, even, lip stuck out in defiance, scolding him and shaking a finger at his laughing tricks.

"How long is she going to stay here?"

"Exactly as long as she wants."

"When will she stop being frightened."

"Who knows. Patience makes the daisies grow."

"She is always shaking her finger at me, even before I do anything or say anything."

"Good for her. She is a courageous girl."

"A courageous girl? Ha. That's impossible."

"You don't think girls can be courageous."

"She's so little."

Now it was the grandfather's turn to laugh. Michael scowled. He had overheard Jonathan and his grandfather discussing the advantages of sending him away to a boarding school, with a more demanding program and social activity and felt dismissed.

Later in the afternoon, Michael played with Maggie, teasing her with a piece of cooked noodle, offering the tidbit and snatching it away again when the dog tried to grab a piece. Maggie barked with a short, sharp protest, and in response Michael kicked out his foot, catching Maggie in the ribs. A different bark — a yelp of pain — and instantly, from behind, Michael flew forward and hit his head upon the ground.

Julia had appeared from nowhere and rushed at Michael with all her might, not slowing at all, completely disregarding her own safety so she too hit her head upon the ground but she recovered first. Holding head in hand, she turned in a sitting posture to look first with anger, then bewilderment as Michael did not move. "Don't play more tricks," she warned with a shake of her finger. Even when she and Maggie prepared to leave and seeing Michael inert, did Julia return and look at the expression on his face.

Blood trickled out of his nose and his eyes were shut. Julia raised her head to the sky and let out a cry of anguish, much like Maggie's cry, and set out for the house, for the grandfather and her probable banishment from her shelter and home.

The grandfather couldn't make sense at first, of Julia's sobbing and explanations, hearing, "I killed him. He's dead. A potato or two. He's so dead. I'm sorry…"

"Who's dead?" Then, "Michael?"

Julia nodded, unable to meet his gaze.

"Show me."

Julia led him out of doors, to the path where Michael still lay in the same position.

She cried out again in a wail, "I didn't mean to kill him." Her lamentations abruptly ceased mid-sentence when with his grandfather's hand in the small of his back, Michael sat upright again with two hands over his eyes.

"Oh. My head," he said.

Julia's mouth dropped open.

Michael turned at the waist and regarded Julia with a new found expression of something almost like respect, and smiled with the corners of his mouth upraised, saying groggily as if in sleep, "She could play professional rugby."

"She thought you were dead. She wanted to go to the police."

Michael explained to the grandfather how she acted to protect her dog.

Both turned to look at Julia, who stood, eyes downcast disconsolately to the ground, arms held stiffly to the side. And only after they began to laugh at her did she raise her face again, confused at the turnings and abrupt reversals of her fate today, first in one direction and then another.

Asters and roses.

In the following week the grandfather left on one of his periodic trips to San Francisco, in this case he absent-mindedly used Julia's language to say as she did that he'd go into the world "where there's murders and mayhems," making the usual arrangements with Jonathan to spend mornings and afternoons at the house and for Bernard to spend a few hours with Julia in the evening. In this way, though uneasy in mind, Julia had become gradually acclimatized to the prospect of the grandfather not on the grounds of the house, which was of course one of the major reasons for these trips.

To Jonathan he explained, "She doesn't leave the

grounds of the house. She refused to see a baseball game, to shop, to visit any other town. And I fear if I dropped dead one day, she would take it badly."

Michael, on the other hand, encouraged his grandfather to embark on these journeys, in part for the freedom from the all-seeing, all-knowing presence of the grandfather, and knowing from experience that a trip to San Francisco meant a return laden with presents and odd purchases.

Now having returned, Michael scrambled into the house, up the stairs, and found Julia still greeting the grandfather by pressing her cheek against the leg of his pants and shyly wrapping each of her short, shrunken arms around his pant leg. Michael would do none of those things, he merely looked in several directions for the gifts.

"Alright Michael." The grandfather shook himself free of Julia's embrace and gave her a package. Shaking his head, he motioned to several packages on the tabletop for Michael. Opening the first, he groaned, seeing shirts and other clothes. And equally a groan at seeing in the second a pair of shoes.

"This is terrible. Terrible!" Michael grumbled.

But his prospects improved when in the third, he lifted out a heavy wooden box, then a second, identical wooden box which, opened, revealed a solid, impressive looking microscope. "It's a good one," he said with approval. "But why did you buy two of them. I can only use one."

"The other is for Julia."

"But she'll never use it!" he complained.

"Michael. Whether she uses it is entirely up to her

but I doubt you could share one if I had bought only one." Even Michael had to admit the soundness of his grandfather's reasoning. In the remainder of packages were several score books and school supplies. Having enjoyed the sorting and arranging of the new supplies, he turned and said, "She hasn't moved at all. She hasn't even opened one package. It's un-American!"

Indeed Julia had remained rooted to the spot beside the grandfather clutching two-handed the first package he had given her.

"Open it," they urged. And Julia shaking her head as if rising out of a trance, looked confusedly at them both, then to the package as if disbelieving that the package was for her. In fact, she offered the package to Michael, who snorted through his nose, "It's not mine." Then as he prepared to gather his loot and leave, "She does this every time."

The grandfather nodded, not to Michael but to her, as Julia carefully undid the wrapping on the package and glanced at the clothes within. And the grandfather confessed, "I had to ask a saleswoman for help. But she gathered up everything she thought you'd like to have," and he motioned to his desk, piled high with more packages — and neatly, calmly, found within socks and girls underwear, gloves, sweaters, even a dress, which she eyed partly with skepticism and disbelief, stockings, tights, and a large brimmed straw hat. In another package were games and puzzles, packages of construction paper, artist's tools, and a jigsaw puzzle, a dog collar for Maggie and new food dish, each with her name painted on in cursive writing, for Julia again a watch, shoes, and, to her approval, a pair of small, but heavy duty work boots, a necklace made of chewy candy, a plastic pipe with white handle and pink bowl suitable for blowing soap bubbles. And so on, incredible riches. In the last package, packets of seeds with a set of gardening tools and against the wall, motioned the grandfather, a Julia-sized rake, spade, and hoe, with green painted splines or blades.

Julia said nothing, somewhat overwhelmed and both males in the house laughed at her expression and the mixture of emotions plainly visible in her face as she began gasping for breath. First in one hand and another, she looked at the labels on the seed packets, "Radishes," read one, "Pumpkins" the other, and many others neatly tied in a fat bundle. On top, bulging with the string bisecting the label, "A child's flower garden." On the other side of the bundle, "Tomatoes."

Again Julia leaned her cheek against the grandfather and remained silent, in part staring furiously at the grey-white hairs in his ears and the bushy eyebrows that nearly met across his forehead. Eyebrows of white fluffiness. Still laughing in their usual way, the grandfather shook her free again and motioned that she carry out the parcels, "Go away! Put away your things." And Julia did so, feeling overwhelmed with a surge of contentment, a surge of gratefulness.

In the afternoon, spade and trowel were already put to use and Julia, having studied the directions on the packets very carefully, with borrowed ruler had measured the depth of each seedling, damping back the earth she had upturned. Satisfied at having followed the recipe, having liberally watered the patch, she rounded up a lawn chair and sat at her garden periphery as if to wait the months needed for the blooms, keeping her eyes, silently, focused onto her furrowed ground.

Upstairs, Michael covered his mouth and laughed to himself, while the grandfather standing behind slapped him on the head, motioning that he keep quiet, as both watched throughout the afternoon, as Julia remained rooted, as it were, to the spot in her chair, looking to the instructions again time to time as if expecting instantly that the magical garden would sprout, perhaps as quickly as the tales she read about Jack and beanstalks.

Near midnight, the kitchen door clicked open and Julia peered out, head only, looking in one direction and another, then seeing no one about stepped quickly down the steps in borrowed shoes, too large, and hurried to the patch of ground she recently tended. She knelt at the patch. From a pocket she brought out a flashlight and with two hands pressed at the switch. And with this beam of light she bent low again to examine the furrow of radish, yet seeing nothing no matter how low she bent. Sighing, she pressed the flashlight to shut, and trudged with scuffling sounds from the shoes to the door and shut the door behind her, giving the handle a reassuring shake from the inside. Bernard had once left the kitchen door open after leaving for the evening and Julia in her insomnia discovered this with a great sense of fright and the next day had reproved him with a barely audible voice, hardly daring this imposition but so worried about the lapse of security that she felt compelled to speak, "The door was open yesterday at night."

Luckily for Julia, the radishes sprouted first, rapidly,

and only within a week did the first green ribbons poke out above the very carefully tended earth, unfurling a bit more each day as if with a flourish of arms. Julia frequently lay on the ground studying the process, not as biological specimens, as Michael would, but as living and tender creatures which needed sustenance and tending. For this reason, for her own private reasons, the need for the radish nurturing and protection aroused a great deal of anxiety within her, so that sitting at the dinner table, focused elsewhere, both grandfather and Michael could see her brows knitted and mouth tightened in silent concentration on the radish plot beyond the door.

She studied the sky for omens, built a lean-to for shade which could be temporarily moved as the sun moved if she felt the sun too hot for the green fragilities. She dreamt, the grandfather mused, of radishes.

Thus with some relief sitting on his bench several weeks later, Julia sat beside the grandfather and presented to him in the palm of her tiny hand, a runty radish smaller than an eyeball with something almost like reverence so that her lip trembled as she averted her eyes while presenting her gift.

He accepted the radish and with pocketknife trimmed the reddish hull and cut into pieces, gave one piece to Julia and ate one himself. In this way in the following weeks, with her pocketfuls of harvest presented individually or at dinner time, they ate the fruits of the vegetable packets with a great sense of accomplishment, and if the grandfather tired of eating the bitter vegetables he gave no sign. Julia herself had given no indication of her first reaction that morning when, deciding the time had arrived for the harvest, with a sharp, decisive tug on the first radish, held aloft she then burst out in an ebullient dance of joy, held at arm's length above her head, she twirled beneath the radish in a herky-jerky spontaneous moment of celebration.

Harvests of broccoli, celery, squash and pumpkins followed, first in small quantities, then increasing so that in the years to come the household would never lack for vegetables. Silently, without speaking of it, Julia felt for the first time she contributed directly to the household economy and with each successive year maintained a studious and dedicated effort to providing these vegetables. If she worried, even a decade later that she might be turned out of house if a harvest failed, she never gave a sign, but the garden plot grew in size until a decade later plots had consumed most of the land in back, and she could sell her surplus for a hefty profit.

She had strewn the *Child's Garden* seeds in a fallow plot near the grandfather's bench and in spring the bench acquired a nimbus of gold and red, of gladiolus and mums, and on the cow field a profusion of cheerful daisies. Thus what had been a neglected yard for the book reading pair, with Julia's efforts transformed itself in the successive years to a blooming field of Julia's pride and an expression of her glories, and appreciation, and grateful thanks.

Julia's undersea world.

Julia presented her week's homework to Jonathan. She spent an inordinate amount of time on her current diorama. Made from a larger than usual boot box, the box top had an unusual addition, a twistable lid made from a plastic pickle bottle lid, so when turned in one direction or another by the viewer, on top, the contents in the middle of the box also turned within the box. Inside an undersea view — in the foreground, seaweeds and long eelish grasses falling vertically and undulating, and beyond the grasses brown kelps with bell-shaped flowers, and flat, pickled leaves. Suspended from the lid and free to perambulate when the lid turned, beautiful translucent blue jellyfish and an octopus with arms so light and gauzy they flew up animated when twirled, golden perch with eyes open with wonder, a whale, not to scale, drawn as if swimming furiously with body twisted with effort.

"That's a very wonderfully drawn scene, Julia," conceded Jonathan. He wrote in red pen on the lid, "A + +."

"That's the first A plus plus I ever got," gushed Julia later, when showing the diorama to Maggie. "Once I got an A plus, but this was a specially good diorama." Maggie nodded.

Another of the grandfather's successful presents, compared to the failure of tennis racquet and archery set, Julia hating weapons, was a homemade moccasin kit where she could and did carefully trace her foot on the supplied paper and cut out a moccasin to fit her foot and with supplied awl, stitch together the suede components for the finished shoe. Julia would in fact all her life long, continue to buy these kits though the mail and would supply her own footwear.

No matter how numerous the exercises or rudimentary or complex the arithmetic, Julia persisted in counting or figuring with her fingers, perhaps as a sign of lack of confidence. But she was proficient enough, Jonathan reported to the grandfather. Jonathan had learned in time that more concrete details made lessons easy for Julia to comprehend. After illustrating addition, subtraction, later multiplication and division and soon algebra, illustrated with examples of buying fruits and vegetables from a mythical store named Fruitland, Julia gave a spirited demonstration at dinner one night of her newfound abilities to figure tax rates.

"You can give me a fruit to buy and I can figure out the tax for you," she offered.

"Alright then," answered the grandfather, looking to the ceiling for inspiration. "I heard that Fruitland has a special sale on apples."

"What kind?"

"These are Granny Smiths. They cost forty cents per pound."

"That seems high. I thought you said they were on sale."

"That's right. I forgot," he conceded, "The vegetable manager made a mistake, the correct price is twenty cents per pound."

Julia looked concentrated and thoughtful, hesitant at correcting the grandfather, "That seems low."

The grandfather threw up his hands, "Fruitland apples cost thirty cents." He waited and was gratified to see Julia's head nod in approval.

"We need ten pounds."

"That means," Julia frequently copied the grandfather's habit of looking to the ceiling while reckoning figures, "The subtotal is three dollars."

"That's exactly right. And the tax is five percent."

Her fingers work and rather quickly and pleasing to the grandfather the result was returned, "Tax is fifteen cents and the total is three dollars and fifteen cents."

"That is exactly right."

Julia's face reddened with pride and she ate the rest of her dinner in a pleased and flushed state of euphoria.

"You know, I had been thinking, I wonder if you

could do me a favor." Her head shot upward, all ears, at this possibility."

"We sometimes order our groceries by phone, you know, or by leaving lists in the cubbyhole for deliveries in the wall outside." In the indifferent manner of the grandfather and Michael who have never bothered to shop for food and before Julia's arrival had occasionally run out of food and were helpless and uncertain about how to deal with this dilemma, the grandfather had years earlier happened upon the happy practice of establishing a weekly account at the O'Dell grocery store in town, and a regular delivery was made to a basket beside the house gate.

"Would you order and figure the accounts for us?"

Julia nodded her head vigorously. And seeing this the grandfather brought out a packet from his pocket, "This is yours too. I opened a bank account for you. I told the O'Dells that you can order all the food you want for us. That way, Michael and I can better devote ourselves to the nothing that we do."

Julia agreed, and this responsibility expanded her world greatly and became a responsibility borne, not heavily, but with solemnity and careful attention to detail. This was a fortunate decision for all, as suggested by Jonathan who narrated in detail Julia's very practical bent for numbers. She proved, too, a shrewd negotiator and had a good nose for bargains. The O'Dell store soon acquired what they called the Julia price, which was below retail and near the wholesale value of their goods, as Julia on occasion ventured into the store to establish costs and lists, bent on driving a good bargain for the grandfather, and frequently argued down the prices of goods, not with

Mrs. O'Dell who learned to flee at the sight of the small but defiant Julia trudging along the road, wire basket in hand, but from her daughter Madeleine who was first amused, thinking Julia five years younger than what the grandfather regarded her relatively true age. In time Madeleine looked forward to the bargaining sessions with great enjoyment, bouts to be anticipated and savored.

Learning the useful combination of savings when buying in bulk, Julia would at times stagger home under the weight of fifty cans of fruit juice, a favorite of the grandfather's, or forced to drag behind her, as if dragging a sled, whole boxes of spaghetti or some grocery which she was yet unable to make, grow, or create herself.

Julia's expertise with coupons became adroit and exact. She explained to the grandfather who expressed bewilderment at seeing her open a pouch filled with sorted coupons, "A coupon is no good if it makes you buy something that you won't use and sometimes a coupon lures you to buy something that is priced higher in the first place. So you have to be careful."

Madeleine O'Dell used the time, as Julia inevitably examined the store receipt closely, not trusting the register, to examine in turn the wonderfully eccentric shopping girl.

By this time Julia had grown somewhat but remained small for her demeanor and seemed younger still by several years than her true age. She still walked with a self-conscious limp, and tended to move slowly perhaps to better disguise the limp. She spoke rarely to others except to inquire about a price, and had never spoken a needless word in the O'Dell store. Naturally in the small town rumors swirled incessantly about the private Hardy clan who alone among those long-timers in the town had no regular dealings with others, except with the chess-playing doctor, Bernard Rush. Only a vague remembrance of the snow battle remained ten years ago and out of sight the Hardys mostly remained out of mind.

On the other hand, Rudy Waters, grey-haired owner of the hardware store, easily wilted under pressure of Julia's cow-eyed, insistent bargaining. "Aiya!" he'd groan, part in appreciation and enjoyment, handing to her packets of flower seeds, lent her tools right off the wire racks on the wall, despite the sign above the rack, "No Tools to Lend." Julia, on the other hand, remained careful to bring back each tool, punctual and clean, those tools needed only on occasion such as post hole diggers. He carefully preserved boxes for her which could be made into dioramas. She suspected that Water's motives were not entirely altruistic, in her suspicious way, but why he would behave so remained out of her ken. She simply accepted his largess with appreciation.

In front of a mirror Julia did not recognize her own reflection. On seeing a scrap of magazine advertisement she did not comprehend that the perfume model was related to her in any biological way. The hand that held the diamond jewelry was not related to the same species of reddened and dirtied hand so lately dipped into a good, rich steer manure. Julia often wore boys clothes into town, and a wide brimmed hat, and her face and arms, scrubbed haphazardly from bird bath beside the gate before running out of the gate, were usually smudged and grimy.

Though she wore the castoffs of the Hardy men,

past and present, she came to buy new clothes for the grandfather and Michael as she saw fit, as manager of the household, and though her judgments of wear might have seemed old-fashioned to a modern American consumer in California of the time, her subjects were equally indifferent. Julia had become a firm believer in quality, saying once to the grandfather, "The clothes I buy have to last a hundred years for the next poor girl who'll live here after me." She had judged good quality more worthwhile in the long run than cheaper goods, tempting though they might be, having thrown away many of Michael's sneakers quickly, seeing them unrepairable. Lately she had taken to buying goods via mail order, though she trusted and preferred cash, since some of the better goods she wanted were not in town and she remained unwilling to travel. Having mastered the checkbook and credit card receipts, the abstractions of the accounting balanced her relief at not venturing into the town. Plus, she ferreted out a bargain equally well by mail, and counted herself lucky to discover on occasion she saved by mail order in not having to pay the state tax.

The grandfather watched through the window as Julia appeared, lugging a pail of peas, one shoulder bent lower than the other under weight, and sat on a brick in bright sunlight, shucking the peas. She had wet a cabbage leaf and placed this on her head as hat, and while he watched, with the patience of Job, the sun altered course and Julia then in shade ate her hat, and continued with her shucking until the content of pail had lightened to empty air.

While Julia shucked peas, indoors Michael set down

his book with a thunk, moved, excited at his reading. The passage from DeFoe's *Journal of a Plague Year*,

> *...it might be distinguished by the party's breathing upon a piece of glass where, the breath condensing, there might living creatures be seen by a microscope, of strange, monstrous and frightful shapes, such as dragons, snakes, serpents and devils, horrible to behold.*

He ran downstairs to find his microscope and a glass slip, hoping to infect himself with the plague, holding hope of seeing the frightful shape beneath the cover slip.

Julia had never taken well to book learning, but this was not for lacking intelligence. Book learning was simply not in her element the way a duck would not naturally take to wearing a coat and tie. The lessons were borne well, and had become amiable enough to her, comfortable in time with Jonathan's oddnesses and eccentricities, especially if she brought in a snack or two during a tutorial, but her heart wasn't particularly engaged in lessons, especially when compared as inevitably she was compared to Michael whose abilities were prodigious, who liked nothing better than to sit motionless on a bench, turn inward and parse some argument in his own seething mind. And Michael needed no snacks.

Perhaps her book learning was stunted on the very first day of Jonathan's tutorials when in her first attempt at public spelling she spelled *pig* on the diorama, with three g's, and Michael's laughter caused her a great pang of distress and embarrassment. She sat back in her chair and stared miserably at the child's dictionary to discover her mistake. Later she also came to regret her spelling of pige, pigg and pigge.

While Michael was learning differential equations and integrals, Julia remained at a stage where she happily made dioramas out of shoeboxes and colored paper, illustrating the animal and plant kingdoms. "I wonder," Jonathan once said to the grandfather, "She knows the answers but parts with them reluctantly. As if she doesn't want to give anything to anybody, and seems to feel that it's best or safest to live as a dumb mute."

In time Jonathan simply acknowledged that Julia learned in a different mode than Michael and on the grandfather's suggestions, taught them differently at least while Michael remained at the house.

Jonathan began to work with both Julia and Michael on natural selection and its evolutionary consequences. In the pedagogical method he adopted over time, by trial and error, he taught the same subject to both, using different modes. Michael learned genetic theory and selection in abstract depth, while Julia made experiments using the same wrinkled and smooth-leaved pea plants once used by Mendel himself. Michael brooded over the lessons silently, working out consequences of selection on human behavior, and wrote several lengthy reports, while Jonathan arranged for Julia to calculate statistical results much as Mendel had done and conclude her report with an extravagant diorama. She nodded her head at hearing the explanation of heredity. She knew this already by her experience in the garden, instinctually, but had trouble with the genetic mechanisms which were harder to visualize on human scale. Jonathan had acquired patience enough, though, and decided to wait a year for the discussion of the special molyballs DNA or RNA.

"This is my last day on the library bench," Michael said at the afternoon's end. Tomorrow he would venture into a boarding school.

"You will fare well," said Jonathan.

Michael shrugged his shoulders.

"You've sucked out all the knowledge from my brain. All I have left — that you haven't soaked out of me — are some Childe ballads and Gershwin songs. The silly ones with the moon-swoon rhymes."

"I can't wait to go. The school has a big library."

Michael went away to a private school in New Hampshire. Julia briefly glimpsed him wearing the blue coat and gray wool pants of the school uniform and then he was gone. He often wrote and told his grandfather that he meant to return home at holidays, but eventually years passed and Julia felt she was not fated to meet him again. The grandfather, on the other hand, visited the school several times per year.

Michael Hardy on this last day at home, the grandfather decided, had grown too proud and austere, sometimes rather unpleasant and scornful too. He was undeniably intelligent, though perhaps narrow-minded and focused as a consequence of his energies that burned brighter with a sharper focus. Perhaps he behaved so because of the social isolation of the household, and that he had fewer interactions with others that might have softened his brittle edges. Julia once said to the grandfather that she thought "Michael's shoes were tied too tight," and he laughed.

Abhorring sentiment Michael barely paused to wave goodbye to those two people who had shared several years of sequestered though pleasant solitude. Twisting around at the train station he merely nodded his head, saying, "See you," and said nothing at all to Julia. Then was gone. Julia would not see him again for eight years.

On the occasion of her eighth springtime in the gardens she stopped in the same spot on the path where she once stood in the wreath of whirling leaves to reflect upon the changed circumstances of her life. With Maggie standing between her feet, she mused, "Oh Maggie. Think how different our lives have been. Just think how down a different path we could have gone."

Maggie nodded her head sagely, sharing the sentiment.

Rain.

Constantly busy in her maintenance tasks, the moving, cutting, hedging, washing, snipping, pruning, and eating, fully occupied the eight year expanse of time since Michael left the house in Napa. Julia busied herself in part to overcome a deep dragging down of feeling at sensing Michael's absence. She did not believe she would miss him much — he had been more of a tormentor and teaser than kind, more capricious than thoughtful.

Her task immediately at hand was to replace the babiche seat on an old side chair. The grandfather, moving more slowly these days, with eyebrows even more bushy if possible, had thrown out the chair because the wicker seat had torn, and also in fact because he had never liked it. Julia, inspecting the garbage with her usual thoroughness cried out, "This is just right for me!" When the mail order replacement strips arrived, she set to its repair.

She wove the straps into a mat then wove the straps again into the lattice of the frame. Her first attempt using only glue failed. When testing the seat, the straps gave way and she fell through, wedged firmly into the seat frame. On a second attempt she believed that stronger glue, thin nails and thorough weave would hold and smiled at her own efficiency. Lowing herself onto the chair tentatively, this time the straps held. The seat now good as new. She had tightened the wicker interweave rigorously and believed it would hold for at least twenty years, long enough to serve the next girl that would live here at the house. The grandfather came into the tool shed, waiting quietly while Julia methodically put away her tools, tidily, each into its accustomed place. They walked out together towards the kitchen door.

"You shouldn't be too upset when I tell you this," said the grandfather in way of preamble and he shot a glare at the chair reappearing in the house, "but I've got to go to the hospital." Julia was not upset because she had expected this. She was oblivious to matters which did not concern her — fashion, current worldly events, matters of good breeding or etiquette such as the distinction between soup spoon and the salad fork. Rather her attention was thrown completely upon those few matters which touched upon her life or the life of the grandfather; central of these the health of the grandfather whom she observed avidly. And the signs of illness were unmistakable though she lacked training or experience. Small hesitations, a flash of pain in his face on rising or walking. A pensiveness and hesitation before speaking. Since Michael finished his prep school and enrolled at a university, the grandfather remained a massive and kindly presence in Julia's life, upon which she fixed her entire attention, and she did not like the tone of signs she could read as easily as the signs of weather or the health of her tomatoes. The consequences of this were unimaginable, and horrific, but not unexpected. By this time, after all, the grandfather was over eighty years old.

The first visits to the hospital for chemotherapy required at most a few outpatient visits. But this second month he was required to move into a hospital room for more than a single weekend. Julia had dutifully ferried his pajamas and books, and his old armless bathrobe, from house to hospital on hour-long walks, the same bathrobe which donated its sleeve to Julia at her car accident many years earlier. Within a month his condition had worsened and he was to be moved by helicopter even further from home, to a cancer institute in Palo Alto. This was the first time in ten years that Julia had to leave the Napa city limits, and she collected her belongings for the helicopter journey. Jonathan had received voluminous instructions on the care and feeding of Maggie, which amounted to one can of dog food per day and fresh water. In fact, her preparations came to naught. The Hardy family's grandfather died quietly in the town hospital without fuss.

He had lived from near the turn of the century to the present day, fought for civil rights, presided over the change of law in the passage of decades, then spent the last fifth of his life in near silence, tending gardens with the tiny Julia, who arrived in his life unexpectedly and who became the best comfort in his last years.

Michael reappeared barely in time to greet his grandfather from behind a hospital window and remained in town only until the day of his funeral. At this time Michael had not been polished by Eastern coast culture. If anything his appearance was more scruffy, his lips curled into a sneer, his manners more gruff. He retained an abhorrence of sentiment and would not admit to possessing feelings or emotions. Made dizzy and faint by the antiseptic smell and glare of sharp fluorescent light during his first and single visit to his grandfather in the hospital, he could not bear to sit for even five minutes in the ward and refused to return, staying in his old bedroom though not appearing for meals.

Julia's last conversation with the grandfather had nothing of the mighty or significant in it, and had she known it would have been her last moments with him, she might have prepared a speech, tried to sum her appreciation or thankfulness. Instead they talked with animation and affection about the current tomato crop. They talked about Michael and how he was doing in school. He had asked her, "Would you like to visit him at his school?"

"He lives far away."

"You can help him. He'll need help."

Julia laughed at this.

"Ahh, but you can help," he said. "Would you promise me that one day you'll visit him and help him?"

"But why would he stay away from the house. Nobody would stay away for long. Our house is so wonderful."

"Oh, you know Michael, he doesn't appreciate things as they deserve. He'll be lost for a few years or a few decades. But you can bring him back to his senses."

"I can't bring anybody to their senses."

"You are, both, responsible for each other."

She looked at him quizzically, uncertain, and part disbelieving.

The grandfather's funeral attracted little attention. A short obituary. But Julia would have preferred this had she a choice. For the service indoors at the town cathedral, Julia tied up Maggie with a piece of string brought from the house, and tied the end of the rope to a spigot, allowing Maggie the reach to lie in a shady spot on the grass nearby if she wished, and took out her water bowl from a floppy bag. After fussing with her companion, she learned that she missed the service entirely, so rescued Maggie from her confinement. They walked together in melancholy thought to the cemetery, a peaceful and leafy place. While the burial service took place, Julia walked with Maggie past rows of cypress and the rows of neat markers, each a dry stone symbol of such emotion and feeling buried into the ground. Then remaining in the background, with Maggie panting from the exertions of their walk, Julia found a leafy branch and fanned the dog with heaving chest.

Jonathan looked thoughtfully, as he paused in his eulogy, as he recalled, oddly enough, an image of Julia's little bird-like hands carefully counting out shrunken peas into piles of equal number, so carefully as if great consequences depended upon the result. The difference between his two students seemed never so magnified as now. He could see her lurking at the far edge of his vision, partly hidden at times by a family's stone crypt or skirted among the cypress.

From their perch near the cypress, Julia pressed her mouth flat in an expressive gesture, suppressed, and said to her companion, "That was such a nice funeral. I'd like a funeral like that one. No one was fighting." Then uttered a quiet, "Oh, oh," seeing Michael break free of a group of sympathizers and heading in her direction. However, he was intercepted by a shrill looking old woman whom she did not recognize. This woman grabbed Michael roughly from behind and began berating him loudly, so that Julia could hear the hostility in her voice but could not differentiate the words.

Julia sighed, "I guess there was fighting after all."

This woman was Michael's old aunt Katherine, on his mother's side, who had attended the funeral purely out of spite and to vent the rage she felt for twenty years since the death of Michael's mother, "I waited," she howled, "I waited all these years for vindication. Vindication! It is!! That man dead! Look at the problems you've inherited by growing under the influence of that man." Onwards she droned, not releasing her grip on his arm. Michael looked upon her without emotion and said at the end only a few words, the last he would speak to herself or her family, "Goodbye, Aunt." She turned and made a gesture something like a dog throwing dirt behind itself.

Julia had brought Maggie in tow, and hid behind one of the canopy poles, as if the inch thick pole could obscure herself and dog. She felt a morbid sort of fascination at Michael's appearance, having not seen him for years, though keeping his old image in mind throughout the interval, now startled at seeing the same presence in person.

His visage to Julia seemed frightening. She knew innately that he had increased his reading, increased his introspection, of unchecked and undiminished naked consciousness which she avoided herself by playing with Maggie or long immersion in weeding and fish emulsion. His eyes were black, rather then the Hardy brownness, speckled with orange, which she used to look into and admire as a smaller child, seeing the same inflections in the grandfather's eyes. She felt uneasy in the presence of this blackness, because his eyes, despite his glance directed towards her from across the gravestones, seemed closed to her and thus she did not know what kind of person he had become inside the older appearance he now possessed.

So to her relief Michael did not return to the house that evening. He caught a ride to the airport and returned directly to his college. She did not speak to him or was required to look at the stone façade of his face again. He did not say a word to her during his brief return home. She thought, "Better this way. Better to part in silence. He would have put gum in my hair or laughed at my dioramas." At the same time some part of old Julia came back to life and she relived her life, especially the first days of her life at the house, beginning in the wreath of leaves and earlier, and she felt as if she were breaking apart again, that the carefully preserved fragments of herself were breaking apart again and fissuring. Feeling anguished that Michael was angry with her, and he being possessor of the house and grounds, she intuited that he wanted her to leave. Feeling shocked and startled at this realization, Julia sadly climbed into the triangular space beneath the stairs, and arranged a blanket around herself, and fell asleep among the sacks of potatoes and onions.

Bernard Rush held his infrequently used briefcase in one hand, and put up another hand to wipe sweat from his forehead, and after a few yards paused to wipe his forehead again, each time switching his black leather case from hand to hand and walking up the road's grass-trodden shoulder and occupied himself in this way until he paused at seeing an approaching figure, vaguely familiar, on the other side of the road leaving the house. He nodded once in an absentminded, friendly though generic greeting, continued his forehead wiping then abruptly stopped as if jolted back with a chain, and turned his head again to his walking neighbor.

"Julia, wait! Where are you going?"

Julia had been walking past him on the road's opposite side, in the opposite direction, wearing a canvas coat, walking boots, and in both hands carried a sack bulging with some packed goods, potatoes, sandwiches, dried apples. On her head was a wide brimmed straw hat. She set down one of her bags, and waved a small white palm at him, in a wagging way, then picked up the bag again. Maggie appeared behind her having paused to sniff a roadside marker and hurried up again.

"Hey!"

Her eyebrows rose, and she squished one side of her lips against the other, in an expression of questioning.

"I'm on my way to see you. Where are you going?"

She pointed to a direction straight down the road, in a gesture that meant, he divined, anywhere, nowhere in particular.

"Great good God! I was on my way to see you this minute! And where would I have found you if we hadn't met here? Did you think you had to leave the house?"

"It is Michael's house now and yesterday he was angry at me. He didn't even want to talk to me."

She seemed to speak reluctantly, as if embarrassed at explaining herself, "I wrote a letter to the Sonoma nursery, and I asked for a job. They hadn't answered yet so I have to ask in person. I will try to find a place to live when I find work too." Her body shook at this thought. Her voice both brave and frightened at the same time. "Maybe I could find an orphanage or I could wash dishes."

Bernard opened his case with a pleasing snap of the clasp and rummaged through the papers within, "The grandfather spoke to you, I'm certain, he's said repeatedly to me that he did, that he would tell you he'd leave the house and the grounds to you. He did so. Here are the papers. You own the house. You own all of the property."

Julia wasn't listening. She felt too miserable.

"Stop. Sit down. I mean it. Sit down right here. You're not going anywhere. That would be a disaster. What if I missed you by five minutes?" Bernard put a gentle hand on her shoulder then held her still by a single finger.

Julia did not raise her hands to accept the papers. Instead, as if to steady her own hands, from a bag she took out a sandwich which she offered half to Bernard.

"Let's go back to the house. I insist. You don't need to wash dishes in an orphanage because I suppose you are now the richest woman in Napa county." She seemed, not relieved, not happy at this news, and Bernard had to actively restrain himself so strongly did he want to put his arms around her, but he also felt she would be alarmed or frightened at a sudden movement. She seemed posed between life and death. "We'll meet tomorrow, come by my office tomorrow and we can arrange the little, official details. Let's turn around." He made a circular motion with his finger. Julia turned at the waist to look at the direction from which she had hobbled and her eyes watered. Bernard turned her with a firm hand, "Go home. Go back to your home." When Julia seemed doubtful, he prodded her into motion using a jabbing gesture with his case and walked beside her most of the way back along to the house.

They returned along the road Julia had followed, in her slow and methodical limp, having turned her back from her aborted trip into the world but at the closed gate, Julia turned at the waist, sensing that the doctor did not follow her. "Go on," he shoed her forward with a gesture, an underhand wave of his fingers, "I'll be in my office, and we'll go through the details in the morning. Why don't you walk out and see me then?"

"What about Michael? This should be his house. If I asked him I thought he might have let me live in one of the back sheds and I could care for things while he stayed away, but he didn't stay to talk and I thought that was my last hope."

"Michael did receive half of the house but last year legally gave up his half to you. That's part of this package that I came to show you. The house is completely, fully in your name. Some of the books and personal belongings still belong to him, but I'm certain he doesn't care much if you sold them all."

"Do people sell books? All these books have stayed here for a hundred years or more."

Rush asked, "Will you come by to see me tomorrow?"

"I...will."

Julia waited until the doctor's blue coated form disappeared among the winding wall of trees at a turn of the road, then turned to face the house again. She swung the gate open with a grunt then closed the wooden door behind her again, beside those rhododendrons she once knew so well, and feeling more secure while alone in her new kingdom, reacquainted herself with the birdbath. At her elbow the aged concrete bowl, rain-washed and water-filled. She cupped the rim of the saucer with her hand and almost inaudibly whispered, "Hello bird bath."

She let her hand drop and walked, shyly to the square inside the wall, a slot to the outdoors, and touching this too, she said, "Hello mailbox." Maggie trotted into the yard, walked up the steps, and curled into an oval, nose to tail, in her accustomed spot beside the door as if she fit — a piece neatly into its puzzle space. Julia walked up to the door, and paused midway, bent to the slat and said, "Hello, stairway."

She paused at the doormat, and bent to retrieve her key on the ribbon, left an hour ago with painful regret under the doormat, the long antique key given to her by the grandfather long ago and placed it around her neck as she had done every morning for the past fifteen years.

She held the tarnished, heavy metal and rolled it between her fingers as if it were a small, thin cigar, "Hello, key. I didn't think I would see you again, but maybe, oh maybe, I'll never leave you under the mat again."

Indoors she knelt at the doll-like dishwashing station built for her many years before, smiling only inwardly at her memories, saying in the softest, least audible words, "Hello dishwarshing sink." Later she covered herself up in the pampas grass by the old clothesline, so the grass parted to admit her, hiding her face so that if she showed any more emotion at all, it could have occurred at this time while she lay in the grasses and no one saw it but the grasses themselves.

Julia and Madeleine.

A frugal shopper. Bane of storekeepers.

"I do understand interest and compound interest too!" insisted Julia, in a conversation with Bernard Rush.

"The grandfather left you money in the bank and the value of the land and house is considerable."

"What I mean is that I have to raise more money than I spend, isn't that right? Or, eventually I'll have to leave the house or sell the house."

Bernard sighed, "In theory yes, but practically speaking you'd have several centuries before you run out of money at the rate you spend it. You are very frugal. You know that."

"Yes, frugality is a good trait." Julia stubbornly insisted on financial conservatism, which though Rush didn't discourage he tried to persuade Julia to relax a bit and relent on her worries about solvency. Julia continually asked his advice on financial matters, since the grandfather died, reaffirming the knowledge she had gained in the previous years, but needing reassurance that once again she would not be displaced by some error, "How much does everything cost? Taxes, electricity, dog food? Everything for a year that I haven't been paying myself for the past few years."

"Even for such a large estate you spend practically no cash. At most," seeing her impatience and her need for a specific sum, "Let's say six thousand dollars per year."

"Then that's how much money I'll earn, more if I can, to keep Maggie and me solvent."

For Maggie, Julia had woven a wreath of purple flowers around a piece of wire and tied this into place on Maggie's neck in place of her old frayed dog collar, which once had arrived in a packet brought from the city by the grandfather long ago. "Why do you need an old dog collar when you stay near the house anyways, eh Maggie? Now with your wreath you are a true May-dog." And added, squatting low to be at eye level with her interlocutor, pointing her finger sternly in admonishment into the intelligent, discerning though aged eyes of her companion, "Stay inside the house boundaries since you don't have a collar anymore. Or you'll be catched by the dog catcher." Maggie nodded in agreement. Both understood very well how the world would treat a stray.

The nearest store for her list of errands was the general shop managed by the O'Dell family. Since a new drug store, part of a national chain, opened a few blocks away customers had dwindled and Julia had lately capitalized by bargaining for their goods, and gaining good deals because her patronage had increased of late. Julia remained the sole customer in town who bought in quantity and the O'Dell's long relied making the weekly delivery to the cubbyhole in the wall of the Hardy house. Since Roserie O'Dell assigned her daughter, Madeleine, to deal with the fierce though infrequent customer, Julia began to enjoy her shopping much more greatly. Madeline remained cool as a cucumber, was not fazed by Julia's logic and insistent ploys, knew the value of her goods and both learned they could settle on a fair price with a minimum of squabble and without rancor.

At hearing the bell jostling its warning, Madeleine looked up from her seat behind the register and smiled. She had been reading a book which Julia craned her neck to see but could not. Madeleine shared with Michael, in Julia's view, the impractical habit of reading obscure books. Julia did not mind picking up her favorite bound copy of *The Glory of Roses*, now and again, mainly to look at the scrumptious pictures but she recognized Michael's frequently changing moods seemingly brought on, she believed, by reading a book which he liked or which made important sense to him, enough to create its own tumult and restlessness in his mind.

By this time Julia was about eighteen years old or so, several years younger than Madeleine, though her habits and small size kept her appearance boyish and scruffy. She continued her habit of wearing patched men's clothes, wore caps of many sorts, colors, shapes, continued to walk in the lee of a wall and in shadows in town and never in the center of an aisle. She looked at Madeleine surreptitiously with her head turned athwart, curious at the differences between themselves.

For she believed this book-reading girl possessed a kind of elegance completely absent in herself, who by a gesture or slight nod of her head communicated wishes and intonations more subtle than Julia could catch, who did not use a word when a gesture or expression would suffice, a raised eyebrow, a smile with a slight movement of the corner of her lips. After her shopping trips Julia sometimes would practice a Madeleine-like gesture in front of mirror, raising first one eyebrow then another, but the effect seemed comical and she would laugh at herself. She had seen how passersby in the street would turn to look at Madeleine, how people would look into the store windows if Madeleine sat behind the register or how the boldest would enter the store and rummage among things, only because Madeleine had been present in the store and not another of the O'Dells.

"Do you have any girl's clothes?"

"Me?" Julia felt caught off-balance by Madeleine's question. "I have a catalog with lots of girls clothes. I could order clothes for a girl. Do you need some?"

"But do you own a dress?"

"Once I tried one on but I didn't like it."

Madeleine narrowed her eyes at Julia's head appraisingly, rummaged behind the counter and brought out a comb. She motioned that Julia approach and she combed out the knots in Julia's hair.

"Your hair is beautiful, if you'd only comb it now and then."

"Why?"

"Who cuts your hair?"

"I do myself." Julia smiled with undisguised pride at her thriftiness.

Madeleine, however, and alarmingly to Julia, frowned, leaned forward and ran her fingers through the knotted hair. "I'll do your hair tomorrow."

"If you *do* hair, what do you *do*?"

"Oh, I know, you won't show up. Okay, sit in the corner chair." Madeleine spoke with a tone that forbade disobedience and partly out of curiosity Julia bit onto all her ten fingers at once and let herself be guided into the corner. Madeleine disappeared into the back storeroom and returned with a bowl sloshing warm water, a comb and scissors. She wet Julia's hair with an unceremonious dunking, slashed through the knots, cutting out the worst of offenders, and began to cut and snip.

At first Julia tensed, suspiciously turned her head needing to watch what Madeleine did behind her head, but gradually relaxed especially as Madeleine repeatedly slapped her lightly on the side of her head telling her to sit still. Julia settled, kept her head rigidly in the position that Madeleine molded, and merely swept her eyes wide to the right or left and in time the sensations of haircutting became a bath of pleasant sensations.

"Oh this were strange," said Julia.

"You talk as if you were in a medieval book."

"Medieval is before the Renaissance."

"I can't tell if you have a stupendous education or have a terrible education."

"I never did go to a school."

"How did you get by?"

"First I started in popup books. Then regular books. Then I grew peas."

"Ahh."

Julia said, shyly, "This feels very nice." The snipping scissors interested her, alarming her when approaching her ears and yet pleasing a sound both soft and sharp at the same time. She narrowed her eyes, trying to separate the softness and sharpness with her ears but could not distinguish a separation between the sounds. And in this time Madeleine had finished, "Voila!" she pronounced with a flourish of her hand.

"So soon!" suggested Julia, feeling mildly disappointed that her haircutting ceased so abruptly and without warning. "Did you get every last piece?"

Madeleine brought out a second hand mirror and showed Julia how to look at the back of her head, but Julia had too much trouble managing to coordinate the task of looking first in one mirror then another to see the back of her head. Madeleine tried too, but in the jumble of arms and multiple mirrors they couldn't manage to fix an arrangement where Julia could see the back of her head. "Oh, take it from me, your hair looks very nice."

Yet even from the front Julia had to gasp in astonishment, and her words caused Madeleine to laugh aloud, "I never had my hair cut straight before! It has never been so short, above my shoulders. I suppose this is a practical haircut. Sometimes when I weed a plot my hair drags along in a furrow."

Then Julia was beset with a thought that caused her to frown and she said aloud, "Poor Madeleine, you must be lonely that you cut my hair for amusement."

"Maybe so. One day I'll leave this town."

"But that would be terrible. Who knows what kind of creatures you would meet with. I heard stories that would curdle your milk. In the old days only gods would travel. People at home would open up their doors very carefully and they would ask the travelers, 'Are you a god?'"

Madeleine laughed, "Gods or Mormons on a mission."

"No fooling. It's not safe to be a wanderer. Stay at home with a good supply of food. That's my advice."

"But if I'm lonely that would not be good…"

"The best thing is to stay home and be content with nothing. I mean, not *nothing*, but very simple things. If you have no wishes at all it's easier to be content. The secret is to be happy with nearly nothing. Then any other thing becomes special. Me and my dog, we're easily amused."

"Well, I agree, wishes can be terrible. More terrible than the need for traveling. My life is full of wishes, but Julia, what will happen to you if one day you start wishing for things."

"Oh, I hope that day never arrives."

Jonathan often visited when in town for no specific reason other than at noon muffins regularly came out of Julia's oven. She diligently ate a half dozen muffins per day but begrudged him nothing. She had brought out the tin, trailing a wisp of steam behind her as she walked to both Jonathan and Madeleine who had spent the afternoon with her in the orangerie.

Madeleine had said to Jonathan as they came through the gate, “To me this house is like a time machine.”

“A museum of natural history.”

Julia had been adjusting and repairing her old Mud Puppy bicycle. From time to time, though she was too old and dignified to ride the bicycle, she uncovered its tarp and gave the chain a good coating of light oil. She smiled at seeing her visitors, smiling, in part, proud of her industry and self-sufficiency and willing to show the work to these visitors.

She glanced up to see Madeleine bent over a catalog of roses and noticed, easily, an ease before books that she shared with Michael. At once a strong similarity arose in her mind between the two of them. Both Madeleine and Michael were taller than average. Both shared a somber, imposing and introspective exterior that some people found interesting and quixotic yet simultaneously forbidding — as if in a glance one might wish to speak to them, for example to ask the time, yet something within their expression or depth in their faces deterred this sort of familiarity.

Madeleine had grown within the year to gain a tall, willowy type of elegance, the grace of a cedar tree or leafy cherry wood, as Julia was wont to use arboreal metaphors, equally at home in silk blouses or a simple low waisted dress, with her long bare arms which Julia envied with open petulance and admiration. She felt that the men in town were irresistibly drawn to her and, at the same time, felt a loss of confidence that inhibited many from approaching her.

"Do you think she is beautiful?" she asked Jonathan.

"Yes, Madeleine is beautiful. But, you'll laugh at me, don't forget that you are too, Julia."

"Ha!"

If Madeleine's demeanor could be described as plant-like or pensive, Julia herself would be less plaintive and more appealing, not by appearance but via a visible kind of raw emotion and honesty. In comparing the two Jonathan believed that Julia's kind of beauty was not classic or photographic, as Madeleine's but Julia's face expressed fleeting, honest emotions that ran like so many schooled fish, in a darting tandem across her face, the honest and appealing expression of anxieties and fears that others would obscure and disguise, but not Julia. He felt that despite her air and proud boasts of self-sufficiency that she was secretly vulnerable, that that half-hidden vulnerability gave her an appeal that tugged at his heart, crusty though it be. Since she came to his table in the library for tutorials, as a little girl, she never developed sophistication or gained a capacity to disguise her feeling and thoughts so that their visible countenances were always evident in her face. Jonathan often felt a bit astonished how appealing this felt to him and how rare this characteristic was among the people he knew. Julia never lied, never spoke an untruth. Once, in a later year, Michael softly said to her that he believed he could read her thoughts by pressing his hands onto her face, and letting the expression of her thoughts on her open face melt into his fingers, as if her thoughts were as clear as Braille letters that he could read by pressing his fingers gently onto the closed recesses of her eyes.

"Fresh lovely muffins," Julia announced a trifle

unnecessarily as both Madeleine and Jonathan had already taken one each out of the tin, "Today is ice cream day. Who wants to help me with the ice cream. Someone can help me turn the crank." She waited but her companions avoided her eye and kept their concentration focused on the muffins. Shrugging, she herself, alone poured into ice cream pot rock salt, sugar and cream, and happily if monotonously, began the turning the crank. Moving herself with pot into the pergola, sitting in the shade of ivy and azaleas interwoven into the trellis overhead, she quickly tired and called once more for assistance but Maggie lay afield, asleep, and Madeline and Jonathan were finishing even her own share of the muffins and studiously avoided her eyes once more. Yet she was driven to continue, muttering how all the ice cream would be eaten by herself alone. When finished at last, well after noon, she put the pot of cream into the freezer and ran to the creek to wash off her exertions.

Jonathan watched Julia's face carefully, "Would you like to travel?"

"Well, I can't at the moment. I've been saving money for a milk cow." Jonathan felt nonplussed – he'd been a frequent visitor in the past few weeks and Julia's abrupt manners were well known to him. He struggled a bit to speak but failed. Julia turned to scrutinize him more closely, and her face clouded at seeing an unfamiliar expression on Jonathan's face and instinctually backed a step, bending backwards slightly at the waist at the same time, as if to add a bit of distance to herself and Jonathan. Jonathan looked momentarily somewhat strange as if he were choking on a piece of food.

He blurted in a gasp as if involuntarily, before she could manage to remember the first aid. He cried out in a sad and pitiful voice, "I love you, Julia, and I want to marry you."

Her hand rose up reflexively, as if defensively, as if his choking food would fly out at her. "Oh that's a terrible thing to say. Please don't say that again." She instantly regretted not having something more polite to say. But what she blurt out impulsively was honest enough, something recognized by Jonathan. She thought that if he had a snake bite she could suck out the poison but simply didn't know how to manage what he spoke, felt uncomfortable and stammered.

"I understand." He turned and left the yard, the house, and the town. Went back to his own peculiar, desolate house north of the City and then even further eastward.

If Michael Hardy felt a pang of surprise at seeing his old tutor walk into his laboratory he betrayed no surprise, nodding *hello* noncommittally and saying nothing. Jonathan seemed formal also, motioning with a nod of head, asking if they could walk outside and talk. They walked in silence to a grass enclosure beside the biomedical library, the dark frosted glass of the library wing in sharp contrast to the patch of vibrant grass on which they stood.

"I wanted to talk about Julia."

"Julia…Julia, oh yes. What has she done?"

"I wanted to marry her. I asked her."

"Congratulations." Michael had continued to walk though Jonathan stopped in his consternation.

"I visited her at your house."

"It's not my house. It's her house. I believe I don't own a single part of it."

"It's more complicated than you think. She said *no*. I upset her."

"The house? Well, I think I remember that in my grandfather's will that half of the books officially belong to me but I don't need them."

"I mean Julia. How I upset her."

"What about Julia. Is she in trouble? What has she done?"

"I came here because I thought you ought to know the dilemma…"

"You have to speak clearly and plainly. I have a problem to solve back in the lab. I'm nearly at a solution."

"She didn't want to marry me, at least I thought so. She avoided the topic."

Michael stopped his pacing at last to ponder on this last point of his old tutor. "I remember she would be easily upset. I don't think you can blame yourself. She thinks things over very slowly. I wouldn't be surprised if she takes her time. I remember she had always been reluctant to make changes of any kind."

"I'm almost twenty years older than her."

Michael did not speak. He could not think what to say. He half-smiled at Jonathan's predicament, after all he was only a few years older than Julia himself, "I haven't thought of her in years."

Abruptly he turned and confronted Jonathan so closely that Jonathan stifled the urge to step back, to retreat to a more comfortable distance as if Michael had spoken too loudly or animatedly. Jonathan had arrived and spoken so quickly that he yet hadn't taken the time to look closely at Michael whom he hadn't met for several years.

Michael spoke with eyes narrowed and concentrated, quietly and with reserve, "I'd ask Julia what she wants and what she feels comfortable with. If she wants to marry you then of course she will do so, and I'd help both of you any way I could. I must confess, though, that I don't understand why you've flown all this way to talk about it."

Jonathan felt a cold shudder at what Michael said, not so much for the content of his words but an odd, blank expression on Michael's face. Something dead in his face. Not a good face to offer advice about marriage.

"You must have come for another reason too. Do you have business in Durham?"

"I've been more than a little befuddled lately. I don't like this. I don't like emotions. Suddenly I feel as if I had been washed and dried with sharp nails. I'm feeling very anxious."

"Don't let it be catching. Go back to Napa. Or Stinson. Is that where you bought your house?"

"Before I do, do me a favor."

"Of course."

"Go back yourself."

"To Napa? No. I haven't time. Goodbye."

Michael stopped himself and looked askance with some irritation on his face but Jonathan's expression had solidified. "Go back to Napa for a few days. Don't you owe me any favors?"

Julia's astonishment knew no bounds and she stood on the topmost cellar step, rooted as a sapling in her shock. One or two thumps from above caught her attention and she came out of the cellar, construction paper and scissors in hand to investigate, to discover a stranger, an unfamiliar young woman in her kitchen. Her mouth dropped open.

The woman smiled, nodded in greeting, and then behind her an older Michael appeared, "You got my letter?" He seemed a complete stranger and only his familiarity with the house suggested his identity.

The blood had drained from her face and she became a little unsteady on her feet. Seeing this, the young woman stepped forward and helped Julia into a kitchen chair, saying, "My name is Wendy. I work with Michael in Durham. You seem surprised and I'm sorry if our visit is unexpected. I wouldn't be surprised if Michael forgot to let you know in advance."

Julia recovered, momentarily, and rose up again, backed to the cellar entrance, picked up a bag of sugar and a crock of wooden spoons, as if to preserve them from the depredations of the visitors and disappeared down the stairs again.

"She seemed surprised."

Michael nodded.

Wendy cooked a simple dinner and then afterwards it was her turn to be startled when the cellar door thumped open and a very determined Julia emerged, who turned off the tap in the sink with a single motion of her wrist. Puffing out her cheeks, she made a dismissive motion with her hands.

Wendy had retreated a step or two and Julia waved her hands again.

In the dining room she asked Michael what this meant. And he had to search his memory, "I suppose it means that she still washes the dishes. Let her wash the dishes if she wants."

"I don't understand. She seemed very fierce. I didn't even understand how to light to stove anyways."

"I'd forgotten some of her eccentricities but it's coming back quickly."

"I don't believe you or anyone else can forget someone looking as beautiful as she does."

"How does she look?"

Wendy arched her eyebrows and gazed at him with some skepticism. They heard more thumping in the kitchen and Michael entered to see Julia seated at the table, eating small bites from a sticky bun.

"Would you like to join us in the dining room?"

She stared at the table and then her bun, alternatively, without raising her eyes.

"Jonathan asked me to visit. If he hadn't I never would have come. I tried to give you notice. If I forgot I'm sorry, but I'd swear I mailed the letter. We'll be leaving in the morning."

Still Julia said nothing, taking small bites from her bun, in a methodical and mechanical rhythm.

"I've forgotten this house and all of a sudden, coming back here, my head had been flooded with many memories. You've worked so hard here. I feel so much fondness for everything I've seen. But really we never spent much time together. I'm sorry for intruding."

Still Julia said nothing.

"You look very well," then in an instant he felt awkward and stilted. Said nothing more. He left Julia to her bun at the wooden table.

Madeleine and Michael.

A dress made of cedar leaves.

Michael's face rarely reflected his thoughts — though now it twisted into an expression of puzzlement. He had sat at desk motionless for several hours then burst into quiet, rapid activity, scribbling rapidly with a pen, then later as if plunged into an abyss of too much thought his face turned immobilized and neutral again in expression. Neil Goodham, his lab mate, said that Michael seemed demonic at times, brimming with ire and wrath. The earth outdoors turned on its axis, the room grew quiescent and shadowed and he remained motionless again.

A voice spoke up out of the darkness to startle him out of the stasis, Neil's sensible voice called out, "Let there be light!" Michael blinked as Neil flipped the switch and the room flooded with brightness.

"Let's go. A mixer tonight for the biochemists. It's my party. I spent the money. You gave me the idea for this and the name for it. I'll call it the *molyball* party in your honor. Everyone attending dresses as their favorite molecule or something like that. I made a mitosis suit with the extra face on the back of my head, and an extra pair of arms and legs. That's funny, isn't it? Wendy says it doesn't make biological sense. But do I care what a woman says who's dressed as an egg with little sperms attached to springs, wiggling all around her?"

Michael groaned, and rubbed his eyes.

Neil added, "Go ahead and mingle. Drink an aperitif!"

"Why are we here. You lied to me. You told me my oligo arrived in the mail. Where's the package?"

"I lied. It was the only way you would attend the party."

"You know what I think of parties."

"Aren't you listening? The personification of the absent-minded professor. Look at them, the two women. They're new grad students, one in biochemistry."

Michael focused his eyes on the women.

Neil added, "The blonde woman is Mark's sister." Michael didn't look at Mark's sister but rather the woman beside her and without thinking walked up to the pair and introduced himself.

"This is my friend Madeleine," said Mark's sister. The

two women, had been holding hands and dropping their gesture, momentarily, as Madeleine, newly introduced, took his hand in a firm and masculine grip. Her friend, Frances, Mark's sister as he always thought of her subsequently, was a blonde-haired, vivacious woman about twenty-four years old, confident and self-assured, wearing a bright red cashmere sweater, dressed to stand out in a party. Frances spoke with a fervid and animated tone in a chatty way and used her hands to emphasize and punctuate her expressive conversations. Michael found himself following her conversation only by the motions of her hands. Even the rings on her fingers caught the room light and flashed hypnotically in his eyes.

Madeleine, slightly younger, spoke not at all but waited patiently and innocuously behind Frances during the whole conversation that ensured and appeared not even to look beside her or beyond the small circle of friends beside her tonight, in her element, also, and not uncomfortable, but gliding, speaking when necessary, seeming to be more of an observer than actor. Her friend Frances, to use a Julia-phrase, seemed to be the bell-cow.

"Madeleine says she knows you and that I wouldn't be able to get you to say three words." Michael grimaced and shook his head without comment.

This evening Madeleine wore a subdued paisley dress of dark reds and ambers and winter growth greens so it seemed to Michael that she stood in the sterile and synthetic room as if representing a throbbing and living forest or a thicket of tobacco leaves, deep-hued as if the colors were burnt into her, as if she were dressed in cherry and mahogany and other rich-grained woods, then well watered leaves were set atop the wood, not orderly or neatly but all mixed up and distressed. A strand of hair in her bangs would not stay in placed and curled up like a dark, wooden ribbon. Michael heard her say in answer to another's question, "I'm in anthropology. I've come back from a site in South America." He searched his mind idly for an interesting tidbit that he could use to begin a conversation, but could think of nothing.

He motioned for Neil to come nearer and bent towards him to whisper, "Did Aztecs live in Peru or was it the Incas. Why am I thinking of Aunt Lucy in Peru?"

"Aztecs in Mexico. Incas in Peru. And I have no idea who Aunt Lucy is. Maybe a kind of Incan mother figure."

"What's this?" lit up Frances, injecting a jolt of energy into their whispered conversation.

Michael edged away and found his new acquaintance Madeleine glancing at him surreptitiously who quietly, easily, said, "Aunt Lucy was the aunt of Paddington the Bear. Paddington came to Paddington Station in the children's book from Darkest Peru."

"Now I remember. That's all I know about Peru. That's woeful. That's not enough to hold up my end of a conversation."

"What do you think," asked Neil to Frances, "Don't you think Michael the austere calculator is interested in Madeleine? I can hardly believe it."

"He's not good enough for her. He's already got such a bad reputation. All brains and no humanity. He's too dry and — I don't mind talking to him. He's interesting enough but he's not kind enough for Madeleine. Madeleine deserves better."

"He doesn't get out much. Give him a chance. He really sleeps during our lab meetings. He works hard and he's smarter than the rest of us combined."

"He's too structured and too rigid. You know the kind."

"You'd think he lacks all social skills but I don't think so. He really can surprise you at times but then who really knows what he's like inside. I've worked with him for almost ten years now and he's never talked about anything personal." He could not judge how Michael thought about Madeleine partly because the room light was dim but also because of Michael's habitual aloofness; he could hide feelings and their expression better than anyone else he knew.

"What does he do now? Does he already have tenure? He seems too young."

"Oh, well, the whole sub-department is a spin off from one of his out-of-the-depths-of-sleep comments. He suggested a precursor neurotransmitter that could be transformed into a family of odd receptor subtypes with a simple mathematical transformation, and suggested a tie between neural connection complexity and the complexity of immune recognition. Now, for example, the Brain Institute and the AIDS Institute are working in a close collaboration that no one imagined even last year. That is two major discoveries in two different fields in only two years."

"I heard him give a talk. He was supposed to talk about the dopamine receptors and instead talked about knots in understanding or something like that."

"He tends to wander and follows what interests him

at the moment. But that's how discoveries are made. We follow him like seagulls follow a fishing boat."

"But a person like that isn't good for Madeleine. She doesn't need an academic, a loveless relationship. I'm fond of Madeleine and want the best for her."

"Well you'd better break them up now before its too late. They've already gone off by themselves." Neil realized he couldn't recommend his friend to the women, being unsure exactly what kind of person his friend really could be; except he felt certain that Michael lacked the requisite social skills and could not ever be a kind person or a thoughtful person. To describe Michael now at this party and his behavior would be, Neil thought, to be in a state of offhandedness and inattentiveness. Yet to Neil, Madeleine too was behaving slightly odd but he couldn't be certain. She seemed to be someone alone in a room full of people.

A blue-suited man, with craggy face, turned to glance at her searchingly as she passed and focused his eyes again on another point in space when Madeleine turned her head in his direction.

At home after the party, Madeleine thought long and hard about Michael. Clearly he did not recognize her as one of the children in Napa who had thrown snowballs at him, one winter's day long ago. Though her teeth were brushed and she felt calm enough to fall asleep and not pace beside the bed and she often did, she sat on the edge of the bed with elbow on the same end table which held her books, and brooded to herself chin in hand. After a few minutes, she rose off the bed once more and stood before a full length mirror tacked upon the back of her closed bedroom door. Restless at churning thoughts, she reassembled her appearance earlier this day, pressed the same paisley dress against her body, "Who are you?" she said to her reflection. "Who do other people think you are?"

Madeleine remembered her second specific memory of him. In the winter of her tenth year, her father drank himself unconscious and fell beside the old road abutting the cherry wood fence of the Hardy house, near the imposing amber gate and was not found until the next morning, frozen solid and lifeless. Michael Hardy himself showed up in the police station with the news that her father was found slumped upon the roadside.

When Madeleine arrived, trailing her shrieking mother and relatives she watched Michael answer questions, very sparing of his words, with the most enigmatic and indecipherable expression she had seen upon a human face, so much that she strangely believed that he was not a human himself, as if he were an alien hiding in a human body and observing the situation in the police station as if he came from another world so different that the body gestures and facial expression denoted quite different meanings to him, so much so that her own strangenesses and enmities towards this town and life melted away and intuitively in her heart she said, "Here is a person who can understand me. Here is person who is as lonely as I am." He looked at her and his expression changed, to something stronger and more obdurate in her own mind, so he looked as a tree would if it had come to life or as if the face of a rock outcropping came to animal life, it was difficult to describe, she felt a rush of water sweep over her, a warm oceanic water, a bath water that jolted and comforted both. She smiled at him, from her position opposite in the room. She smiled meaning to say, "I know how you are. I know how you have always felt and I feel similarly." But in this terrible moment she saw that he had dropped his glance so her wish to convey this to him was lost. For some unfathomable reason her mother believed the Hardys caused her husband's death, but the police refused to charge them for any crime.

Michael reappeared in town again at her father's funeral. He stood in a darkish, ill-fitting coat far away in the crowd of townspeople. Despite the distance Madeleine recognized his black hair and brown eyes and enigmatic expression. Even in a crowd he seemed both distinct and solitary.

At the party with Neil and Frances, after she had talked about Paddington's Aunt Lucy, she said, "You don't recognize me but we come from the same small town in California."

"I lived in a little town called Napa."

"In the sixth grade I used to ride my bicycle past your house on my way to school. Sometimes I'd spy on your yard and the people there. Until the movie theatre arrived your house, and the packages that went into it, was the closest thing we had to regular entertainment."

"I never spent much time in that town school. My family more or less had a hard time of it."

"Not by everyone."

"Not by everyone," he conceded.

They found themselves outdoors on a redwood patio. Somehow they had walked, in a way unknown to themselves through the floor of the party, through dancing couples, and chair and tables, to be alone in the dark.

Michael thought, curiously, How did we get here? But Madeleine was not listening, she was watching a movie of her own memories in the dark in her own mind.

They began to stumble upon each other at the same places on the campus and spent more time together. Talking and silences both came easily between them, a first time this was so to either of them.

On her first night alone with Michael, many months ago, Madeleine marveled at the strange behavior in her bed, as he approached her, felt his body join hers and she spoke aloud, involuntarily, "How far gone am I, how strange life is!" She wanted to share her feelings about this expansion of her experience but Michael's eyes were closed, engrossed in his own internal sensation, processing his own thoughts and experience and rather surprised, that she was as physically close to another human as could be possible and simultaneously, in her lifetime as an adult, had never felt so forlorn and solitary. Again the thought, "How far gone am I?"

She turned his head towards her, with her own hands and looking beyond the expression in his eyes, a dreamy and satisfied mixture in the brownness, the cow-eyed irises, speckled with orange, and told him with her own expression that she wanted him to understand something, but Michael seemed embedded too deeply in himself. She didn't know what else to say, how else to reach him, and felt a desolation sweep over her, and the loneliness, a quaking and shaking from the inside seized her, sank its teeth and shook her to the point she felt disoriented and lost her bearings. She hugged herself with her own hands but felt nothing, felt comforted with the warmth of Michael's hands as they held her, his palms and warm fingers.

Later in the evening, she sat before the bedroom window at her writing desk and idly leafed through the bills that had accumulated, pushed away her checkbook and lay her head on the desk, pressing her cheek on the cool papers.

Rain drummed on the glass panes at the bus stop and Madeleine huddled within the bare shelter, glancing out from time to time hoping that Michael would remember he meant to pick her up after his day in the lab. A rhythm of buses arrived and departed, and each group of passengers in successive buses declined in number. Night had fallen, the rain became more intense and Madeleine felt more forlorn, holding hope that Michael would remember her this evening. But he hadn't changed, or else she hadn't yet permeated into his consciousness enough that he would be looking forward to an evening with her, she believed. More than an hour after they had agreed to meet, Madeleine caught a bus herself and found her own way home alone for the evening.

Sometimes Madeleine would sleep beside Michael when he took a noontime nap in the lab. Accustomed to his habits, the lab worked quietly around him, and when Madeleine too wanted to nap he added a cot to the corner of the room, and they lay quietly in their corner for an hour or so in the middle of each day.

Sometimes she preferred to lie on the grass in an atrium between buildings and in the shade of trees. She would sometimes decorate his sleeping body with pebbles of various colors, arranged in lines or circles on the sinews of his back visible through the shirt. She scratched his back so in his sleep he'd turn, to better arrange pebbles anew on his stomach. When her seizures would be stilled by this pebble arranging then she might sleep also and she pressed her nose against his shoulder and the grass.

"Madeleine!" he called, "Madeleine." She did not appear. He searched in the entry, in the library which doubled as their kitchen, or a large closet with a window in which she hid with shawls and blankets to read when the idiosyncratic Durham weather warmed enough that she could read in the winter warmed by sunlight. He found her at last in an upstairs bedroom with a heavy wool blanket pulled over her head. When he drew back the blanket he saw that she was trembling and shaken, "Why hiding? Why trembling," he asked, silently. Then aloud, with a budding sense of inadequacy, "Have I forgotten something. Did I do something that I shouldn't? You have to tell me."

She answered only with a twisting of her lower lip and lay back into the blanket.

Madeleine continually marveled at the occasional, though undeniably happy moments she felt in observing the nearness of Michael's life to hers. She sometimes spoke aloud to herself, "Oh life is so peculiar and wonderful." But when near to one another Michael's eyes as often as not were closed and didn't respond to her searching glance.

"What can I do?" Michael would ask when he saw Madeleine huddled in her woolen cap pulled low over her eyes. He could see the external signs of her distress and sadness, and often responded with offers of external help. Aspirin. Sweaters. Even his friendly hand, which gave her much pleasure when held firmly in her, sharing intertwined fingers, couldn't mitigate the pains Madeleine would sometimes feel, because sometimes, as she felt, something was missing in his response. "It's not your fault, I know. I knew before we began to live together what to expect."

"Is it sympathy? I want to understand. I feel frustrated at times because I can understand book learning. But nothing in my life has helped me with what you need. It's unfair for you."

"Some things defy analysis," she admitted. He felt she needed some kind of new limb which he didn't yet have to provide comfort and solace, and felt that growing a regenerated limb would be painful for anyone even if it were possible at all. She added, "Even if I understood I'm not certain I could explain. And even if I could explain I'm not certain it would do any good."

This day in an empty, sandy field spotted with desultory patches of grass, variegated like some ears of corn that appeared now and then in vegetable stands, almost as ornaments, some patches of grass yellow and corn-hued, others, almost blackish, Madeleine liked to buy such ears of corn and keep them expressly because of the orphaned kernels with their imperfections. She put daisies in Michael's hair, tucked behind his ears, all those she could reach within her prone position and pull from the ground without leaving his sleeping embrace. When stilled and near sleep herself, when emotions slowed to a stasis and manageable murmur, warmed enough by the sunlight and the regularity of his breathing, she too began to nap, fitfully at first, holding onto his hand until her eyes closed as his and she dreamt of corn kernels.

Julia encounters a new feeling stronger than her ordinary feelings.

She tries to squash it.

No doubt the biggest worry of the year for Julia was the annual property tax. Since the grandfather's death this was the largest intrusion of government into her life. Bernard Rush reassured her that he could pay the tax easily out of savings but as the grandfather made this an annual rite of irritation, sometimes looking to the wall calendar and smiling at Julia, saying, "It's that time of the year to curse our national government and its system of taxation," so likewise Julia sometimes smiled to herself and muttered deprecatingly under her breath, "*It's tax time.*" Much of the year was a scramble to raise cash for the bill. Selling herbs and packets of spice to Madeleine's store, selling cartons of vegetables and fruits, from the back yard trees, in town. Not long after she assumed responsibility for the house finances, did Julia realize that simple sales of fruits would be insufficient. One of Jonathan's economics and accounting homework problems asked her to invent a company for which she would respond with proper accounting and report writing. In this way she invented a company which sold home-made jams and jellies, called *Maggie Jams*. Delighted at her invention, the grandfather asked, "Why not make this a real company? Wouldn't you like to sell your jams in town?" In this way *Maggie Jams* became a real entity, with Julia's involvement as sole proprietor, cook, salesperson and accountant. Several weeks of the year turned the kitchen in a mass of boiling jars and sugary jam-making sessions. Peach jam was created early in the season, strawberry jam to follow. Within the town many people grew to anticipate the jam season, buying Julia's jam in queues so that *Maggie Jams* turned a steady profit.

In this way, with other projects too, each year Julia managed by thrift and with great relish to present herself in Rush's office with boxes full of carefully rolled coins and neatly pinned bills.

"I tell you every year that I can pay the bill out of accounts," said Bernard and he waited expectantly for Julia's traditional response, with his hand turned upwards in a flourish.

"The damned IRS. They get me every year!" said

Julia ritually, as the grandfather would and they laughed together in fond memory of the grandfather.

Bernard laughed inwardly to himself too since Julia didn't realize how she mimicked that grandfather in other, more subtle ways, for example, how she adopted his habit of pounding her forehead with a fist, at the side of his head above the ear.

"Well how are you."

"Next year I may sell a few more cartons of peach jam. I may start to advertise so the peach moves more quickly. The strawberry always does well even without advertising. I don't make plum anymore."

She turned out the study light and wandered through the rooms between the study and her bedroom, one by one, trailing her hand upon the objects in the rooms she preferred best, sofas, end tables, bowls on low shelves that in the past she reached by tiptoe to investigate with such awe. She walked through each room turning out a light or seeing a particular thing to its proper place in her night time ritual, saying *good night* to the house, and *thank you* to the house.

When she had brushed her teeth and washed up, her worn copy of the *Glory of Roses*, with dog-eared pages and scribbled scholia, waited for her on the nightstand and she climbed into the high bed and covered herself with the woolen blanket. She said, "This is much nicer than a root cellar though the root cellar can be nice," and pulled the blanket completely over herself so that only her face and her hair, and her fingertips remained exposed to the world. She arranged the book on her knees and flipped from one page to another very contentedly.

Before embarking on a short excursion into the woods she packed a bag with supplies, oranges and crackers, and kept a spare sandwich on her person the same way some people keep a spare tire in the trunk on a driving trip. She said to Maggie, "Let's gather up some onions for dinner." Maggie had aged and her wiry tail had acquired a sort of arthritic tilt, so that in wagging the tail it moved only a bit from side to side in a stiff motion. While walking on the expedition, Julia munched on the crackers absentmindedly as she hurried through the grounds of the house and yard intimately familiar to her and folded the crackers back into their waxed wrapping when after a half hour she reached the grounds of the woods which required closer scrutiny.

To her own delight, Bernard mentioned that the land adjoining the Hardy property was for sale — though a century earlier it had belonged to the Hardy clan — and Julia bought it. Here a gardener long ago had mixed native trees with eastern beeches in an intriguing pattern. The unknown predecessor had in the wilds of the woods pruned the lower branches of the beeches and raised the leafy canopy to an impressive height and this, one of her more recent discoveries, had become one of the main objects of her recent energies. Perhaps a carriage path passed beneath the branches though she couldn't know for the overgrowth. To her right the weald rolled downwards to the beginnings of the creek a mile upstream from her bathing glen. In summer the slope was sheathed in bluebells.

At one point she paused and bent low to the ground to pull out a stalk of potato. She came upon evidence in these parts of the remnants of a long neglected garden grown here in secret — pentimento of a garden that must have been very beautiful. Seeing tarragon, parsley, sage, many herbs not native to the region. Adjoining the herb garden may have been planted a series of hedges, laid out as a panterre in earlier days. Further east lay her favorite exploring grounds which had long ago been cultivated by a Hardy ancestor who had been homesick for the east or perhaps the Dordogne because she or he had planted hardwoods and an extravagant expanse of rain and mist loving flowers, bush roses, sweet William, sweet alyssum growing at the feet of yew and black pines, even a row of linden.

If she were to restore this carriage path it would be a colossal undertaking, the largest single project of her life. The thought occurred to her that she could raise a small troop of children, or at least one small hard-working child, who would do the majority of hard work. She was after all, aging, though gracefully. She could lie on a settee or ottoman cushion, out of doors, and shout instructions while they lifted little buckets of dirt or turned over the ground with little spades, wearing small plastic boots and dungarees. The thought of children, from herself, had never occurred to her before, and the novelty, the newness and the vividness of this idea affected her a little more strongly than she could have imagined, needing to sit a moment on a turlock and catch her breath.

"Aren't we silly, Maggie," she said to her companion who stiffly settled at her feet. "We're bachelors for life together and happy bachelors too." Still, as she rose again, steadying herself with a single finger on the mossy outcrop, she couldn't help but wonder how difficult it would be to make a little cherry wood wheelbarrow for these industrious children. It would have to be the size of her breadbox with handles that she would turn on the hand lathe.

Tramping off the trail, she took a quick look and discerned a few sickly remainders of the lindens which might be nursed back to health. An expansive plan for regeneration, of herself and the new property, took shape in her mind. For the next step she required only a few small children and the cherry wood wheelbarrows and felt determined by evening to have a plan for the wheelbarrows.

In the potato patch she harvested an armful of the spuddy roots, leaving half again to grow, smiling pleased at her discoveries this day. On her return home she would skirt to the south where she knew of relict, hardy patch of onion. She would fry onions in a pan with butter, with cut potatoes browning separately, and her mouth watered at the thought of it. Tomorrow she would make onion soup. Because she did not want to exhaust the patch, like the potatoes, she would still buy red and brown onions from the stores in town, but saved her favorite recipes for those wild onions and other vegetables she found on walks in the new barton.

Beside the creek, about a hundred yards to her right, an unexpected swath of asphalt appeared peppery thorough clumps of unmelted frost. She hadn't seen a road in this part of the landscape so felt alarm at the intrusion — she parted the rushes grown in abundance beside the road fed by runoff from a drainage flue, and let the green stalks rest against her neck so that only her disembodied head remained visible from outside the boundary of the grounds and from the road. Then with a swish and whisper of the reeds, she disappeared again. Somehow in her absence on this edge of the property a whole new road, a highway had appeared by some mysterious process which she would have liked to have witnessed, as if a large insect dragged behind and unrolled in its wake an instant path of asphalt and painted line.

As she turned onto the tarmac and walked further along, potatoes and onions dangling from her hands and draped over shoulders, an uninterrupted vista appeared before her where the road straightened and rose spindly towards the horizon though, thankfully, without a single car on the track. To Julia the road was a sign of blight. Even this innocuous sign of human life unnerved her, causing a shudder in the coat, though she was still unaffected by her exertions or by the temperature of the day.

She returned to the undergrowth beside the road immediately on hearing scuffling noises, cries of a creature in distress, and around a bend in the highway came upon a roiling mess of children. Two larger boys punched a shrunken little boy, who by the time she arrived seemed to admit defeat merely by lying prone and face down, jerking upwards now and then in response to a specially hard punch. Nonetheless he did not cry out consciously. Julia could hear only the impact of the punches and the quiet *hup hup* of his, involuntarily, expelled breath. He did not cry out! Despite her timidity, instead of running she watched even with a budding admiration at the runty boy. At last the bullies tired, as if the beating merely became exertion to them and they left, muttering insults and a few parting kicks.

The runty boy remained inert but Julia felt,

sympathetically, this was feigned and after a few minutes of silence boldly ventured onto the road and squatted by his side.

He did not look up, only flinched at hearing footsteps.

She poked him gently with the rounded snout of a potato.

He moaned a bit.

"Little boy," she said in a voice that in its gentleness made him turn around and peek through the space under his arm thrown protectively over his head.

She helped him up and walked with him in silence through the barton, down a ravine and upwards through the dense thicket of poplars to the familiar grounds of the Hardy house.

Jasper the boy was six years old, and Julia now twenty-two, according to the grandfather's estimate and accounting, yet neither seemed taller or heavier than the other. Quick to be surprised, they unconsciously surveyed their surroundings seeking — as if inevitable — trauma and harms and dangers. Both uncomfortable hearing even a loud noise.

As they trudged round the hillock at pond and the house came into view, Jasper gasped, and Julia with undisguised pride said, "You can visit me if you like. I live here and care for all the gardens and the house."

"It looks like a magic house, like a house from a fairy tale. But someone will find me and then they'll beat you up too."

"Well, we have to be tricky and hide out all the time."

"I try to hide but I get found out."

"We have a guard dog."

Jasper looked down at his knees to see Maggie panting at the exertions of joining them on the hillock, doubtfully.

The next morning, Jasper roused himself early, crept along the street and rapped quietly on the gate. He knocked and hid beside a tree, and knocked again.

At last a small, unseen green door, the grocery chute, opened beside the gate and a suspicious face showed itself. Julia's eyes scanned up and down the empty street, with pursed lips in annoyance, that vanished at seeing the laughing pair of eyes barely visible beside the wall. She had squinted into the sunshine, caught sight of Jasper and motioned that she would open the gate. A few moments later the gate opened and Julia stood small and shy in the much greater height of the gate. Her mouth smiled but her eyes were squinty still and welcoming.

They soon developed a routine to minimize their exposure to the world. In the morning Jasper would knock at the door of the gate. Julia opened the grocery chute and he would crawl into the yard. While Julia prepared breakfast, in the kitchen, he sat at the table to read the almanac and sipped the tea she set at his placemat. Julia looked at him, sidereally and wondered at the miracle — how even before she could lathe up the handles for the cherry wood wheelbarrow, a child appeared in her kitchen.

She introduced him to the usefulness of gardening hand tools and that very day they began work on the carriage path gardens. Throughout the summer both become sunburnt, healthy and cheerful.

By the summer's end, Julia noticed a change in his behavior, how familiar he had become to the kitchen, how he walked in unannounced, poured himself a cup of orange juice, how he had lost his fearfulness, at least while on the grounds of the house. He opened a battered cigar box from his seat at the table, and showed her the previous day's catch in exploring through her woods and the ghaut — several flowers, a bug, and shells and a rock with fake gold ore in a blotch on one side. She looked at the flowers and named them; he wrote down the Latin laboriously, letter by letter. After a particularly long name for the insect she mentioned, "That's also called a doodlebug."

"Oy!!" Jasper cried. "Why didn't you say that first. That's easier and more fun to spell."

"Sorry."

When she returned with a fresh load of clothes brought in from the line, Jasper's mood had changed and he now sat, chin in hands, downcast, staring into the polished wood of the table.

"What're you thinking?"

"Nothing really, I don't know."

"Let's do something different today."

"We already did everything."

After a moment of reflection, she tapped Jasper on the head and said, "I know just the thing." She hurried to the tool shed where she had stored some of her favorite treasures and under a canvas tarp uncovered her old Mud Puppy bicycle. "Strange," she thought, "it's so small. I remember when it was as high as my forehead." Nonetheless, small as it was, the bicycle would serve for Jasper and she added the training wheels that long ago Michael removed with the magical crescent wrench.

"Ooh," he sighed, "this is a nice bicycle." He approached the bicycle with appreciation. Julia knew his family was one of the seasonal workers in the vineyards that lately had become prosperous, though Jasper was thought too runty to labor in the fields, as Napa had grown almost fabulously wealthy with the popularity of its wines.

"I know how to ride a bicycle," said Jasper, "I don't need those," he said with ill-disguised disdain, condescension, "They're for little kids."

"Wait for three minutes," she found a wrench and removed the training wheels.

He hopped onto the seat and promptly fell to one side. When she reached out to support his balance, he snapped peremptorily, "I can do this!" so reflexively she held out her hand and memories of Michael's impatience and temper flooded back into her mind, partly with a bit of annoyance, but also to her surprise partly with some fond remembrance. Michael had terrorized her, when small, but in seeing Jasper she considered that perhaps he was not as terrible as he seemed and Michael perhaps was more ordinary than she imagined.

"Maybe I forgot how the bicycle works." And looked up to her with mildly recondite eyes.

"Put your feet on the pedals," she directed as gently as she could and when he nodded in readiness she pushed the bicycle from behind until the trembling ceased and the bicycle rolled forward straight and true. The momentum lasted a few yards and when he lost his balance and fell, he lay down face into the mulch, much like his accustomed manner when getting beaten by other kids, looking back towards her with a glance from under an arm thrown over his head.

"Patience makes the daisies grow," Julia reminded him.

Jasper persevered and after a short break in the afternoon the persistence was rewarded and he learned to pedal around the yard unassisted. Soon he had worked up the courage to disappear from sight, rambling beyond the yard into the trails in the river woods, reappearing momentarily as he pedaled furiously past the doorway and away again past the irises and headed towards the clotheslines, shrieking all the way with happiness. He never seemed to tire of this and Julia laughed with him.

Durham, NC.

…*much learning doth make thee mad.* —Acts 27.24.

On the same evening that Julia and Jasper put on a puppet show of Bible stories for Maggie's entertainment, Michael Hardy became the youngest member of the National Academy of Sciences and was invited to a dinner with a subgroup of its membership to receive a medal to honor a discovery he made in mathematics a decade earlier. His math function was only recently adapted by others to describe anomalies in the behavior of fleeting "proto-elements." This helped to explain the decay of unstable elements that themselves were created under pressure and heat, for example, in a large bomb or possibly in the center of the sun. Michael used hafnium as the basis for his calculations, and only in the past year with the construction of the world's largest cyclotron in Europe did his predictions come true, which no one believed realistic at the time he offered them. The most useful component of his theory was a calculation method created for the derivation of his theory, a simplifying math with an aesthetic component like the Hamiltonian in physics — it simplified calculation and allowed a whole field of scientists to see better what before seemed only a bewildering set of complexities. Younger scientists used his theory to grapple with, among other things, a question like, why, out of all possible worlds, did *this* world of elements result, with oxygen to breathe and water everywhere?

Michael began his speech in the habit of past lectures, by tracing the history of his problem and the personal path of thinking that led to his particular solution. At one point in his speech, he pressed his notes against the podium with an audible sigh and sought out a friendly face in the auditorium. Not finding one in the glare of lights, he folded his notes in half and felt himself split in half. He had been thinking of Madeleine and her awkward behavior lately, her refusal to speak with him, her moving out of Durham, her accusations, all true, how Michael seemed inadequate for a shared life together. He felt as if an axe had riven him in half and he faltered in his speech.

The pudding.

O world! Your loves, your chances,
Are beyond the stretch of any hand from here.
A touching dream, to which we all are lulled,
But wake from separately.

Philip Larkin, *The Building*

Madeleine's rare occasion of a smile became contagious. Even the new arrival at the clinic, a Mayan woman newly arrived to America and frozen stiffly in her chair, legs too short for the floor who did not speak a word of English — with deeply furrowed face from a lifetime of work — broke into a sunny smile at seeing Madeleine's happiness.

"What's up with you today?" asked the visiting medical doctor, who distributed inoculations once per week and received in turn pamphlets which Madeleine had translated for the clinic from English into Quechuan or Tzotzil. The medical worker had known her for six months since her abrupt return to the country. Though admiring Madeleine for her work ethic he had reserved doubts about her ability to enjoy herself. He thought she was too brittle for emergency work and, then, was surprised to learn that she had worked in the clinic for decades.

Thus his curiosity at seeing the curtain of formality and distance removed to reveal such color returned to her face, to see her body seemingly animated with silly, cheerful energy.

And his spirits crashed a bit at hearing from her, "A friend from college will visit for a few days."

"A male friend?" She nodded her head affirmatively. He had been working up the courage to ask this mysterious, formal woman to dinner but felt his chances diminished, if not dashed. "What's his name? What does he do?"

"His name is Hardy. He's a research chemist. But he's been on a sabbatical."

"I haven't heard you mention his name before. Why so suddenly?"

"He called me right out of the blue, very uncharacteristically." Madeleine looked to the floor as if a switch had been flipped and she was no longer able to communicate. The medical worker could get no more information out of her.

Madeleine hadn't been entirely honest. It was Michael who received a letter in the mail from her, asking him to visit her in San Francisco. He had learned several years earlier from Neil's lab gossip that Madeleine had become pregnant and brought a baby into the world while working for her dissertation in her Quechuan village in darkest Peru, but before the birth had been deserted by the father. So ran the gossip (mainly third hand from Frances to Neil to Michael but sometimes even further afield). He heard no more until the arrival of the terse letter.

After a short flight to the City he found himself plunged into a dense mass of people arranging themselves into a chaotic mix or jumble, feeling irritable as he rode the escalator out of the subway system into the city proper, partly sensing after an absence of crowd and bustle in his quiet life that he had once again joined the flux of humans in their perpetual movement. He felt he could not walk without jostling somebody rudely, though no one seemed to mind when he turned to apologize. Then in the way of modern acclimatization after a few minutes he became inured to the crowd and no longer turned to apologize. He walked for several miles through progressively less crowded streets, through the weekday traffic in Golden Gate Park, trudging along the road's median strip beside parked cars, bicyclists, skaters. In time he passed through the park, across Fourth Avenue, waiting patiently at each stoplight as instructed by the electric signs until he found himself at an airline office and remembered according to letter instructions that Madeleine lived in a flat beside the office on the shady side of the building in back.

He climbed the steps, pushed a button near the door. The door opened and after a moment of quiet scrutiny, he was ushered inside. After perfunctory greetings, Madeleine left him, hearing a crash within and a girl's whimper. Michael followed but stopped short on Madeleine's heels at seeing her daughter. His heart nearly stopped. Because the girl's epicene face seemed to resemble his own so strangely, remarkably, in a way he would have been hard put to define — perhaps because his face male and hers female. He found it odd at times to look at a face and see how with such little alteration that a male face could have been female, and vice versa, for the existence of a tiny curl of DNA; how like the pentimento of older paint beneath a finished painting one human template, neither male nor female, lay beneath all faces.

Madeleine interrupted his musing to say, "This is my daughter Louise." Then in slight change of intonation and movement of head, as if to a child's puppet, "Louise, say hello to my friend Michael." Louise did not say anything but held up her hand, which had a pink and bruised knuckle. Michael bent to look at the simulacrum, the doll's hand in miniature and soothed it within his own grip. He looked at Madeleine expecting her to speak but she in her old way of searching his face, answered as if she did not like the expression on his own face for the moment, silently answered that she had no intention of answering his own unspoken question. He accepted this for the moment.

"How old are you?"

The girl held out three stubby fingers, emphatically chirped, "I'm four!!"

Madeleine shrugged and set her daughter onto the

floor. Louise hopped away into the adjacent room with exaggerated jumping steps.

Immediately Michael asked, "When was Louise born?"

"More than a year after I left Durham." Her face altered itself into something unreadable, some expression indecipherable.

Now it was Michael's turn to shrug his shoulders, "How have you been? I haven't heard any news of you since the pudding."

After traveling to the countryside out of Cuzco for her dissertation research, the graduate department lost track of Madeleine. Her research was nonpolitical. She studied how the Incan languages and grammar reflected women's status. Originally she began in Central America with its many, related Mayan languages, but as a kind of control she spent the last few years in Peru, and Bolivia, but mainly Peru.

While learning languages and volunteering in the local clinics, political violence broke out again, and as a Western woman she was suspected of leftish leanings by the government, and of cultural pollution by the leftists. Terrorist violence resumed in the region following a year-long period of peace, which had lulled the country, even the world, into complacency. Bombs exploded in the capital, airports were closed and briefly the whole country became a closed camp. Even when communications were restored, no word from Madeleine was received for several months.

Out of the blue, as they say, Michael received a travel-worn letter without return address, a letter in her usual terse way,

Michael. A cholera epidemic has killed one hundred children in my town. I hear crying every night from the women who live beside me. For lack of clean water. I try to understand human life and it defies my understanding. I simply don't believe any longer that reason or analysis can deal with this, so I struggle on trying other methods.

Below a few crossed out sentences as if the letter was meant to continue, and simply nothing else as if interrupted unexpectedly and mailed by mistake.

Michael consulted a few sources and mailed a box with a portable water filtration system addressed to Madeleine and the name of a small town south of Cuzco. Impulsively, he went to a corner store and bought several cartons of bottled water and dessert pudding. He mailed the pudding in a separate box with the same vague address. Before mailing the two boxes, he returned to the corner store and bought ten gallons of household bleach, and mailed all three from the counter of the post office.

The woman in the post office looked at the address, seemingly vague and nonspecific, without a single number on the label and shook her head.

"Just mail it please." And over her protests the boxes were shipped away.

"Your boxes did arrive. Because by the oddest chance I knew the wife of the shipping clerk in Cuzco, the packages were saved for me and they arrived in my town by cart."

She had been much changed since he saw her last;

she appeared gaunt when before she seemed elegant and fashionably thin. Now with haunted eyes instead of eyes lively and dark. To Michael who was not prone to poetic images, she seemed transformed, even transfigured if that was not too much of a romantic word — less of a physical appearance than before and more ethereal this day, as if each waking moment of the past forty months in that country had been spent in intense thought, in an intense scrutiny and internal examination.

He did ask when he learned the names of the towns, Trujillo and Piura, where she had lived, for more details of her life but she didn't answer and changed the topic. She did once say in passing that she thought the bleach probably saved the lives of hundreds of people. He said to Neil — after Madeleine died — how Greek tragedians dealt with horror, for example Medea's killing of her children, "When something occurred so fateful and terrible at the culminating moments of the play, those moments were never seen in the way modern movies glorify trauma — they always occurred offstage. It took place off-stage behind the *schema.* This way the unseen appeared even more terrible. And this was why Madeleine's life, to me, seemed all the more terrible. All the more terrible because the world only knew that the countryside was populated when she arrived and it was empty when she left and she never spoke about it."

Madeleine didn't seem to mind the abrupt changes in her life. She never resumed her dissertation and worked as a poorly paid clerk in the Divisadero medical clinic. She listened to music, she and Louise taking turns choosing the records they played on an archaic electric turntable with built-in, raspy speakers in the side. Michael learned how she snuck into the symphony building downtown when the symphony practiced before concerts. She cajoled Michael into volunteering at the clinic. He helped with assays, collected blood, analyzed genetic tests for chromosome damage. He bought a centrifuge for the clinic out of his own pocket, and in only a few weeks the director transferred more authority and decision making to both Madeleine and him. In this way he quickly found himself assimilated into life in San Francisco and nearly forgot about his previous life in Durham or his desultory travels, all over the world, that occurred in the interim. Julia, in Napa, remained only one hundred miles away but much more distant than that in his mind.

Madeleine mused that eight years had passed since she and Michael met at Neil's *molyball* party. She looked into her bedroom mirror and saw changes in herself, lines beside her eyes, creases betraying the passage of time, aged hands and arms that were weaker and more frail. "I never thought I'd reach old age, even middle age, but look how it happens while you're not looking. I'm so glad." Michael too was aging, which Madeleine only too mischievously and gleefully, pointed out, and for confirmation she sat on the edge of the bed, where he lay prone, poking at his waist where he had gained some, little weight. Michael sat back, watching with open eyes a patch of light, reflected through tree leaves onto the wall. She said aloud, "How strange and foreign you are. As strange and foreign to me as the day we met."

"Am I the same, am I unchanged in all that time?"

"No, you've changed in small ways."

He had tucked his hands, as if cold, into his arms and

remained lost in thought, wandering in some fathomless space far from this room. So she lay behind him and wrapped her hands over his and fell asleep. Each pressed against the other and each lost in their own separate realm of thought.

Michael saw how she stood at the desk window, wrapped in a towel, hair wet, and she bent into a momentary posture over a ceramic bowl, arranging pears to her liking, bending straight upwards to look at them again as if from different perspective then bending low again. The air seemed very still to him so that her movements seemed encased in syrup, slow and heavy.

"What pattern?"

"I don't know. I'm not so aesthetic that it makes sense to me."

Her hands swept over the pears upsetting the pattern so the topmost fell onto the floor and bruised, "I don't like pretty things any longer. I like grim things best, grim like you. Grim like me. Grim species are honest species." She sat on the bed beside him again and pushed out her lips in a comic way, "Pretty things are not for me anymore," and she curled one of her arms into Michael's, as if to say he was a non-pretty thing that contented her.

Madeleine as usual was late for her shift at the clinic and yelled at Michael to answer the door. He opened the door but nobody stood outside. Had she begun to hear imaginary noises? She swore the bell rang at the door, or a telephone rang, but to Michael these seemed phantom noises. An ambulance siren wailed faintly in the distance, the sounds of a motorcycle drifted over several buildings. "Do you hear the ambulance?" asked Michael.

"Yes, I do," answered Madeleine, "but the sound is fading, it's fading, now it is gone."

Madeleine sat quietly in the passenger seat, hands folded in the pockets of her sweater, and silently watched the streets of the sleeping city glide past the glass, the city mute except for an odd pedestrian, walking likewise with hands in pockets. Michael parked on the street beside a car dealership, one of several in a row on this avenue. They walked amongst the shiny and forlorn cars on the lot. Madeleine, on nights she felt ruminating, liked to shop in the car lot near midnight when they could be alone. She peered into the darkened interiors with her hand, shielding her vision from the falling beams of light overhead, from lamps spaced sporadically through the lot, studying the details on the invoices pasted to the interior window of each car. She appeared at one point, beside him, and braided her arm between his, "Which one do you like best?"

Michael walked a little further for awhile, then pointed to a dull and anonymous looking sedan, a box on wheels, "No one would steal that car. I could park it outdoors, with the engine running and door open, and at the end of the day I'd find it in the same place."

Madeleine returned from work and much like any day kissed him. But today his perception seemed sharpened, as if from a sense of impending danger and he looked at her more carefully than usual. The realization struck him, "She doesn't look at me when she kisses me. We are living in the same space but by rote." And, regretfully "How did this happen again?" When he mentioned his train of thought to her, rather than reacting confrontationally, Madeleine to Michael's surprise seemed pleased, more pleased than she seemed for weeks, saying she was grateful for his sympathetic thoughts and to keep up the good work, then she lapsed into silence again. The complexities of thought, the sorts of complexities of sorting what another person thought, in response to his own thoughts, his thoughts in response to her thoughts, and so on, seemed bewildering to Michael. It was, he thought with impatience, but humor too, how much more complicated life became when one considered the thoughts and wishes of another person.

Jonathan had dropped by Madeleine's house for a visit, and in answer to his query for Michael's whereabouts, Madeleine pointed backwards, "He's brooding."

Michael nodded, staring through the window as Jonathan said, "I'll go to my beach house for the summer, and I'd like to invite you and Madeleine and Louise if you'd like. Madeleine says preschool and the babies' coop has a break this upcoming week. Besides, I need a ride. I'm stranded in the city." Michael shrugged.

They packed a few, half-filled bags for themselves, a mountain of luggage, parcels and duffel bags for Louise and her accouterments, and they embarked on the short journey to Jonathan's house near Stinson Beach, north of the city.

On the journey, over the Golden Gate bridge, while Louise pressed her nose against the window and counted pylons aloud, Madeleine asked, "How's Julia doing?"

"Julia?" Michael was momentarily distracted counting pylons silently with Louise.

"Don't you ever think of her?"

"Of course. But I'd say she is a constant and steady and never-changing kind of person. Wouldn't you agree?"

"She's more complex than you think. You take her for granted."

"Not by me," said Jonathan. "I asked her to marry me last year."

This news was met by a silence that made him nervous, so he immediately added, "She pretty well reacted like you now. Then she pretended it was a joke. And when I insisted on talking seriously, she said *no*, she wouldn't marry me, but thank you very much. I haven't seen her since that very minute."

"I had no idea you were so taken with her," said Madeleine, "But I can understand why. I sympathize. Jonathan doesn't underappreciate her, Michael. I'm not surprised. When one thinks about it, she's an old-fashioned catch, worth a bunch of money, and pretty to boot."

"What surprised me was what she said. I'd asked her, *Why not*? Why not marry me, I wanted to know why not. You'd never guess what she answered."

"Well?"

"She said she had to marry someone else."

"What?" cried Madeleine, truly surprised, though Jonathan couldn't tell if she were laughing or felt somewhat more somber. "And what did she say?"

"You know how Julia can be. She pressed her lips together and closed her eyes. When I pressed her for more info she put her hands over her ears and bent over to hide."

"Well, well."

The blooming crocus.

Back to the ghaut and river's woods.

Julia trudged beside the road, with steady and measured pace, glancing backwards time to time as if she feared to be surprised by the occasional car or truck that roared along the road, and paused on the uppermost point on a hill. A piece of broken pot or clay shingle lay nearby and she used this to scrape mud from her shoe. And walked on. She made a circuit of the entire property, grown substantial enough that an afternoon was needed, and a task she performed almost weekly. Now home, gladdened, feeling more secure for having made the circuit.

Maggie poked her head slowly around the gate post, sprang forward and hobbled, as best as she could through the gate.

Now Julia ran forward and mutely hugged her dog. "Oh, you're an old dog," she said.

Though happy to see her house reappear in sight, she frowned at small evidences of maintenance and growth that had gone derelict in her absence since she passed that way last. Julia dropped the grocery bag which held her lunch, and bent to unroll one of black woolen stockings worn, mistakenly, in the morning. She sat in the porch chair, moved to the edge to bath herself in sunshine, and scratched enjoyably. In bare feet she stepped into the loamy black earth and pretended to fall into the high-grown primroses. Sweet scents and greenesses soaked into her ears, her nose, her chest heaved. For a long time thereafter she lay among the primrose, causing Maggie to poke in her nose from time to time, lying still except for wiggling toes.

The primrose stalks were bright green, as if flushed through with the hue of new rain grass, a color that existed on the earth only in young grasses immediately after a full rain — the color would vanish by the next midday.

Once in the past Maggie had been a spry and energetic, protective young puppy, then in later years a stately and dignified pet, now only recently had she turned creaky and arthritic — a bit like a dignified matriarchal mother-dog, though never actually a mother with pups. For the past year Maggie's joints had stiffened and walking became painful and difficult, so Julia had constructed a cart, outfitted with rug and water dish holder, for use in wheeling her companion into shady and warm spots in the yard at different parts of the day. Often, because the jostling in the cart also seemed uncomfortable to the dog, Julia often simply took carrying Maggie in her own arms, to gently set her down onto the porch in the morning, and indoors later in the afternoon on a cushion and blanket in a place of honor in the kitchen. In July and Augusts of the year Maggie slept comfortably on the porch all night. Julia had briefly considered construction of a small, narrow-gauge railway that would have provided a smoother journey from one sun spot to another, but in the end judged that project too impractical. Maggie like Julia herself appreciated the simple and natural way most of all.

One morning in summer Julia wandered onto the porch for mail and found that Maggie had died. She had fallen asleep on a rug and not woken up. Her eyes were closed and her body stiffened into an awkward position with shoulders thrust forward and hips turned obliquely to the side. Julia stood idly by, overcome by a reverie of memories, saying softly, "I should have paid more attention to you yesterday. I should have paid more attention to you all year long." She knelt beside the dog's body and stroked the old fur whose hue and texture were as well known to her as the back of her own hand, "What a good, kind dog you were."

In the afternoon Julia constructed a mortise and tenon casket made of good maple, and she laid Maggie onto one of her favorite sweaters, and filled the casket with Maggie's heart-shaped dog license, a bag of crunchy food, a blanket for warmth, a box of dog biscuits, a squeaky toy, a bone wrapped in cloth napkin and her old dinner plate. She buried Maggie behind the golden knoll with a small gray rock as headstone.

The lamaria necklace.

Not hour by hour / But grief by grief the day passes.
—Pablo Neruda, "Initial"

Jonathan Gunn's house was an ancient one, unrestored Victorian wood, dilapidated and shorn of friendliness. The eaves broken, windows blackened. The yard overgrown and weedful. Michael was struck when driven up the path that this appeared much like the house he grew up in before Julia's arrival. Before her energy and work ethic transformed the dreary Hardy house into its own bright world. As if reading his thoughts Madeleine beside him at the same moment touched his shoulder, "Julia needs to spend a year here."

Michael knew that Jonathan rarely ventured outdoors when not working in the city. He resembled Michael, at least the past Michael, in seeing no real purpose in the outdoors except as a storeroom for objects for study.

After walking indoors, Jonathan immediately sat himself at an upstairs desk, book in hand, chin in palm of hand, already having left his new visitors to fend for themselves in the house, to make themselves comfortable. Michael was again struck with a thought, "Is this what I seem to be, to others? Am I rude to them? Is this what I will become?"

Michael and Madeleine often walked together mornings in the woods behind the house while Louise slept, usually striking inland towards a series of low, steppe-like hills, looking like an egg-carton turned upside down. They would hear a rumble, a low timbered pummeling from seaward which Madeleine avoided instinctually, without asking its origins. Around them in the hills was a scattering of runty shrubbery, nothing taller than their knee, "It feels," said Madeleine diffidently as if speaking alone, "as if the earth is so young nothing has had time to grow taller than these." Michael said nothing but felt the wind lift the hair on his forehead, felt the coolness of the oceanic air in his eyes.

"Walking in natural surroundings is supposed to be elating, isn't it? Haven't we all agreed in this century to say that beautiful nature restores the soul?" They walked onwards and below, more inland, began a grove of redwoods, second growth, no tree taller than twenty meters. "Yet nature red in tooth and claw or something like that. We think about competition and natural selection with animals, the food chain, one animal eating another. I think it's true even with plants: they crowd each other for sunlight. Their roots push and shove each other for veins of water, minerals. Some wither. Some flourish. All is selfishness. But it seems all the more terrible because these struggles take place in plants without voice. All the agony voiceless and mute."

Madeleine rambled on in a poor mood, and Michael trailed behind, wishing she would be more cheerful and feeling later somewhat despondent that a change of scenery, a few days among the celebrated redwoods and Jonathan's otherwise bucolic house would do Madeleine good and lift her moods. But none of this had such an effect, Michael and Louise, instead, played games with each other.

When she and Louise were alone Madeleine once startled herself by turning towards the roaring noise, a roaring she was never certain if external or internal to her own mind — uncertain if the roaring took place within herself or not. Louise followed dutifully in her hopping, mincing steps. Madeleine made a faux bow, glued onto a barrette for her daughter. Happy at receiving this, Louise ran skipping ahead, sometimes walking on her heels, throwing out her hands for balance with ribbon in hand, holding the ribbon aloft to the winds, later walking with her feet turned outwards and walking with bow-legs. They rounded a strip of redwood and saw a gray level expanse open in front of them. At first Madeleine thought they had wandered to the edge of a desert, then saw strange foam at the edge of sand, and realized that the gray was made of water. A vast, unimaginable expanse. They stopped at the gray edge, in surprise. Louise raised one hand frozen in midair, frozen in her astonishment.

"Ocean."

"Ocean," questioned Louise, emphasizing the nice *ssh* sound in the word. Repeating the word to herself as if needing to memorize the sound, as if the repetition would link the word to the astonishment and fix it for her own enjoyment in her mind.

Three gray feathered gulls dove downwards in a line as graceful as the inner curve of a shell and Michael marveled at the communication that their synchronicity required, wondered idly how that was possible. In a similar way he thought of the coordination of a flock of birds that turned mid-air with a oneness of mind as if a single organism turned, as if all members of that group of gulls were single fingers on a hand.

Two of the gulls hovered above the waves and the third caught a breeze in its outstretched wings and remained motionless in the air as if frozen into place, meters above the roiling sea caps. It remained in that spot while his brethren flew from behind and past, until with invisible motion of wings resumed his flight and rapidly flew from sight.

"Look at the ocean," motioned Madeleine, "I'm so proud of myself for seeing it. When you get right up close to it, you can, look, how it's monotonous and so varied at the same time."

"Some people live here and see the ocean every day and they'll never admire it so much as you."

"I always felt afraid of it somehow. Even looking at the big blue section of ocean on a map. It'd make me feel nervous. I preferred the nice colors of a good solid continent, oranges and greens and browns. On the other hand it may be sometimes good to turn towards one's own fears, to confront them or at least look them in the eye," explained Madeleine, as she and Louise and Michael now chose the ocean's edge as the preferred destination for their continued walks.

Sometimes venturing barefooted into the sea itself, Louise shrieked at the cold dead grip it took on her ankles, raced back up the slope of sand and let the wave chase, then courting danger she would race down slope again to dare the wave to give chase once more.

"The wave has a calm moment at the very crest, when it stops at the high point on the sand, when it seems to stop or pause and it seems very soothing then," said Madeleine to no one in particular.

One day on a walk along the beach, which seemed bereft of visitors, Michael busied himself on the shoreline — kneeling on the darkened edge of sand where wavelets of water washed over him — as he worked on a project for Madeleine. Great quantities of kelp and sea grape lay strewn upon the sand that in afternoon gathered black clouds of flies. Taking a single strand from the bunch, he laced it around his wrist and examined it closely and chose to make a necklace from it. A *lamaria* necklace he called it. He bit into one edge of bulb and fit into it another edge of the strand, looking strong as surgical tubing into the hole, knotting one end. And placed the necklace, leafy, salty, around her neck. "Thank you. It's very nice," admired Madeleine, patting the unexpectedly delicate, gold-veined leaves in place on the slope of her bare shoulders.

Louise hopped up and cried, "I want a necklace too."

"Let's make another one. I'll show you how." But Louise pouted, "It's not the same. I don't want to make one. I want you to make one for me." So Michael complied.

"Now when I say, *it's very nice*, I mean something more." Madeleine fumbled with her words as they returned to the house and simultaneously held tightly to her new necklace and door key. The return to the house never was so invigorating as the walk outwards. "You once asked me if I ever felt happy and I remember saying that *no*, nothing made me feel happy. But I felt happy when you put this necklace around my neck."

"Then," Michael added, "I ought to make a necklace every day."

"It wouldn't be the same. That's the trouble with living, nothing comes so easy."

"I suppose not."

Michael and Madeleine rarely spoke these days, though not unhappily. To Michael's view of things they had become accustomed to one another in the time spent together. He could intellectually recognize Madeline's sporadic dips of mood in which she disappeared entirely from sight. He inquired, he fumbled at the awkward moments when she seemed to live in genuine distress but she never asked for help. He had a sensation that she simply slipped away from him and that the slippages were beyond her control also. If he could help her, he felt, he needed to be an entirely different person, he needed to grow a different appendage, like a third arm or a third leg that understood and could comfort, but frustratingly these moments with Madeleine only seemed to point out his own inadequacies. Not that she blamed him for inadequacy. He could grow the comforting appendage, he thought, only in a process of incredible pain, in some way that women underwent pains in childbirth, but of course in the winding path of his ordinary life he could undergo no similar transformation wrought of pain. In fact, if anything, their life together was entirely too comfortable. And in the comfort of their lives dissatisfactions and dissolutions were only to easy to ignore.

Prodded in this way, awkwardly, and feeling that these impulses to aid Madeline were not originally in his character but with gradually more ease and familiarity, Michael became more attentive, began to share more of their mutual lives together, to make necklaces for Madeleine, and when, demanded, for Louise. Necklaces from daisies, roped together, golden dandelion. Madeleine flushed and pleased as a cream puff, with tiara of roses, leis of gladiolus, garlands heaped around her neck, bracelets — blooming flowers behind her ears, in buttonholes and bulging in her pockets. While Louise delighted in every material thing, Madeleine took Michael's necklace-making as a gesture of his own willingness to bridge the gulfs that separated them originally.

"Louise is due back for the start of kindergarten next week," said Madeleine with mouth half open to let the oatmeal cool. Louise ate on, enthusiastically, spoon held in five-fingered grip, unsuspecting. As if the profusion of flower bracelets, necklaces, crowns and even dandelion dress that fell apart at first wearing, that Michael had assembled for Louise earlier on an early morning walk, seemed to compensate for all failures in her mood at breakfast, Madeleine spoke less but the mood in the spare house seemed lightened.

To celebrate, or rue, the impending departure Michael had gathered a large collection of firewood and that evening he set a small fire alight, arranged in a pit dug into the sand. They gathered to eat their last dinner in a mournful mood.

Michael had forgotten what fire smelt like, its primeval nature, an autonomic and enervating nasal smell in it. He stood as close as bearable to the fire and took in the smoke and brine. The smell of blood returned to his head, enlarged it. The smell of the blood washed through his temples into his nose, and sickened him, woke him, invigorated him. He, as if punched in the head, looked beside him at his fellow picnickers illuminated with flickering streams of light with a different sharpened sense as if all his previous life were a dream and he had only recently come to life. Madeleine watched Michael as he frowned, mistaking the frown for sadness, and she became sad herself and felt herself slipping out of her grip in the moment.

Madeleine had begun the process of packing Louise's clothes and belongings into the pile of bags that had somehow been surgically packed full on arrival. "When we arrived," she said, "all this once fit into the bags. Why won't it fit now?" She felt a quick, corrosive pang of frustration that wounded her, and Michael put a light hand on her arm, which she yanked away impulsively. Something self-harrowing, a burrowing sensation within her, was at work here simultaneously. She meant to say, "I want to be alone right now," but said in its place, "Leave me alone," and the tone which she, mistakenly used, stirred up real anger in Michael which she had not seen before, an indignant anger rose up in his craw and they argued vehemently. Louise stood nearby, in hallway, with hands over her ears, grimacing to herself.

Michael needed a few hours to himself, to calm himself, to sort through a mass of conflictions in his own mind and later found himself sitting beside Madeleine on the bed where she hadn't stirred. He folded a few small shirts. She refused to look at him, but in trying to match up a few of the small socks, her hands shook, and she put down the socks again. Several pairs matched, the rest were odd-colored singlets. She often felt sympathy for the singlet socks and never threw them away. When Michael tossed out his unmatched socks, she sought them out and kept them for herself in a clothes drawer of her own.

Madeline's angry mood had melted. She put a finger under Michael's chin and lifted his face to examine it. He had not aged gracefully, she thought. His face was more haggard than his soft life and comfortable circumstances would seem to permit. His hair already peppered with gray which did not give him a distinguished appearance as gray hair some times gave men, but made him look as if he had simply aged too quickly. He still had the quick and adroit expression of intelligence but now with the awkward elbows and large hands of adolescence without youth. Yet as his features hardened, grown craggy and lived-in, he seemed more handsome. How unfair! Madeleine had struggled all her life to balance disregard of her looks favoring an attempt to become a balanced, inwardly substantial woman, but admitted privately to keeping watch at all times of small changes in her own appearance. Rue, feigned inattention, obsession. That was her life. If she admired anyone in this regard it would be Julia, who seemed truly feckless, diffident, to appearances. But Julia herself lived much like one of the sad orphaned socks Madeleine kept as a kind of novelty pet. A perpetual singlet. An isolated ward in her fenced world, in an isolation that Madeleine would have found terrifying. Terrifying to be alone, not only in her own mind but alone, physically, in the world. Not to wear necklaces made from seaweed. Not to feel another person's breath in her own nostrils. Madeleine moved confined in the fence of her own skin, a prisoner in a wider world perhaps, but free to try with all her might to break down those fences. Did Michael think the same of himself? How did Julia live? Was Julia happier than either she or Michael?

Madeleine stretched a sock between her hands, rubber band style, and shot the sock at Michael's face. But it fell short onto the pile of unfolded clothes, and Michael was jolted out of his own reverie and smiled at her attempt at humor. She had not minded loneliness in the past. Only with Michael nearby, since his arrival in San Francisco, did she realize that loneliness was not an ordinary way to live but a confinement unique to herself, unique to the choices she had made earlier in life perhaps. At seeing Michael and Jonathan talk for hours on topics common to each other but not to her, and awareness at the awkward reach for conversation she had with him, at dissatisfaction she had with baby words and time spent with Louise that did not assuage her questing, a bitterness and pitiless shaking rose up, filled her lungs, made her dissatisfied at being a single person, not joined inwardly with any other single person, with sharp painful edges where her own self ended. As quickly as a burp, her mood dived again.

"You're so dull these days. Why did we come here anyway. I could sit and home and stare at a wall and be just as entertained."

Michael turned his eyes to her but didn't rise to the baiting.

"Understanding you requires too much thought and energy for me." She tightened her lips.

At looking at him sitting on the bed, folding up Louise's little pants, again the fear that he would leave her alone with her own thoughts began to frighten her again, a chemical rushed through her veins, heightened her fear, alarming, rosy in her face and arms, but not her hands which begin an imperceptible quaking, a shaking from within. She reached for his arm, and pressed so tightly that her fingernails cut into his skin, and a stream of blood ran down and dripped from his elbow on the laundry, onto Louise's tiny pair of purple pants.

Louise ran into the room, crawled across her mother's lap, hopped onto the floor and ran out again, while Michael and Madeleine looked at the other.

"I'll take Louise and visit Julia in Napa, in the last few days before preschool. Would you like to come too?"

He shrugged his shoulders, "Doesn't the preschool

begin tomorrow?" He smiled at Madeleine's feigned doubt. "I'll stay on with Jonathan a few more days."

The pair of fugitives from preschool had visited their grandmother's house, then as quickly as was felt polite, marched through the town to the old-fashioned rural portion, left old-fashioned involuntarily since Julia had kept buying up property and left it unimproved and they stopped marching in front of the slightly forbidding wall and gate of the Hardy house. Louise ran her hand over the rough stones of the wall, humming to herself.

Madeleine held onto a brass fitting on the gate, and used it to make a resonant knocking on the closed gate, though it hurt her knuckles, and let Louise continue to knock with a stick found on the roadside, for a good long time. Silence reigned within, and they took to yelling out their names, Julia's name. Louise shouted, "Help help oh help!" And they laughed together. When they tired, Louise suggested climbing the wall, but Madeleine began to walk around to the back, climbing over a low wall at another edge of the yard, which extended an unexpectedly long distance. And soon, with rising noise in the distance she understood their neglect. A great roaring rose out of the side area of the grounds. A mechanical, diesel roar.

When arriving at the closed kitchen entrance of the house, Julia still appeared nowhere in sight, not indoors nor in the sheds or in the grassy knoll or swimming pond. As they hunted, feeling certain she'd be somewhere on the grounds of the house, they felt they were playing a game. Then they heard the odd metallic roar again, in the distance but took no notice, until it snarled near and they could hear a new sound of gears grinding as a clutch was let out too early and at last the putter of a large engine in low gear growling louder as it approached. The mystery was solved when with a heavy odor of diesel fumes Julia appeared perched atop an old, blue Ford tractor, which Madeleine recognized as abandoned town property, years ago. She had got it running somehow. She had tied her hair into a red kerchief and smiled down upon them from her high perch, clearly enjoying herself in her interrupted solitude. The smile instantly turned into a frown at seeing strangers beside the house.

Madeleine stepped back and held Louise close by the shoulders as the tractor rumbled up nearly up to their feet. Julia did not let out the clutch until Madeleine's breath held and she closed her eyes in fear, then the tractor turned expertly and parked neatly parallel to the shed. She climbed down. Madeleine saw she wore some old pants of Michael's or his grandfather's which had been patched in the seat and knees and a nearly new chambray work shirt spotted with chaff. Julia approached, squinting cautiously at her visitors then smiled cheerfully at last recognizing Madeleine close up. Madeleine smiled too at seeing Julia in good health and spirits, adding, "I like your car."

"I ordered the parts by mail order catalog and learned to fix the engine from a book called, *How to Fix a Tractor*." Clearly proud of her achievement but frowned at saying, "The gas mileage is terrible." Frowned as if imaging what sort of tinkering would improve the mileage, "But it rides better than you'd expect." Then, "I'm looking in the Truck Trader to buy a backhoe."

Madeleine walked around Julia's new convenience,

uttering sounds of admiration, and Julia with her brusqueness came to the point, "What do you want?"

But Madeleine was not put off by direct talk, not discomfited, "To visit. I'm home visiting my mother. Do you remember I used to live nearby?"

"I cut my own hair now since you left."

"I see. I can tell!"

"I like my haircut."

"You have a smudge on your nose."

Julia shrugged, "I think it grew there a year ago. I can't seem to get it off. It's like these spots on my hands. I acquire spots." Then, oof!

Louise ran up and rammed her head into Julia's stomach.

"Louise!" Surprised more for her approaching a stranger than the rudeness. Louise generally stayed away from strangers but surprisingly now struggled to rummage in Julia's pockets as if they had been friends for an eternity.

Julia held Louise by the head, in the palm of her hand with a stiff arm, looking suspiciously at the little girl's wrestling attempts, barely taller, barely stronger than the little girl herself. Then after a few moments of suspicious surprise, relented. At last Julia did not seem suspicious anymore, "Let's go the orangery where we can repot some gladiolus." She took the little girl by the hand, who then skipped and hurried in larger steps to keep pace with Julia's rapid steps. To Madeleine they seemed children of same age and temperament.

Despite the rancorous introduction, Madeleine knew from Michael's stories that an invitation to the orangery was the surest sign of Julia's trust, for it was her favorite structure on the grounds of the house. The metallic infrastructure of the interior was painted by Julia when still a little girl with an odd color, her favorite, a lime, greenish aquamarine which to Michael's reminiscing, represented a type of mythical sea creature. It was basically the single exception to her otherwise muted choice of colors in her long refurbishing and maintenance of the grounds. Other walls and furniture in the house were finished in their natural hues, or with natural wood stains, or else subdued blues and brown and nice pale, rubbed reds. It had seemed to Michael that painting the orangery this bright, individualistic color was a proclamation of sorts by Julia that the orangery was "her own." It was either in the orangery or root cellar that she like to sleep best when she was a piggy girl with the upturned nose. It was in the orangery that she nursed her baby roses and cuttings, and it was here that the bulbs fresh out of the refrigerator were brought preparatory to their dunking in the dirt of the gardens. Impatient in winter to begin an early start on vegetables, she started seedlings in pots each year. Despite twenty years of hard work in dirt, she had never tired of being witness and shepherd to the miracle of plant's life, as if her astonishment at seeing her first packet of radishes poking out of the dirt had never ceased to amaze.

After leaving the orangery, each new bulb spent a day or so in broad flat pans on the stone balustrade in front of the gabled walls to warm up then to be plugged twenty inches underground as part of their phoenix-like burial. Many panes of antique glass were set among green-painted iron. Grown upwards along the inner walls were long fingers of shrubby roses, not as a water-fall but a water-rising.

Madeleine said in surprise at seeing these, the wall of upward rising roses, "I thought roses only grew in a bush shape." Julia shook her head and pointed. On an interior wall the blooms stood out in a ravishing display of their shape against the contrasting flatness of the leaves, glass and iron trellis. Her favorite wall without roses had always been the brick behind the orangery where cascades of wisteria flew downwards in bunches of grape. She pointed this out to Madeleine and Louise, modestly adding they looked particularly well at this time of the year, mentioning that she called this wall, "Niagara." When Madeleine came round the wall and saw Niagara for the first time she involuntarily stepped back and exclaimed, "Oh my!" Louise stood under the cascade and childishly raised her arms in glee, as if she could lose herself in the rain of blossoms and color and scent.

Beside the wisteria were a few furrows, with dry-looking weedy plants protruding. This was Julia's small herb garden. A few shrubs were surrounded by a fine mesh net to keep out aphids. In this plot she grew Chinese chives, rosemary, sage, scarlet salvia, fennel with nice yellow flowers in bloom at this time, a type of Italian parsley, tarragon, basil, thyme, curly parsley. At dinner time she'd walk here to pluck and snip and pinch off those leaves she needed for her sauces.

Within the gabled hut, Julia pointed out the various tools and materials of her trade, the spades, an adz, chisels to chamfer boards, and odd trench digging implements. Some were miniature and jeweled, whose handles were worked with bits of colored tile. The little girl bent often, with hands clasped behind her back, to examine each in turn, describing some with exclamations of delight which in turn pleased Julia to no end. After talking with and observing the little girl for a few minutes, Julia had quickly lost her composure and reserve and smiled at the girl simply out of pleasure with her company. She asked, "What's your name?"

She didn't ask, "Who are you? Who is your father?" seeing a strange resemblance to Michael in the little girl's face. It did strike Julia with a melancholy pang or two in her heart to see such a reminder of Michael, whom she had not looked at or talked to for years.

The girl's eyes widened in alarm at trying to speak clearly. She tried to locate the word for her thoughts. At last she grasped it in her mind and then her lips fumbled in trying to form the syllables to the words. "My name is Louise." Hearing her lisping voice Julia felt a sudden pang of kinship. She awkwardly touched the girl's hair and Louise instinctively moved in, forcing Julia's embrace. Louise began to suck her fingers with contented, closed eyes.

Madeleine opened her eyes, brought down her arms, "Your flowers are beautiful. Do you grow vegetables?"

"Vegetables? Do I have vegetables?" She took Louise by the hand and hoisted her atop the tractor and invited Madeleine on board, motioning that she stand behind the open driver's seat and hold onto a pole for support. Madeline smiled at seeing Julia's straw seat cushion, and the box of Kleenex strapped to the yellow metal dash, with a straw box attachment that held bits of old meals. Beside the seat a water cooler and larger wooden picnic box were strapped to the vehicle engine compartment. Julia had removed the keyed ignition, and to start the engine she merely had to poke at a large button beside the wheel, on which she had painted a smiling face, and the engine chugged into life, huffing at a low murmur. When she stepped on the gas pedal the murmur altered into a roar, and she drove the tractor forward over a low berm of grasses beside the orangery then further afield into the paths beyond.

In a few minutes they rumbled through a grove of white-barked trees and with clear pride Julia pointed out the orderly rows of vegetables she had planted, no longer a simple garden, but on the scale of a small farm which now provided her with the self-sufficiency she had craved since she was a little girl. As they drove past, Julia pointed out the rows of radishes, asparagus, tomatoes, cauliflower, eggplant, garlic, parsley, wide-leaved Bibbs lettuce, and winter beets, cabbages, broccoli, different colored peppers, "I hope some of them are sweet!" she called out above the snarling engine. "And there," she pointed, "are kale, Swiss chard, basil, mealycup sage but most of that is potatoes. Potatoes! I'm a potato woman."

The tractor chugged along, noisily but cheerfully, at a snail pace.

"You might ask," shouted Julia, "*Do you have any flowers?*" Madeleine nodded as if yes that would have been her next inquiry.

"Yes indeed," Julia answered herself, and pealed off in the tractor to her left, with great contentment, causing Louise to tilt half out of Julia's lap, and at the last moment before falling out, Julia reached out with calm absentmindedness and pulled the girl back to safety.

"Whee!" shouted Louise and her mother didn't notice. Her mouth had opened into an o-shape at seeing the next portion of Julia's work, further afield from the house, in land Julia had bought and finished, seeing the refinished carriage path and stand of young lindens, at the beauty of the scene before her. And beyond Julia's private flower gardens, a feasting of flower that no one else in the town had yet seen for themselves.

"Here to the left," shouted Julia in mock docent voice, "are dahlias and hydrangeas, narcissus bulbs that haven't taken yet, and those are called Kent pride iris. Very finicky. I ordered them from the Burpee catalog but they're not faring well I think. They are supposed to have a rusty color. There are impatiens.

"To your right pink peonies, Canterbury bells and some dull things called Sweet William which I planted because I liked the name but next year I think I'll pull them out. Sometimes the dullest flowers come with the nicest names. That's clematis on the lattice frames, around it — hostas and bunny ears —"

"Bunny ears!" shouted Louise with pure delight.

"Bunny ears" affirmed Julia, liking the name. "Sweet peas too."

"Sweet peas!" Louise took to shouting out her favorite names.

"There are columbine, erigeron, those are the pasty white stuff, and sage stuffed around the sides. The white flowers are alyssum mixed up with snow-in-summer."

"Snow-in-summer!"

"Poppies on long stems, and shrubby cotoneaster." Her fingers jabbed right and left.

Julia smiled at seeing Madeleine's appreciative face,

"I probably would like to visit gardens in England. I read about English gardens and according to my books this is partly Englishey."

The tractor made a circle on a gravel patch and they returned to the orangery. Madeleine asked as the engine was poked to shut down, "How long?" Meaning how long had it taken to change the yards so much.

"Oh long. Gardening at least teaches you patience. You want to see your hydrangeas bloom but after you plant them you have to wait through the growing season and sometimes several years pass. You have no choice but to wait. And sometimes they don't take and you suffer heartbreak." She saw Madeleine's smile at her use of the term.

"Yes heartbreak" she continued with a tone of defiance. "I might be alone but if the hydrangeas don't take that's exactly what I feel." Madeline climbed off the tractor and lifted Louise from Julia's arms. Beside them a deep lot of flowers with a wide hedge of grassy lavender. Some of the lavender, more untended at the edge, had grown up in unruly, rounded and knobby clumps.

When indoors again, Julia made sandwiches from bread with an aroma that grabbed Madeleine by the throat and gave her a good shaking. She hadn't smelled good homemade bread for a long time, years even. A bean soup warmed up in a crock on stove. Madeline admitted, "You eat well here. I feel ashamed of my mothering and cooking skills."

"Nutrition is important."

Louise was tearing into her sandwich with a good appetite, something Madeleine did not always see. Louise turned to Julia with a mouthful of half-chewed sandwich, mischievously, opened her jaws wide to show how much she could cram in, and Julia too did the same, making Louise laugh and spit out some of the sandwich onto the table, pounding the table top with her hand.

"Louisa!!"

The girl covered the spit out mess with her napkin and pressed her lips together in mock innocence. After a moment, Louise bowed to the inevitable, swept up the sandwich mess in the napkin and shook the napkin clean in the compost box as shown by Julia's motioning hand.

"Michael wanted to know how you are."

"You can say, *Julia is well, thank you.*"

"I don't know why he doesn't visit. Isn't this is his own home too?"

"He doesn't think so. He left here a long time ago and I think he doesn't feel as if he belongs here, at least as much as I do. He doesn't have roots like a tomato. He's more restless and modern." Julia frowned as if this were an impossibility, motioning with a sweep of her hand, then shrugged. "I tried to leave here once but I couldn't. My roots are here. My feet are dug in here."

"Why don't you invite him back here for a visit? Maybe he feels this is now your home and not his. Maybe Jonathan too. You could have a dinner party."

"They don't need invitations. This is their home as much as mine." Yet simultaneously her mind filled with the novel idea of a dinner party. The idea of guests in the house was simultaneously appealing and appalling. She could light the lamps in the paths, as had been done many years past. Guests could mingle. Sounds could drift over the trees, as if they were so many wistful spirits of this house past, the spirits, as she remembered them when she was a little girl who would be eager to resurrect these memories. The spirits would hover to hear again sounds that passed unnoticed in their human lives, from a time before Julia had lived here. She always had been curious who lived here before she did, curious who had built the house of which she had become so fond. The clink of plates that clack, a person's quiet breathing, floor boards creaking under the weight of a walking foot, most of all the wordless noises of the human voice — sounds Julia rarely heard even for years at a time in this house — murmurs that meant happiness, doubt, regret, and odd guttural sounds meaning yes, or "I don't know," and sadness, bewildered uncertainty, contentment. Many sounds she would have liked to hear, sounds not made only by herself. She would like to smell friendly smells not made by herself, to see things not made by herself. To be filled up merely with the imagined sights and smells and sounds, as if this house were once again filled up with human presence and human life, made her smile involuntarily and happily.

Even on the short crunchy walk on gravel back to her car with Julia and Louise in tow, Madeleine's mind filled with pensive, pessimistic thoughts about her return to San Francisco. Louise sang to herself, happy with the soup and sandwich and sights of Julia's gardens, helped herself into the back seat and pressed her face against the window, opening her mouth, flattening her nose and tongue against the glass. Madeleine motioned for her to stop saying, absently, "That's unsanitary." She paused, keys in hand, turned around and to admire again the house and environs, "This would be a good home for a little girl who is all alone. Who didn't have a mother."

"It *has been* a very good home to a little girl who was all alone," said Julia.

Madeleine grasped Julia arm, the arm so thin that Madeleine's hand encircled all of it, "Do you love Louise?"

"I do."

"Do you love Michael?"

"I don't hardly know him."

"Was he ever kind to you? Ever? Or was he always mean to you, playing tricks and acting remote?"

"He was always the same. He never changed. He was never *mean*-mean. But he was rarely nice." Yet at this Julia paused, as if summoning from someplace within her, a dredging operation when the weight of the object dredged were heavy and stubborn.

"Once he was nice and I nearly forgot it. When I was a little girl I had a bicycle. The bicycle had training wheels. I rode the bicycle every day for miles and miles, always in the yard. After several months I saw a picture of a bicycle without the training wheels. No one ever noticed that I had grown up but still had the training wheels. A whole year had passed. And at that time, then, I didn't understand how a bolt and nut worked.

"One day Michael used a wrench and took off the wheels. Now I was happy and I said thank you. But he didn't leave. He waited because he knew I would have trouble riding at first, and though he didn't say a single word to me the whole time, he ran behind the bicycle while I rode in a circle on a garden path, until I found the balance and could ride the bicycle alone. He was patient and tender that day but he didn't say a single word. That was the only time he was tender. I was about eight years old."

Madeleine watched her face carefully and kept her own face composed during Julia's recital of Michael's meanesses or lack of meanness. And in a quiet voice that broached no doubt, "You love Michael." With some wistfulness in her voice.

Julia insisted, "I don't love anybody bigger than myself. Why would he like me? He doesn't know anything about me except I wash dishes like a maid in this house." Then, "I did once think how I'd like it if he were blinded and had to limp home with his hands patting all the walls and doors trying to get in and I would care for him. Or if he was crippled. Then he could use the chair with wheels on it, and have a rug on his lap, that's in the attic. Or if…." And her voice trailed off as if her mind wandered with a long list of crippling injuries that he could suffer by her thinking it.

"But it doesn't matter because I'm already an old lady. An old lady who's very happily set in her cranky ways. I spend all my time puttering in the yards here with a watering can, talking to myself. Maybe I'll become a beekeeper and wear a funny hat or goggles. That life is rich enough for me. I can tell you."

"Michael thinks he's prospering in the world. But at the same time he's growing more empty, and older, at the same time. Nothing will persuade him to leave academics, that empty, meaningless race of rats." Madeleine felt bile rise in her throat, felt she probably wouldn't stop herself once words came out, "Michael likes to study and analyze things. He analyzes but feels nothing. That kind of life is impossible here in a place like this. You've made this house into a complete thing of beauty. And where can we find beauty in the world anymore. At this house, so many beautiful, thoughtful things," she gestured with a sweep of her arm, "there's nothing but good feelings here. Nothing to analyze, everything warm and affectionate to feel.

"Michael can change. Michael is strange enough, he is strong enough. If he's wise enough and not *too* smart."

Julia nodded her head, "I hardly talk to people. I think I understand what you're saying. If Michael would do that then I would love him, even if he wasn't blinded or crippled."

Madeleine laughed, "At least, before I send him this way, perhaps he can change like that, perhaps a miracle will cause him to become a better and kinder kind of person."

By this time Louise had tired of her neglected faces in the window, faces of protest and impatience, and slapped the window with the flat of her hand demanding that they leave.

"The empress calls and off we go."

Julia shrugged her shoulders and whistled aimlessly with her wetted lips in a feigned indifference, having begun to feel a little nervous and awkward at the turn of their conversation, that what she began as a flippant conversation was taken unexpectedly serious by Madeleine the whole time they were speaking.

At the door to her flat, Madeleine did not even pause at entering, so distant in her mind was the possibility that Michael be inside, thinking he remained north with

Jonathan, thinking that he would not want to return to a life with her after their argument. She did not see signs or sounds of occupancy on her approach through the entry. Walking briskly to the kitchen, attempting to make light of what she perceived to be a dismal future, she stopped short at seeing Louise leap onto the sofa and be flung upwards into the air in defiance of gravity, as if by strange force of nature. When she fell back into the sofa, with a handful of his hair, Louise brought up Michael's face from the depths of the cushions where he had fallen asleep.

"Stop that!" she called, but half amused at the wincing expression in his face. Louise patted his cheeks and pressed his nose shut, patting him, pulling on his ears. When able, he said to Madeleine, "Look outside at the new garden area." In her absence Michael had industriously rid the small patch of ground behind the flat free of weeds and had planted some kind of plant, fresh from a carton, which Madeleine could not recognize though only earlier in the day she had received a good lesson in garden plants. While she stood admiringly on the porch, Michael joined her carrying Louise under his arm. She said, "It's fateful. If you only knew what I talked about with Julia this morning."

Michael's new life as a botanist began innocently enough. In Madeleine's absence he wandered among the pines and redwoods, thinking idly about the biology of groves of trees, how in his eyes, he saw not individuals but a system of organisms, a more holistic approach than his usual ever-narrow and analytic approach to things. He brooded and moped until Jonathan in exasperation said he should just go home.

Since returning to San Francisco and to Madeleine's empty flat and seeing that the flat, like Jonathan's house, was at first sight drab and cheerless, he tried to brighten things. He found, to his surprise, poking in the square of weedy ground in back, that he enjoyed rooting around in the dirt. He bought a tray of cyclamen and planted them in separate chunks, and read that they would take well in the shade. He found himself looking through the kitchen window at the cyclamen several times per day, a habit he found amusing, remembering Julia's early obsessions at observing the progress of her early gardens. He bought a pH kit and tested the soil, and altered the composition of dirt with peat. He began to appreciate Julia's obsessions a little differently.

Michael groaned, hearing Madeleine implore him to dress. They prepared to venture into the San Francisco Opera House, in the venerable, gray stone Memorial building on Van Ness. Michael hated preparations for formal occasions. Irritable at having to wear a tie, he complained to Madeleine as she stood in her slip worriedly looking at various dresses in the opened door of her armoire, "Operas are for the masochistic. It's a form of punishment. When it's finished I clap like a maniac, thankful and grateful that it's over."

The greater irritation this evening is that he had forgotten how to knot his tie, having tried several experimental lashings but nothing came out even. And to forestall any more whining, Madeleine knotted the tie for him and miraculously pulled the ends flat and even.

Perhaps he was now irked at her competence, "Why invite me? Do I need to be cultured? Your friend Phoebe loves operas." She pulled him towards her with the even tie ends and merely looked into his eyes, so he quieted himself and remained docilely muted. Satisfied and pleased at his quiescence, she turned her attentions back to herself, twisted up the length of her hair into a twine, and with an adroit motion behind her back, and above her head, she wound up the braid with both hands in a swift gesture that caught his admiration, tucked up the ends into a bun, which she secured with a wooden pin. She paused a moment with fingertips over her heart, as if to quell a qualm, to still her heart that might have raced too quickly for her at the moment.

He had made a present for her earlier in the day which she now brought out to reexamine. In the kitchen, seeing a bag of tiny pearl onions, with needle he, impulsively, threaded the onions together to make a necklace, tying the thread snugly to complete the loop, and now, while dressing, she carefully brought out the onion necklace and laughing placed it over her dress, lifting her hair through the loop in back. Michael was impressed, "Very beautiful."

"Isn't it nice? I love this necklace, just as much as the seaweed necklaces you once made for Louise and me."

"I don't mean the necklace. I mean you. You are beautiful."

"I hardly recognize you anymore. You've come along nicely. You have become quite a thoughtful person, Michael. I love the person you are. You've been like one of Julia's packets of seeds. As if the label were missing, one plants the seeds and doesn't know what will come out of the ground at first."

She had worked into a frenzy at the Divisadero clinic, as if time were running out on some project, as if feeling pressure of an invisible deadline, cramming all her time and attention into the problems of others. While as usual finances were tight, having lost a federal grant, and upwards in her mind keeping alive the need to search for a new grant, Madeleine took extra duties upon herself, being the only speaker of Quechua among the staff, she kept close responsibility for integrating women into their new housing and new lives in the city. Madeleine also began a new medication for her moods and started Louise in a new day school, which she seemed to like, already making a new friend on her first day. Michael had agreed to accompany Madeleine to the opera, instead of Phoebe as he suggested, only because the extra stresses seemed to affect Madeleine in a specially urgent and powerful way that she wouldn't acknowledge. He wanted to suggest they take a vacation and decided that intermission would be an apt time for the discussion, especially if he could wheedle out an acknowledgement that she owed him for going to the opera itself.

Used to seeing her in smock or lab coat, tonight he felt surprise at seeing her once more as she used to dress years earlier, when she reappeared at the bottom of the stairs, having given instructions to the babysitter and calling on Michael that it was time for them to leave. She wore a linen skirt and jacket, with bright silk blouse and the homemade necklace made of the pearl onions. To Michael Madeleine never so strongly seemed a woman of ineffable, unknowable contrasts. His perceptions of her were constantly shifting, never still, unendably complex. She was never the same one day to another. At one hour cutting up cantaloupes and dispensing the breakfast to so many children joking and cajoling, and talking to them in different languages she alone at the clinic was able to speak, and in the next prepared, in elegant clothes, to sit through a three hour opera that she knew by heart and prepared Michael by explaining plot and singing arias the whole week earlier in preparation. A woman of surprises, depths, he thought, an ocean of depths. To appear at once unconcerned, capable, authoritative, commanding, at the same time prone to silent suffering that she bore without speaking, and vulnerable to stings that she alone seemed to be inflicted. Tonight she could have been on the cover of a fashion magazine except the presence of a comical cowlick above her left eyebrow, which Michael thought he should mention but chose to ignore. Thus he felt elated and honored, when she wove her arm through his and they walked closely entwined in body, if not thoughts, on the rain-wet streets eastwards past the, slightly grubby Victorian ladies in the Cole Valley, on their ambling, leisurely walk to Van Ness.

Madeleine tended to become philosophical and heady when stuck in mildly pensive moods, as the charcoal-hued evening, threatening them with detritus of rain cloud and wet street, seemed to draw her into tonight. She pointed to the criss-crossed, silvery trail that snails recently drawn onto the sidewalk, as if with faintly glittering pens, "Maybe these are snail hieroglyphics. Maybe the snails are trying to write messages, to communicate with us."

"*Don't step on us*!" Michael suggested.

"*Or, Don't eat me, I have children at home to feed and support*!" added Madeleine. She frowned, "I was thinking earlier how if I become even momentarily happy I can be struck by a guilty feeling, as if we feel happy only in an exclusionary way. I mean, we are happy only at the expense of becoming at the same time self-deluded."

Michael nodded but felt mildly worried at the direction of her thoughts, busied himself thinking of a light-hearted retort about the snails again.

Madeleine continued, "But I don't want to seem unduly harsh or bitter. I'm afraid that I am happy only at the expense of avoiding unpleasantness or honest suffering. A woman in love, skipping home in her happy thoughts, must be physically unable to see someone lying, bleeding and sick in the gutter. One can't be simultaneously happy and perceptive of other, strong feeling."

Michael interjected, "One doesn't need to be happy all the time. Feelings alternate. Replace one another. And everybody deserves, even needs, those moments of happiness."

"Do you? Do you ever feel happy? I sometimes think you live in an emotional monotone."

"That's not entirely true. I felt happy tonight, walking with you."

"I wish you expressed it more."

"Should I try?"

"Yes."

During intermission Madeleine disappeared into the woman's restroom and kept him waiting until the bell rang repeatedly and the crowd emptied from the auditorium, the last stragglers throwing back their cups of coffee into the rubbish bins and hurried to their places. Several ushers in succession frowned at him and one warned him that he couldn't enter until the beginning of the next act.

Madeleine reappeared, pale and flushed, as if fevered, just as the usher finished her warning, using her right arm to hold onto the elbow of her left.

Michael felt alarm, "Are you not well?"

"Let's hurry," and then to the girl usher who had just closed a side door to the auditorium, "We're here! Please it's not too late," pleaded Madeleine, "that's just the preliminary music and it continues for at least five more minutes. Papageno doesn't appear on stage until then." All three bent their heads slightly towards the heavy paneled door and the usher relented only when Madeleine in her urgent distress made a Louise-like pleading face, and the usher recognizing the source, possibly being a mother herself, laughed quietly and let them pass. Madeleine and Michael found their seats and sat through the next two acts in silence.

On the walk home Michael felt her trembling and touched his hand to her forehead. After stumbling a few more steps she had to admit defeat and sat on a stoop, beside an ornate iron railing, "I felt clammy for a second there. Whew!" Michael leaned into the street and hailed a taxi, and they rode home in silence. Madeleine held onto her left arm with right hand, as before, leaning forward until her forehead pressed against the window, eyes closed. Michael tapped on the window and directed the driver, "Let's go to the hospital," pointing out the most rapid way to go.

Madeleine died.

When I say, My bed shall comfort me,
My couch shall ease my complaint,
Then thou scarest me with dreams
And terrifiest me through visions:
So that my soul chooseth strangling and death
Rather than my life.

Job 7:13-15

On Madeleine's second day in the hospital, she had been moved into the ICU. "It's a simple case of stroke, or so we thought, but she's not responding by recovering her heart function," said a doctor. "We can keep the heart pumping for a short while, but the sooner her heart recovers its old functions the less damage." Michael remained in his coat and tie, having stayed in the hospital without respite since their arrival the previous day, and had Jonathan bring in Louise for a short visit. Madeleine wasn't able to see her, and Louise went home again. Michael briefly spoke with Roserie O'Dell, Madeleine's mother who agreed to watch Louise, and see her to school and back, at least during the next day, when Michael would return home or else alternate with Madeleine's friend Phoebe. Michael was familiar with hospital routine only from his brief time during his grandfather's illness, but nothing seemed different from that time, decades ago. The doctors remote, harried, and unresponsive. All hurried and impersonal.

She propped up her head onto the small stiff pillow and looked at him cagily, mischievously. A few strands of bedraggled hair, made limp by perspiration or fear, curled up in the way her cowlick was wont to do. Michael impulsively leaned over and patted those strands down, licked his own fingers and pulled on those strands so they lay docile again, but in the humid air of the room, soon her hair curled up again. She said, "I was thinking about how pretty it was in Durham when we were there last. Do you remember walking in the horse pasture on the Neil Goodham's farm? I remember walking into the field of fireflies, like walking into a huge black cavern full of candles. All around as if one were swimming at the bottom of the sea with fluorescent monsters and gilded fishes beside you, above you, in all sorts of strange and unfamiliar dimensions. All those dancing flies with lights on their bottoms, flitting, floating, magical. At that moment, of all people, I thought of Julia, and how happy she must be to be in a private land of her own. I understood her then, at least a bit more than usual." She looked above her, beside her, as if in this very room she could see those luminous fishes. And closed her eyes again and gritted her teeth.

She looked upwards, behind her own closed eyes this time, to other fearful emotions still unshaped in her mind. If she could find words for these, to embody them, perhaps they would lose their terrifying force, just as Louise fumbled with the words in her throat trying to speak out. Then she would sleep, she could eat something, she could deal with Louise and the myriad demands of ordinary life, simple to others, insurmountable to herself. She would be able to hold up a glass to a light and not be saddened at seeing how her hand trembled of its own accord, how she had not even the control to hold up a glass to the light unaided, so that the light would no longer appear as a sparkle or corona as evidence of her own incapacities. She dreamt of water, how clear it could be, at the bottom of the sea, as if it were a kind of glass, a mirror which could calmly, serenely, with the placidity of health, reflect back to her images of a world that were no longer agonized to her. In the end she simply tired of her own mind's unceasing and unending and relentless self-ordering, which had become too energized, too frenzied to bear.

Michael mentioned that a heart bypass operation was rescheduled for the evening, but Madeleine would have none of that, as if not interested in the workings of her heart any longer. She caught Michael by surprise by an odd request, "Sing something for me. Do you remember anything from the opera?"

"No, I don't. Mozart is too difficult for me anyways." He thought a bit and then sang in a low and faltering voice something he thought she'd like, part of Wagner's *Tristan und Isolde*, explaining that the song should properly have begun with a short bit by an oboe or bassoon. He sang in that quiet part of the hospital and Madeleine smiled at him. Before he finished, her heart failed and Madeleine died.

Madeleine's face was bloodless, unnaturally pale and ghostlike, in part disfigured by the struggle of her body to extricate oxygen from her failing blood. She seemed neither happy nor sad. She had pressed Michael's hand into her own.

Michael let a scrum of nurses busy themselves around Madeleine's bed, waited first in the room, then beside the door, then sat on a sill by a window at the end of the hallway which overlooked a parking lot, lit in the night by orange bulbs. Earlier in the evening Madeleine had said, "You know, Michael, I trust you with everything. I trust you and entrust you with Louise's life and with Julia's life too."

"Julia Medearis? Why hers? That seems a strange thought."

"I trust that, soon, you'll behave and act in a kind way and in a wise way."

"But I'm neither of those things. I live abstractly. I shirk my personal responsibilities. I have a long established reputation for those things and I won't give up all the time I've spent to develop that reputation. Think of the responsibilities I've evaded because no one believed I was capable of fulfilling those obligations of kindness."

She smiled, with a faint sort of smile as if her external smile for appearances masked another truer smile under that expression on her face, but Michael could feel the second, more honest expression even if he couldn't see it — she could feel that understanding in his presence in the room and it was tremendously comforting to her. "You will change," she thought and let the conversation wither. Madeleine turned her head to the wall. She no longer looked for fishes in the room. She felt herself at the bottom of the sea, under a powerful pressure, what others felt as the daily, trifling costs of existence, borne lightly, exerted upon her a distorting, crushing cost that she could no longer afford to bear. She had borne the weight for years. Now her accounts were running low and she had exhausted herself.

Michael had later become so unresponsive to the persistent questions of the administrative clerks who found him in that corner of the hallway overlooking the parking lot that the clerk looked to Madeleine's insurance information and notified as next of kin, Madeleine's mother. Roserie O'Dell seized the opportunity immediately at hearing that Madeleine was gone, and in the several hours that Michael remained in the hospital, had collected Louise from the babysitting Phoebe, and arranged with the landlady access to Madeleine's apartment.

After further rummaging and furious drawer shaking, Roserie found Madeleine's will and several prominently placed letters explaining what she would like done in case of her own death. In no matter had she mentioned her own mother. Madeleine had named Michael as the father of Louise, named Michael as guardian and her wish in the will that he live with Louise in the Napa house with Julia. Roserie laughed aloud to herself at the thought of this, the impossibility of this, and removed the papers with her as she swept out of the apartment again, roaring to herself in her anger.

Michael sat in Madeleine's apartment, empty of papers and child. Phoebe explained how, despite her efforts, Roserie took Louise and thereafter disappeared. In the meantime she'd arranged for a moving company to take the big pieces of furniture, not that she needed any of it but perhaps to deny Michael the opportunity of acquiring a major keepsake. After a upsetting few days of searching for Louise, calling the police, settling with the hospital for Madeleine's burial, Jonathan visited. He had arranged for Michael's legal help in locating Louise and claiming parental rights. After a brief, one-sided discussion, Jonathan insisted that Michael could do no good in the state he found himself and he was moved into Jonathan's near empty house in Stinson.

"Nothing's wrong," Michael snapped at every offer and attempted solicitude. "Don't think I'm helpless. Remember how you used to insist that I had no feelings."

Jonathan scoffed, "You love your own myth. Naïve self-love."

"How can you cast aspersions on my life. Cast out the log in your own eye."

"We don't need to tear into each other. I'm going into the city. I've arranged for a partnership to take up your suit against Roserie O'Dell."

"Why do I have to do any business at all with lawyers. Shoot all the lawyers."

"To recover Louise."

Michael bit his lip, stormed out of the house. He sat on the slope of beach, on the shifty, flour-thin sand a leg's length above the high tide line. He had gathered several large wreaths of seaweed, and wove necklaces from the bulbs and stems. When he finished a strand, he threw it into the encroaching sea angrily and began another, and continued this past the sun-fall, working in darkness.

After several weeks of furious necklace making, and showing nothing for the labor, Jonathan pretended anger, "You've loafed here long enough, you owe me for the room and board."

"I'll leave today."

"I mean you could be more useful. Neither of us is very tidy. Can you help with the laundry, the housekeeping. If you clean out the yard, and trim back those bushes in the front drive, then we're even."

"I'll call a gardening service."

"I don't want a gardening service. I'm asking you to do it."

Something vague, out of the old relationship between teacher and pupil asserted itself. Jonathan had planned this weeks in advance and had steeled himself for Michael's newly raw aggression. Contemptuously, Michael didn't change his clothes — he angrily roved outdoors, found a shovel, spade and hoe, and charged into the garden, furiously hacked at the overgrowth.

Several weeks had passed and the struggle between Jonathan and Michael continued. Michael worked in the extensive yard at Jonathan's house. Morning and evening, Michael worked himself to exhaustion. He presented a list of supplies for Jonathan and began the task of painting the house. First scraping off the old paint, adding an undercoat and laying two coats of paint over the entire outer surface of the house, a huge and exhausting task, which occupied Michael for several months. When that task was finished, Michael repaired fixtures, fences, repaved portions of the drive, planted new trees. He worked himself into exhaustion and rarely spoke to Jonathan, who returned home each evening very pleased at the transformation to his house. Neither made efforts to speak civilly, and both kept to themselves, eating separately.

Once Neil, from Michael's old laboratory, inquired

from Jonathan about Michael's disappearance, visited and exploded with first surprise, then contempt at their slovenliness, cartons in the sink, food boxes on the floor, "How can you pigs live like this? You're both disgusting."

Jonathan was adamant, "I'm not going to tell Michael what to do anymore. Besides, look at what he's done, I'm afraid he'll stop working. You don't know what a mess this house had been before he started all this work. And I'm not cleaning any of it either." He looked at Michael who declined to answer him.

Neil argued that Michael should resume his life in the laboratories. Michael looked at him with a questioning gaze, while he spoke, as casual and unnerving as any that his own grandfather used to work on him. Neil felt uncomfortable being subject to Michael's intensity, internally feeling unexpectedly vulnerable as if Michael could see every weakness, every poor and selfish thought, every inadequacy of his own lifetime, so he stopped speaking, feeling as if he had no right to lecture Michael. And before Neil left the table, feeling very discomfited, having had no answer to the accusations or weaknesses of his life made bare. Jonathan studied him, amused, having experienced Michael's new-found intensity and anger, made some light comment or banter.

Michael turned that gaze to his food and said nothing, until annoyed at their amusement, at their bantering at his expense, "Neil, I do have a lot of work to finish up in the lab but I've lost interest in it for the moment. You can take up any part of the program if you like. But it's my own responsibility. I'll write up the results and I would have been free anyway to find something else to do. Now,

I might just choose to do other things. God knows I'm not in the mood these days to do any teaching. I'll accept the loss of salary without complaint."

Surprising those at the Divisadero clinic, Michael eventually returned, continued his work and assumed many of Madeleine's old duties, trying to understand her, rarely easily accomplishing tasks she once handled with aplomb but learned in time. He traveled to Peru and wandered through towns where she once worked and spoke to her acquaintances, gaining belated insight into her life, seeing how much she was loved.

The grandfather's funeral, reimagined.

A diorama.

Within the shoebox, open to the viewer without a lid was a funeral scene, much like a Mexican day-of-the-dead vignette kept in Michael's old collection of oddities populated by clay-molded skeletons. But the scene from Julia's imagination was peopled by paper cut-outs, standing upright on a baize cloth standing for manicured lawn, a closed casket carefully constructed from balsa wood. Paper dolls representing Julia and Maggie appeared in the foreground, and a Michael doll in black sweater drawn larger than the other spectators, prominent though set in the background. Wires were carefully glued in place across the top from which were suspended paper angels, cherubs playfully laughing, smiling birds, a stork, a pelican, an eagle. The spectators, besides Julia, Maggie and Michael, included Jonathan wearing his tweed coat, frayed at the elbows, giraffes in the background, whose mottled, velveteen fur was carefully daubed with paint from a sponge, an elephant with trunk raised as a kind of musical instrument, with paper musical notes drawn on white paper, as if the elephant were playing a kind of jazzy flourish while the funeral proceeded. To one side were drawn three little monkeys on the back of a hippopotamus, a prairie dog standing upright on its own molehill beside the excavated dirt of the burial plot, cradling in its arms a large bright diamond. Cotton white clouds were hung high from their own wires in the background and multiple, gleaming chrome suns, five in number, differing in size and placement, made the brightness of the scene seem cheerful.

Old garden roses.

It appeared clear to the doctor, Bernard Rush, and was a source of affectionate amusement, that Julia had unconsciously taken to dressing like the grandfather in small details. She chose the same blue sneakers and nondescript pants and flannel shirts that the grandfather wore for his infrequent jaunts into town. Delighted with her first gift set of boots as a girl, she continued buying the same good quality boot, in the same unchanging size year after year from the same mail-order company though she also kept her old lists of the grandfather's clothes, so practical Julia simply bought smaller sized versions of the grandfather's clothes for herself. Also hand stitched her own moccasins from a template found in her old kit of instructions, used sheets of leather bought by mail, and a heavy needle and leather cord. The very same fuzzy slippers used by the grandfather on the very night of her discovery by the inhabitants of the household were still worn on occasion by Julia in her isolation in this same house, twenty years later, stitched carefully together after small tears, restuffed with batting and cotton patches when necessary, especially when she sat in the grandfather's own chair in the study. To the doctor, she imitated gestures, even, echoes of his old friend and seemed a tribute to the long-dead man. During her infrequent visits to his office, he pointed out these similarities and laughed at her.

"Okay, now, put down the tongue depressors please."

"Can I have one? I could use it in a diorama."

"Yes. Now, cover one eye with this card, and look at these letters on the wall."

"I know my letters. I knew them a long time ago."

"This isn't a reading test. This is an eye test."

"I don't need an eye test. Look, I have two of them."

"If you don't follow orders then you can't have the tongue depressor."

Julia behaved, explained, "I'm creating a new diorama scene of King Kamehameha and the beach in Waikiki. I think the great challenge will be to make some kind of realistic water scene. The tongue depressor will be a surfboard if I cut it back a bit." She blinked owlishly at the squiggles on the wall and tried to pierce through their meaning, to make them clearer in her mind. Then, "Let me try again, I'll do better this time."

"I saw you study the chart with both eyes open. You're going to cheat. Read the very bottom row."

"I wasn't going to cheat. It was harder to see them with only one eye. And the room is dark."

"That's the whole point. To see what you can see and what you can't see."

"I don't worry about what I can't see. If I can't see it, then I just can't see it."

He indicated that she peer into a large machine, with eyeball diopters and levers to adjust. Julia complied but complained, "I can't see because everything's fuzzy."

Rush said, when finished, "You need eyeglasses."

"Eyeglasses!" Then, suspiciously, "How much do they cost?"

"Not much. About six crates of peach jam I think." She begrudged all expense but at heart really wouldn't defy him or mistrust him. She nodded her head in acquiescence.

Within a week her new glasses arrived and in Rush's office in Napa she tried on her pair of spectacles.

"Oooh," she said, remarking at recovering her eyesight with a simple optical contraption, "There's clear letters everywhere you look. I never knew the world looked like this. I'm so glad." Turning to the doctor, she asked, "Ask me to read something to you. Something far away and hard."

He pointed to a billboard across the street, but she felt cheated, "That's too easy, try something harder with smaller letters." So in this way, until his next patient arrived, they played the game of pointing to words visible from the window and Julia reading the messages with great relish.

Julia returned a few days later, interrupting Bernard as he spoke to an elderly woman patient. "Two visits in one week," he exclaimed, "I'm earning more jam than I can eat in a month of breakfasts."

"I was thinking of my carriage path."

"Yes." Bernard filled out an insurance form, absently, while Julia continued to talk.

"I decided that I needed workers to help me. This would be a gigantic project."

"You can put up signs in the union hall in town or put up a notice outside the grocery store.

"I wanted a particular kind of small, child worker."

"You might find a few neighbor children…"

"I mean children of my own."

Rush continued to fill out the form, paused a moment, slightly confused, then when the import of her statement hit his mind the pen scratched on the tabletop.

"Do you remember our talk long ago. You had hip and stomach injuries. Childbirth would be painful and difficult, if not impossible."

"That's what I wondered about, if anything has changed in all this time."

"No, nothing's changed in all that time."

He patted the paper-lined seat and Julia hopped lightly onto the examining table, but upright and talkative. He thought how small she had been when he first saw her, as a bloody, feral child found in the Hardy's back yard, beaten within an inch of her life, and reflected how she hadn't grown much taller or more substantial in all the intervening time since those bad days. Though she obviously was in better health and better spirits, healed over much more substantially by the calming years alone at the house.

"I don't know much about how babies are made even, except from encyclopedia articles. I know you won't laugh at me. But I began to think how nice it would be to have a dependable troop of cheerful child workers, and lot of babies. I decided I could make cherry wood wheelbarrows, and little garden tools about this size." She held her hands apart about a foot's width. "Once I started thinking like that, thinking about babies and the wheelbarrows I hardly have had time or energy to think about anything else."

"Yow," he repeated to himself, at a loss for words, feeling that Julia's stubbornness might make this an issue requiring a long time to resolve and one that might not have a happy resolution.

Michael stood for a moment before the gate with its odd, familiar etchings, to orient himself to the confluence of the unfamiliar and familiar both, growing a bit dizzy at the rush of memories, the apparitions of the half-forgotten past. He stood beside the house at this time of the year which had once been described in a poem as "when yellow begins to show in the leaf." The dense foliage of the maple towered above the gate, the same tree he once hid in during the long forgotten snow battles that had changed him much and beneath the foliage a small patch of rhododendron. Merely by looking and breathing in this place he sensed himself refilled by an ether, a substance made of memories of affections that corrected a wobble or eliminated the "squeak" in his chest that he had been feeling of late in Durham, where he had returned to tidy up the remnants of his old life. So, he believed, it wasn't wrong to be here. Perhaps he should have visited earlier.

The house stood much as he remembered it, he rubbing the side of his head absently, though altered, in mild, barely perceptible aspects. Patches of asphalt had been replaced by gravel, small cisterns had been built and buried to collect rain water. He was unsure whether the changes were in the house or in himself. No grandfather stood above him now, in his thoughts, smelling of tobacco, the strong pipe smoke. Though less active the house seemed more cheerful, in part because of the profusion of wildflowers and shrubbery grown in high and carefree abandon, and the rain gutters swept clean of the rubbish that had lain there for generations, and all of his childhood.

Julia watched Michael approach around the house and gave him a thorough visible examination. He did not frighten her as he did in the past. His appearance had changed much — he seemed both heavier and softer, better mulched, not angry, neither abstracted nor befuddled. He seemed to her to be a mild, calm, more thoughtful man, and not so much the angry, impatient boy. *Oh, Madeleine*, she thought, and a pang of sadness trilled in one of the chambers in her heart, a musical sad note, *this is your work.*

She smiled at him, feeling curious at what he would have to say. When he stood within arm's reach he simply smiled, and she too smiled, but with a smiled stored up with many years worth of feeling, yet inexpertly expressed. Three years had passed since Madeleine died in the hospital and the full span of time had worked its effect into Michael, Julia could plainly see. Oh, Madeline, and the pangs again.

He had become a gardener of sorts and caretaker at Jonathan's house, living in the colossus as quiet as a mouse, as a kind of apprenticeship, he explained, and thought he might visit her in her house too. Perhaps they could trade cuttings and bread recipes. As he spoke, his voice too seemed changed, something different and human in his voice, as if he used his voice not only to communicate a fact a belief or statement, but that something human, emotional or otherwise, lay under, or lay intertwined with, something he had to express with that changed voice.

As a little girl Julia had always tried to minimize her wishes, and lately in her burgeoning middle age still suppressed her wishing, though she enjoyed secretly now and then a small furtive wish that could be instantly sated, but she still possessed the resolve and discipline not to wish excessively. However, hearing this changed component to Michael's voice caused all these restraints to vanish completely, and her heart filled with strong clamors, pangs, ringings, and demands. More fiercely at seeing Michael standing within a breath's distance, her whole body beat out a pang of wishing. She stuck the spade into the ground and let her feelings cool again, drip into the shallow furrow she had dug before he had arrived. With Michael at the house now, the furrow which earlier occupied all her attention now seemed useless.

He approached more closely and stood quietly with her hand awkwardly in his. Suddenly grateful she hadn't been wearing her glasses or else this first minute would have been spent in him laughing at her.

Michael felt suddenly shy, something he didn't recall feeling before. She peered at him with her piggy nose, with the same short-sighted expression, but he was struck anew at her health despite her small size. Julia looked brimming with good health, her cheek ruddy, though teary her eyes still the bright disconcerting blue. This made Michael thoughtful as he remembered how Madeleine had become more forlorn, in time becoming ever more bleak and thin. Julia on the other hand, presented such different, sharp contrast, appearing radiant even and cheerful, in her own element and content. Her arms were burnt from sunlight and her legs, scuffed knees and all, cheerful too, if cheerful legs weren't an impossibility, cheerful too for the children's band-aids carefully placed on her knees.

Michael noticed that only at his own approach did the birds clustered near Julia cease cluttering. They remained motionless on the tree branches but silent. They did not regard Julia as a threat but had become silent in his presence. "I wonder," he began to muse, "if one day I become mild enough that even birds don't fear me any more."

The store managed by the O'Dell family, Madeleine's mother, had prospered in the thirty years under her management, especially as Napa real estate soared high in value when French wine critics began to praise the local wines. The O'Dells began to sell more wine than children's candy and gained wealth.

The storefront had been remodeled and modernized,

and parking spaces installed in orderly rows in the space that had been a laundromat. Within the Chamber of Commerce, Roserie O'Dell was an influential, if sharp-voiced woman. Sixty-seven years old and flush with prosperity, Roserie had moved with her remaining child, to the famous Ruskin house, nearer to and nearly rivaling the Hardy house in size and prestige. But it would be harder to imagine two houses more different — one built in a rural and rustic style with no conveniences but electricity and a gas stove, and the other in the sterile but admired Frank Lloyd Wright style, stark and streamlined, with multi-colored Malibu lighting on the landscaped yard in front. It seemed that one house belonged to the eighteenth century and the other to the twenty-second century.

At this first meeting with Roserie in which he asked to see Louise, things did not go well.

"You are an adulterer and corrupter of children. You killed my daughter. Demanding to see my granddaughter is outrageous. If you return to this house, I will shoot you through the head. If you insist that you are related to my granddaughter, I'll sue you for that outrageous insult. You are a miserable dog."

His silence, even confusion at not knowing the source or reason for this invective, seemed to inflame Roserie to even greater fury until his face was speckled with spittle as her face moved closer to his.

When she had exhausted herself to the point that, when she paused for breath, he added that the only option left to him was to contest custody in court, but that he tried to speak to her in person hoping that something could be worked out quietly for Louise's sake. Her vituperation and scorn resumed and seeing no point in enduring the abuse, he left.

Julia waited for him in the yard, eating a lemon pastry, having set herself in her babiche chair in front of the porch, with a plate of sandwiches on one side and a picnic cooler on the other. She gazed time to time at the backdrop of the Mayacama mountains with dense trees and foliage as it appeared this time of the year. Michael could see it was a lemon pastry by a fresh custard stain on her blouse. When he pointed this out, she rubbed off the custard with a finger and licked her finger, then put the dark spot on the blouse in her mouth and sucked on the stain. The blouse was still in her mouth when she muttered, "Hw d'd i' go?"

"Pretty well considering."

"Will she let Louise visit?"

"Maybe. But more likely not. At one point she threatened me with death."

"Death, eh? Well remember that no one in the town likes the Hardys."

"Eh yes. The next step is to enlist Jonathan and began the legal proceedings he recommended. It'll be a long and involved custody fight."

"If you need extra money I'll sell jam on Sundays again. And I can plant cash crops."

"We'll see. I worked out an agreement with Jonathan while I was gardener at his house. For every billable hour he spends on the case I'll pay back with time at his house. And he said he'll take payment in muffins and jam."

Because Michael had lost the urge to return to the structure of the university, his absence had become an indefinite sabbatical. Since he no longer taught courses, he lost some salary but tenure gave him a basic stipend so he wouldn't lack for money. He allowed his curiosity to be vent upon observations he could collect in the old laboratory he had assembled as a ten year old before leaving for prep school. This small room in the basement was divided part for storage, part for Julia and part, in the dark, little used rear portion, for Michael, outfitted with microscopes, dissecting trays, pins, scalpels, notebooks, wooden cases, tubing, beakers, burners, electrical components, vacuum tubes, transformers, sketches of animals, pressed leaves, ants and insects floating in tubes of isopropyl alcohol, bird's eggs in a dry nest. The walls lined with books, several thousand below the regular library itself.

Because of Julia's housekeeping diligence, the laboratory remained in good condition, not dusty or musty even or mouse bitten. He rummaged, poked and recovered enough of his fondness for investigation to keep his thoughts occupied and too busy to lapse into the doubt that seized him from time to time. In the root cellar, asking permission, he set up a work table for himself adjacent to a table already filled with Julia's work materials. She joked, "If you are a real scientist you should invent a marshmallow that doesn't melt in hot cocoa."

On a corner of the bench, below her framed high school equivalency certificate, was a shoebox with a hole in its side. Michael picked it up and peered inside, and could see a recreation of the familiar façade of the Hardy house, and in front a paper boy and girl, holding hands, with different expressions on their faces. The boy, looking suspiciously like himself, was smiling broadly, joyfully, but the Julia figure more muted in expression, not smiling visibly but seeming content, an odd expression of and Michael searched in his own mind for the term, something that he decided would be called an expression of completeness. He could sense in the diorama, in the paper children holding hands, all the sorts of richness of emotion that he lacked himself. The sense that it was she, remaining at home, tending her crocus and tomatoes, who had after all lived a life of substance and value. With shaking hand he placed the diorama back into its place, and left the room, turning out the light with a quiet click.

Later in the evening, when asked about the diorama, Julia blushed, "I should have hid that one. But it's one of my favorites."

"They're wonderful and it's nice that you've kept them all this time."

"What do you mean *kept them*. Do you think they are only old things from long ago?" Her voice rose with a tone of indignation, "I work on those dioramas almost every night, in secret, when no one's looking. Do you think those are the work of a little girl? I worked on the boy and girl diorama only this morning!" Her face took on an expression of mock outrage.

Still often pensive from Madeleine's absence he noted similarities between the two women without intending too, as if a mind couldn't help but note correspondences the way a mind might pun without thinking or speak in simile or in metaphor. Once Julia arranged a few pears in a bowl, oddly enough just as Madeleine had once done. Though Madeleine arranged pears to suit her own notions of beauty and aesthetic, Julia piled up the pears in a display of substance and as a sign of their availability to be eaten. And throughout the day indeed she ate from the pile without adjusting the pears that remained.

Julia's latest outdoor project was the refurbishing of an abandoned lawnmower advertised in the local newspaper under the heading, "Free to a good home." She said to Michael as she showed him the ad, "That's what I was: free to a good home." And she laughed to herself. She paid kids to push the lawnmower forward into her tool shed, just as they had done for the tractor earlier in the year and there in secret she tinkered for weeks on end, emerging in the evening to consult an auto parts catalog and manual, then disappeared into the tool shed and at times even working into the early evening.

In a few weeks she had finished and the end product looked very impressive.

"Hop on," she urged, motioning him forward to the seat. The lawnmower was the sort where a person sat on top and drove across the yard with a steering wheel while the clippings spewed to the side. He climbed on, pressed the ignition and the engine roared.

"I don't like keys so my ignitions are simple on/off switches."

He said over the chaotic roaring, "I'd like to drive this into town and park it beside the O'Dell's wine store."

"You'll get a ticket. I once asked Bernard if I could

drive the tractor through the town at night, but he said it wasn't a proper licensed vehicle." Michael shrugged his shoulders.

"Good. Could you please mow the outer field of bluebells in that direction. We'll put in a field of tomatoes. I've been thinking of selling a new line of tomato-sauce." In time Michael became accustomed to mowing and tractoring in Julia's fields and unknown to himself when driving the tractor on Julia-assigned tasks he smiled with an expression unerringly like the face given to the paper boy in the Hardy house diorama.

"Look," said Michael. He had returned from a foray into the town to pick up supplies and held up before her eyes, a paper flyer, an advertisement for a flower show to begin in an exhibition hall the following weekend.

"What's a flower show?"

"People bring in their flowers to show to others and sometimes there's a contest and information and food."

"What kind of food?"

"I'm not sure. Cucumber sandwiches and English tea maybe. Served on lace doilies. You have to wear hats and suits."

He realized yet once again that irony was wasted on Julia, "Forget it, any kind of food and you can wear any kind of clothes you like."

"I don't want to forget it. How can you have a flower show indoors?"

"People bring their flowers in pots I guess. I don't know, I only thought you might be interested."

The next morning, rising early and as usual finding

Julia in patched dungarees already at work in the orangerie, she motioned to an adjacent field, "Remember how the far place is a good site for tomatoes. Lots of sun. Would you please mow down the weeds?"

Michael nodded his head, climbed onto his assigned machine and pressed the ignition. As he chugged onto the gravel lane, he turned at hearing a similar, diesel roar. Julia had run to the tractor, gunned the engine and drove up behind him. She turned expertly and entered the narrow path beside him, and with a motion of the wheel, jokingly threatened to push him off the path. When he ignored her, she seemed disappointed and motioned with her hands to pause, and shouted over the hum of the idling engines, "I'll race you to the tomato field. Last one in has to wash the clothes!" He answered by gunning the engine, pulling up the rotors to be certain he wasn't scraping the road to lose speed and left her behind, cackling in a miasmic cloud of fumes and laughter.

Julia's tractor had twice the horsepower, and a real transmission, but he blocked her path and happily puttered along, glancing behind time to time to occupy the whole path and not let her pass. At times he'd let go of the wheel and raise his arms in triumph. But Julia too let out a cackle of triumph and when he looked back again the tractor was gone: she had veered into a fallow field of onion and cut short at an angle, bumping along at a pace slower than a pedestrian's walk. Michael groaned aloud and pounded the palm of his hand on the yellow metal console, the machine chugged slowly and wiggling everything on the dash did no good; impossible to exact any more speed; and in desperate frustration at seeing Julia imitate him and raise her hands in mock triumph, seeing her near the tomato field, he simply let the engine of the mower die and coast to a stop, jumped out of the mower and sprinted across the onion field on foot, jumping the *ha-ha*.

Julia busy enjoying herself had stood upright on the tractor with her hands raised over her head, chanting something to herself, didn't notice his changed strategy, and only when he passed her on foot, jumping once or twice in a smart alecky way, and took off again, did she pause in her antics. She cried aloud too and seeing the futility of pursuit in the tractor, killed the engine and jumped, barefooted, into the field.

By this time he nearly reached the tomato field and without thinking she picked up a hard clod of dirt, largish, the size of her fist and threw it, hitting him on the back of the head, a perfectly thrown, gracefully arched shot that felled him and threw him face down into the loam. Julia had run after him, but instead of stopping, she ran into the tomato field, jumping up and down in the same spot, in her bare feet, with her fists thrown up into the air excitedly. She won; no clothes washing for her today. But not having Michael to share her triumph, gradually a sense that something was amiss stole over her and she returned to the onions to see him lying in the same position.

Her mouth opened in fear. This same thing happened thirty years ago and the same thought returned — that she killed Michael! When she dropped to her knees beside him, her mind was a confused jumble of wondering how to call the ambulance, and what she'd eat in jail, and pity at seeing Michael's life end before — and he turned over and caught her by the waist and pulled her down into the dirt beside him, her face landed in a wet patch of mud, and face down, he pinned her down with his legs and conked her on the head with the same clod of dirt on the back of her head. Bonk bonk bonk.

"There!" he cried. "How do you like that!" Bonk bonk. The clump broke apart and the crumbs sifted into her hair. When he finished his shouting of indignation, the field lapsed into silence, and he could see her shaking beneath him, her shoulders shaking in silent laughter. After a moment she turned and he began to laugh too, when her eyes blinked open and as if wearing a mud pack, her face was smeared with a coffee-colored mask. He fell beside her not laughing, but smiling quietly, he leaned forward and kissed her on the lips, and after wiped the mud off his own lips and made a yucking sound at discovering that some of the mud from her face transferred itself into his own mouth. Julia lay still and smiled, almost dizzy, and her hand sought his.

The Napa Garden Show.

Julia stood at a kitchen counter, coaxing cloves of garlic out of their paperish wrappings with a pound of her palm and the flat of a knife. "I've been thinking about that flower show you mentioned. I was waiting for you to wake up. Would you go and tell me about the flowers?"

"You should go yourself. How can I describe flowers. It's like describing music in words."

After a pause, the obvious compromise, "I don't go to town anymore since it grew so much. I've never been in a crowd of people. Would you go with me?"

"Of course."

If Julia felt pleased by this, it was not only the

affirmative answer but the rapidity and the certainty in his reply that assuaged her nerves.

"If I can't make it, what will you do? I mean what if I get nervous and want to go home again?"

"We will find the nearest exit and walk home."

"If the crowd is too large and confusing?"

"We'll be the very first people in line. When the doors open we can run down the aisles and leave before the hall fills up."

"When does the show begin? In an hour?"

"We can leave right now. I'll find my shoes."

Julia waited beside the closed gate in front, and when Michael strolled up with tickets, she nervously sought his hand. He waited while she locked the gate and gave the latch a good shake, and waited again until she found his hand again. Then cried, "I forgot to bring food!" With genuine distress.

"Remember there'll be food there. The cucumber sandwiches and English tea. I have money. Or else, if you prefer and get hungry we can find a door and we'll walk home for lunch."

They walked along the street and Julia kept to the inner part of the sidewalk away from the street. In the exhibition hall, she did seem to lose some of her apprehensions and studied the placards, soaked up much information and found herself relaxed, even enjoying herself while seeing many flower species and garden inventions that piqued her interest.

At first she walked and mutely observed, then took to grabbing Michael's arm, "Look at that!" "Look at that!" Always conscious of the stares of others in the town who saw her only infrequently. Julia quietly gathered pamphlets, learned interesting fertilizing facts, watched sprinkler displays that kept all the water in plastic cases, and she tapped each of these cases with her knuckles in admiration at the water-integrity.

"Look how much they charge for a sandwich," she scoffed, "Who would pay that much?"

When they returned home, she closed the gate behind her with a satisfied smile at the click of latch. "Now I don't need to go to the town for another year. Sometimes when I leave this house I come back only thinking how everything I like is right here inside the walls. Does that seem strange?"

"No. I think I can understand you better now than I did when I was a little kid."

Julia looked through an upstairs, dormer window at the moment a bolt of lightning lit up the sky then began to count the seconds before the peal of thunder whipped towards her ears. Michael could see her lips move as the seconds mounted. A second scorch of lightning followed and he could see the light reflected on her face.

She had been looking at him strangely now. He felt she was about to give him a harangue about something and actually felt curious about the subject.

"Always tell me truth," she said at last.

This took him by surprise. Not what he expected.

"Usually I do."

"Yes, usually you do, I don't know why but everything is changing for me. When you'll go back to your home everything will be a little different for me here in this old house."

Michael paused, unable to answer because it hadn't

occurred to him that he *would* leave but knew nothing to add at the moment.

She sat in a green wing chair in the library and read all evening, squinting at the text in the dim light. She read a recent gift from Michael, a lavishly illustrated book called *The Wild Garden*. Often her eyes would ache and consequently for relief she'd bring out the *Glory of Roses* again and gaze upon the colored, scrumptious pictures for comfort, a reliable comfort book and a classic.

Julia rummaged through a kitchen drawer, looking for the vegetable parer when she brought out a photograph and gave an audible gasp of pleasure. In the photograph she recognized Michael and beside him was a grown up Madeleine O'Dell. They were very close and together as if awkward in their proximity. She turned the photograph over but the paper side was blank and empty.

Her first reaction was partly pleased at seeing Madeleine again after many years but a second reaction was sadness at the recollection of her absence. She placed the photograph back into the drawer. Then she took out the photo again and lightly stroked her finger over both persons in the image.

Moving among the sparse crowd, perhaps, had given Michael a flu and Julia whose health had been stupendous and hale grew alarmed at the sneezing, watery eyes and fever. "Don't worry," he cautioned, "I'm going to bed to rest."

Soon Julia too began to sniff and rub her nose also.

By the evening her nose was red and runny and she had begun to cough.

"I've never been sick before so I can't be sick now. But I think I'll take a little nap." At dinner her place at the table remained empty — this alarmed Michael. To his knowledge she had never missed a dinner, even been late to a meal. In fact she regularly appeared well before the food in a habitual eagerness. Not in her room, not in the upstairs bedrooms at all or in the house, it seemed — then Michael found her rolled up in a nest of blankets in her old hiding place under the stairwell.

He uncovered her face, after first peeling away a blanket and finding her feet in woolen socks, and at the other end found her closed eyes. His hand on her forehead felt the heat. Sweat.

"What's happening to me?" she muttered through closed mouth, eyes closed.

"A flu, I believe. Are you comfortable in here? I can barely stretch out my legs."

"Oh, it's terrible. I'll never go to another flower show ever. Besides I don't need as much room as you do."

He folded the ends of the blankets back over her head and patted the lump of her head again as he closed the hutch door behind her.

Bernard Rush looked at the bundle of blankets, and Julia within, in the cubbyhole and said, irritably, "Julia go upstairs and into a bed."

"I'm dying. Can't you be nicer to a dying woman?"

Bernard made the same mistake as Michael and chose to open the end of the blanket bundle with Julia's feet, then wrapped up her feet again and searched for her head in the bundle. Became frustrated, "I can't stand upright in this box."

At last he looked at her face, checked the dilation of her pupils and lymph nodes, felt her forehead and motioned to Michael who took Rush's place in the hutch and lifted Julia in his arms, blankets and all. He managed to wiggle her out of the cubbyhole and carried her upstairs in the cocoon, despite her protestations.

"Where are you going? Oh I'm dizzy. Michael, I'm hot and cold at the same time."

Rush asked her for symptoms and Michael explained about the flower show.

They stood by the upstairs window and Michael looked upon the scene, the Mayacama mountains, the spare, washed out colors looking for all the world like one of Cézanne's watercolors of the French countryside. At this time of the year the countryside seemed part desert, spare and skeletal.

Bernard explained to Michael, "She hadn't ventured out of the house grounds for several years. She conducted all her business, if necessary, at the postern door, you know that little wooden mail slot in the wall. She likes to think that her jam sells well at the fair, but I arrange for kids in the neighborhood to do the actual selling in the booth she created. Becoming sick won't encourage her to leave the house more often."

"I've seen her sneak into the cemetery in the early morning, almost every morning while she thinks I'm still asleep. Don't you know? She sits beside the grandfather's grave and lavishes flowers around the marker."

Rush smiled, "Well that makes me feel better."

Michael added, "She works the ground for almost

miles around, even ground that doesn't belong to her." He motioned towards the back of the house, towards the carriage path which was land whose purchase was arranged by Bernard, described the patches turned over for her large scale tomato sauce farm, and the fruit trees that she now used for her jam.

"But that land now does belongs to her. She owns it free and clear."

"I didn't know that."

Rush explained to Michael, "Almost twenty years ago Julia mentioned a carriage path in the woods and how she'd like to work on those grounds. Well, I knew they had been Hardy property a hundred years ago and been sold. So I asked if she'd like to own it and she said *yes*. So I bought it, never telling her how much because she'd be fretful. And it turned out that the land has quadrupled in value, increased even ten times in value. All that land south of the road up to the county line is hers, free and clear."

"Well, so this is a flu she has and nothing more?"

"She's not accustomed to a flu so she's complaining. But she'll live."

"I can hear you. Don't you care about my feelings. You're wounding my feelings," piped up Julia from beneath her blankets.

"She's my favorite patient so I'll drop in every day. But it's a flu and nothing more."

Julia lifted the blankets from her face only enough to let her voice carry to them at the window. "I'll be dead before you return. Just before I die I want to be sitting in my chair by the porch."

Rush continued as if he hadn't heard, "In the

meantime, don't you have any bread? Every time I come by, Julia has some fresh bread and jam."

"Nothing like that for two days now."

Julia groaned, and lifted the blanket, "When I'm dead that's all you miss. Bread and jam. Years later you'll be sorry. You'll wish you were nicer to me."

"I suppose I'll have to cook something now for the both of us. But about now a microwave would come in handy. Sometimes I still do like to eat a frozen dinner."

"You can drop by my house any time," said Bernard. "I found a good brand of frozen dinner. The portions are larger and I like the dessert, a kind of cheesecake. When you put the whole dinner in the microwave, the cheesecake absorbs some of the heat but it stays cool somehow. The old dinners I used to heat up had a cherry pie for dessert and the filling would burn my mouth."

Julia moaned and thinking that the moan was too inaudible, she raised her blankets a bit and modulated her moan, a little more softly, so that Bernard and Michael smiled to themselves.

"Aren't you hungry?" Bernard asked Julia.

"I'm not hungry at all. Dying people don't think about food."

Michael brought up a bowl of soup carelessly, Julia could tell, by dripping on the platter and a noodle draped over the edge of the bowl.

"I hope you wiped the floor where you spilled the soup. But take it away, anyways. I'm dying."

"Don't worry about that for now. Just try this."

"Where does it come from? Did you make it?"

"No, but I think it's just as good as your soup."

She grimaced, upset at this effrontery, and challenged, Julia sipped the soap, "That's nothing like a good homemade soup. That's can soup."

Michael tried a sip too, "It's not bad. It's just like your own three bean soup. Maybe better."

Julia made a snorting noise but sipped a little more to be certain, "This isn't a bean soup anyway." She waved away his soup, a dismissive gesture with her hands.

Michael sipped another spoonful. "I like the spices. They're a little stronger than homemade soups. Maybe more subtle."

Julia had turned away her head but remained motionless while absorbing his criticisms, then unable to bear the thought of well-blended spices, motioned that she'd like to try another sip. He brought up the spoon and dribbled a bit into her mouth. Her eyes remained closed and she shook her head in negation at his folly with spices.

He sat beside her, not laughing at her any longer, and the breeze through the window cooled his forehead. He lifted his fingers to better gauge the breeze, and was startled to see her eyes open, watching him curiously. As he lifted his eyes, her eyes closed again rapidly.

Her feet at the other end of the bed stuck up perpendicular to the blankets.

He said, "You have pretty toes."

Again, she remained silent but a reluctant silence as if she struggled for composure, then relented, saying very quietly, "Do you really think so?"

"Yes. Very nice."

"There's a difference between *nice* toes and *pretty* toes."

"Pretty, then." He turns his head sideways, as if to better admire the toes.

"You never talked about my toes before."

"I think they're your best feature." Julia's face underwent a transformation — breezy sunniness, perplexity, doubt, annoyance, "Don't look at my toes anymore please." Julia immediately regretted breaking her deathly silence while Michael remained ironical so her feet disappeared under the blankets again and she turned away her face the better to express a pout.

"Don't be angry. I was joking."

"You're always joking. You're never serious, and you were almost going to say something nice to me."

"I don't know what you mean. It's not like I'm being offensive."

"You've always been offensive. I remember you once were tender when you showed me how to ride a bicycle without training wheels but that was an exception. The rest of the time you were tying my shoes together so I'd fall."

"I don't remember any of that…"

"I remember it all. I have a good memory for those things."

"You have to remember that people change."

"But mean people always remain mean."

"Children behave differently and you can't hold me responsible for what happened thirty years ago. Children are children. Men are men."

"But I do. I never tied your shoelaces together and laughed when you fell."

"My grandfather once told me that he never scolded you, never reprimanded. He never had to remind you to brush your teeth or take a bath and that you never did anything that was unfair." They both paused in their skirmishing to ruminate about the grandfather.

Julia, "It's irritating to be weakened. I hate it. For the first time I suppose I can understand why it irked you, when you had the typhoid fever. I thought it was a defect of character, not to accept fate, even a horrible, terrible fate. But once you've been sick like this, I don't think I could bear it again. I hate the thought that the ugly purple iris is blooming right outside this window. I can't even sit up to see them but I *know* they're blooming without looking and it disturbs me. If I were well I'd uproot them all!"

"Which patch, specifically."

"They're the ones called *purple bearded*, next to the path. I cut them back every year, but they're like a flu. See now I have a new word. *Flu*."

So Michael went downstairs, found a lantern and hoe, and in the circle of light thrown by the flame began to turn up the earth beside the path, scything the broad leaves which in places stood nearly as tall as himself, when a plastic mug sailed close to his head. He looked up to see Julia propped up at the window, annoyed expression on face, pointing to the direction behind his back. Michael pointed with his hoe to the right, and feigned misunderstanding when her finger jabbed repeatedly to his back. Then left, and forward, but Julia's finger stabbed to his rear. He feigned more confusion, but when Julia disappeared and reappeared holding the soup bowl as if prepared to fling it at him he suddenly appeared to understand her at last and point backwards to another patch of the purple iris, and he set to turn over that patch as well. Not stopping until all of the offending irises were overturned.

This work took two hours or more and when finished, his hands had developed blisters. When upstairs to receive approval for his deeds, Julia glanced at his hands and told him to bring back the bowl filled with clean water, and antiseptic.

She washed his hands, spread the ointment on the blisters, and with strips torn from the sheets, carefully, tenderly, bandaged his hands. And kissed the palms of his hands when she had finished. Then she turned back from him and put the blankets back over her head.

Michael said, "Goodnight," and left her in the peace of evening.

Wincing, and at arm's length, Michael poured a can of diluted fish emulsion onto a row of potted plants lining a brick path, watered them thoroughly with the same can, and standing on the path arms held away from his body afraid of the stench in his own shirt, idly wondered what to do next. A plastic cup sailed past his head and landed near to the first of the previous night on the bed of upturned iris, and he could hear the sound of her window closing, as if this would protect her from the cup thrown back at her. He looked up to see Julia's face pressed against the glass, and with small gesture, motioning that he should come upstairs to talk. Michael cupped a hand near his hear, pretending not to hear, but not in the mood for his tricks she held up another cup and in this way Michael admitted defeat and trudged indoors.

"You stink," she said without preamble, "but I like that smell. It's the smell of life."

"Because life stinks?"

"Because life is fertile, and fertility has a stink of abundance." She had chosen her words carefully. "I'm feeling better."

"You're getting better distance with your throwing arm. Your first cup rolled to the irises. The cup you threw now flew the whole distance. Very accurate."

"My joints are still achy. But tonight I want to sit in my chair, so I'm resting for the walk downstairs."

"That's good," he said absently.

"Would you bring up my babiche chair?"

"You want to sit here in this room?"

"No, I just want to look at it."

"Anything else?"

"Would you bring the blue painted clothes chest in here?"

"But it weighs about three hundred pounds."

He looked at her, and realized from her evasive expression, and turned-away glance, that she knew how difficult the task would be, and not certain why she asked it, agreed.

While he wrestled with the armoire, pushing and pulling it through the door on a towel, and setting it into place where directed, Julia tried to slip her next words in an innocuous manner, "There's something else." Michael groaned.

"I was thinking....well, I don't know how to say it," continued Julia, "I'd like to have a baby. Push it a little more towards the corner. That's right."

"Okay?" He lifted one edge of the armoire, and then

the other to remove the towel that preserved the polished floor from scrapes.

"That way the doors open without hitting the window sash."

Michael sat on the babiche chair and wiped his forehead with the towel.

"Did you hear me?"

"I heard you. And I know what Bernard had said to you about your broken hip. That you can't have children."

"I was reading a book in the library about babies."

"The books in the library are all about a hundred years old."

"This was written by a frontier midwife who came west in a wagon train."

"It sounds grim."

Julia's face was flushed and by this circuitous rambling, she sensed a great embarrassment and fell over backwards into her blankets, covered herself up carefully and curled into a ball under the thick wools.

When Michael poured the bean soup into a crock, wiped his spill, cut sandwiches neatly with knife and arranged the sandwiches on the clay plate, first aligned with the edges of the tray, and at last moment nudged the sandwiches to be askew, more of real life in the arrangement than harsh symmetry, then turned his head slightly so someone might have thought he paused to listen, but in fact he turned his head in response to some monition he wouldn't have been able to recall later; he paused to think at the kitchen window downstairs where the frames had been painted with child paints, decades earlier by himself and Julia, a frieze of Grecian athletes. Julia's athletes each carried sprigs of herbs and dallied on the track. A river of memories, a sea of pictures. A rumble of sounds that weren't memories or pictures or sounds in any conventional sense but a strange pulse of unconscious life.

Julia remained curled up in a ball shape under the blankets. She wanted him to believe that she hadn't moved since last night, but, while comfortably rumpled in the morning, she quickly rearranged herself when hearing Michael approach upstairs. He lay on the bed beside her, thinking private thoughts to himself, and held her small pixyish, piggish shape under his arm and fell asleep, while she continued to eat.

He awoke when Julia reached across him to fetch a sandwich, placing one hand lightly on his chest more out of liking the touch than for balance, and sandwich in hand, settled herself back once more into her old position, had arranged his arm over her as before and he could feel the tremors in his own arm of her chewing. Derum, derum. Her heartbeat quivered in her arm, quivered across their skins, into his arm into his bloodstream and into his own mind. Derum derum.

He kissed her on the back of the head, her glossy black hair, and she turned to offer him the last piece of her sandwich which he accepted. And immediately with his cheek full of the sandwich, nestled in his two-armed embrace, she kissed him full on the lips.

"Michael. Michael." Julia poked a finger into his bowl

of soup and licked the fingertip, meditatively, searchingly. "Do you want the soup warmed up?" She wasn't waiting for an answer and continued with her own thoughts, "This afternoon, with the armoire. I was testing you. I wanted to know if you would do something arbitrary."

"I had thought so. I tried to act my arbitrary best. I tried to suppress my complaints." She giggled. Michael twisted his head, in exaggerated gesture as if looking for a sandwich but sank back into the sheets remembering that Julia had eaten them all. "No sandwiches for me," his plaintive complaint to Julia's answer, with fake sympathy, "Poor boy." He eyed the remnants of her lunch and waited for a moment of distraction when her eyes momentarily came unfocused, tore off a piece of the portion of hers that remained.

Eight year old Michael had crawled onto his grandfather's lap and hugged him, with the whole extent of his arms, which didn't quite reach around the man thin as he was. Lower lip trembled, the only sign the boy gave of fear, of disturbance. Michael said with small voice, "I'm thirsty."

The grandfather walked with him to the kitchen. Julia had washed the evening dishes and they easily found a clean cup and saucer on the counter, neatly turned upside-down. The grandfather poured out milk into a cup and mixed in a large shake of Nestles chocolate from the yellow tin. He gave the cup, saucer and a spoon to Michael, who sat at the table, swinging his legs, and stirred the chocolate carefully, then he sipped the cold milk gratefully and sat still with his grandfather quietly in the kitchen until the disturbance within him was quelled.

Michael woke. He was no longer in his grandfather's bed, but in his old room with grown-up Julia napping beside him, breathing through her nose with a quiet, part charming, snorting noise. He remembered the last part of a childhood dream, of being stranded on the moon, looking at the earth, at the blueness. If only I could get back to the earth, he said to the grandfather in the dream, I would live my life differently.

As Michael recounted this story, Julia's face had been overcome by a flood of conflicting feeling, which he tried to follow by studying the changing contours of her face — intense interest and disturbed emotion, a flash of her white, even teeth when she briefly smiled, concern for him and his thoughts.

"I once told your grandfather about my dreams but he made me talk to a talking doctor, a psychiatrist. He asked me if I heard voices, and I said yes, I just heard a voice ask if I heard voices and he wrote something down and scared me. After that I stopped telling people about the dreams."

"What was one of your dreams?"

"I dreamt once that I lived on the moon, all alone. But I wasn't lonely. I ate crackers and jelly. I wore a patched up sweater and blue shoes. Maggie ate puffs of green dirt that tasted like apples. We were happy on the moon."

Michael's smile ceased momentarily, "My grandfather

knew that both of us dreamed separately we were stranded on the moon alone."

"Your grandfather was so funny. I'll tell you the story how I came to live in your house. I left my old house and went to the moon. I really did. You have to believe me."

"The moon?"

"That was a long journey and it hurt. But I finally arrived. But that was only the beginning."

"What happened next?"

The earth viewed from the moon.

"*The moon spirit looked* like a gnarled earthly tree, with branches and spiny twigs for fingers but made of an unearthly kind of silver dust. She served as rules-arbitrator for recent arrivals onto the moon surface. "Look, look," said the spirit, it tapped me on the forehead, "if you live on the moon it's a one-way trip. You cannot return There!!" In a roaring voice, causing me to stumble backwards, the spirit pointed with a crooked twig finger at the blue planet I had flown from, with my nervous dog balanced under one arm, a picnic hamper under the other arm. "There!! There!! No returning from there!! Bad things There!!"

"Please, sir, don't yell."

"Excuse me, don't What!!!"

"Yell, sir."

"Oh, sorry, you're so little. I'll be more quiet and I'll use short words that fit into your little ear very nicely. Are you listening to me Michael? I'm not telling you a story. I'm telling you what really happened to me."

Michael leaned upright and turned his head to her, "Yes, yes."

"Then the moon spirit explained things to me. She said, 'No going back you understand. Ab-so-lute-elee not. Never happened.'

"I agreed. I said that life on the earth was not for me. I tried it but it didn't work out.

"She gave me a pouch full of crackers and a jar full of jelly. And said I could live on the moon, which I did for a long time. And for a long time Maggie and I were very happy. My leg healed up. Then something happened that made me suspicious later how no one can be content with things. I became discontented. I could see the earth in good detail when the swirling clouds would part some mornings. I could see and I was very interested in the lives of children and for the first time I saw how some children weren't beaten or killed. Some children laughed and when they laughed they coughed up milk through their nose, and they were safe so much that when someone held their hand they didn't wince or tighten up. Some children slept in cribs with mobiles and pink stuffed pigs. Some children played and were chosen for basketball teams. Once I saw a girl near birds and when the birds fluttered up in a wave of feathers so beautifully the girl laughed and clapped her hands —

thinking the birds were dancing for her alone. I knew that even though I was on the earth beforehand I had never really lived. Now I had crackers and the nice jam, on the moon, but I wasn't living much either.

"I went back to the moon lady who looked at me suspiciously. She knew what was up. *No returning from there*, she said, but her heart wasn't in it, her twiggy finger stayed curled up in her twig hand. You forgot all the details and the smells and the fears. I didn't, I said. But still I wished to go back. I was sorry."

"But what good is wishing, said the moon lady. Only humans can wish."

"But aren't I a human?"

"No longer. You're a spirit now like I am. You are a foggy breath. You are the clearness in a piece of glass. You are the hole in a donut. You're like the memory of a baby that was never born and was never heard from or knew of. You were anyways a baby that no one wanted." She placed her fingers in the space that a solid Julia would have occupied, "You are wraithy."

"Yes," I said, "all that is true."

"I remember pressing the edge of my hand, horizontally, against my forehead and squinted at the earth, looking with moon sight at the part of the world I had fled from. And what the moon sprite spoke was true. Under the pallor of the atmosphere I could see the cabin I used to inhabit and my old, poor body with the broken legs and bloody nose, lying where I had fallen for the last time. I was half in and half out of a drainage pipe, where I ran but was caught. I was caught by my father and killed like my sister Elizabeth. My sister was killed with an axe and buried under the floor of the cabin next to the foundation of the fireplace.

"The moon lady didn't look at me any more, I think she knew I wasn't meant for the moon anymore, but she tried to persuade me, she tried her best, "You don't suffer any longer."

"I liked to eat fried onions in a pan."

"You will never see cruelty here."

"I liked to hold my sister's hand in the dark."

"Nobody will mistreat you here."

"I liked to talk to cheerful otters that could have lived in a pond."

The moon lady sighed, "Why do I bother with my one-way, no-returning rule."

"I would like to return to the earth. I want to eat fried onions in a pan." I started to groan again with pain and held my legs where the bone stuck out from the skin. Now I was next to the wall by your house and I pulled myself up and leaves blew around me in a circle. I think you watched me from a window upstairs. My life began again all anew."

Julia looked hopeful for a moment and spoke with conviction, "One day, for real, I will see a child laugh up milk through her nose. One day I will hold someone's hand without wincing. One day I will see birds rise up in a pretty wave of feathers."

Michael held her hand and felt a tiny, almost impercetible wince, an involuntary tightening of her fingers.

She said softly, "See what I mean?"

"But that time will come soon."

"Yes," said Julia with a note of certainty in her voice and Michael smiled.

Julia remained melancholy during the dark hours and later added to him, a tremulous and subdued voice out of the darkness while holding his hand, "I was either happy or unhappy for a long time, but gradually I became less unhappy." Then, "I don't think I'm happy as much as I used to be but I am hardly unhappy anymore."

Michael opened his eyes and looked at Julia in shadow, who had turned her face towards his but watched some point in space beyond him.

"What happened to your father?"

"I don't know. I expected him to appear any day for a long time, but he never did."

"What happened to your mother. Where was she buried?"

"I never knew. I was too short, too young."

"What was your sister like?"

"She was older. She was nice but she was even more afraid than me. She kept saying that if only we were good then we would be okay but that didn't happen. She was good but that didn't help her one bit. I didn't believe that we would be okay even if we were good. However, when I lived at your house I thought that I would be okay if I was good. So I tried to be good."

Michael had fallen asleep again with the piece of his uneaten sandwich in his open hand. The bread had fallen away from the cheese, and reaching across his warm and substantial, breathing body, Julia took the cheese, ate it, and left him with the pieces of bread.

She draped her arm across him and pressed her face against the side of his chest. "Who?" she blurted aloud, and Michael turned his head then turned away again seeing she had been lost in her own thoughts. He felt the bread in his fingers and lifted his head and turned to look at Julia. And sat up to put the pieces of bread back onto the nightstand.

"Is the soup very cold?"

"Very."

Michael idly picked up her hand, the little seen hand with the neatly healed bits of missing fingers, and felt a tremor through the hand as Julia couldn't stifle the urge to pull the hand out of his grasp, and realizing this he turned his head, though he continued to hold the hand.

As he released the hand, he asked idly, without much thought, "Were you always left-handed?"

Julia waited a moment or two before answering, "I don't remember."

Twilight morning had not yet warmed the window blinds when Michael awoke to a odd quiver in his arms and neck. Eyes open only, he came to consciousness with the sensation of a strangeness in utterly familiar surroundings, and located the source of strange familiarity, without jolting his head — a tap tap tap from within the bedclothes. And lifting his head he could see the white heel of Julia's foot, sticking out of her pile of blankets, taping and thumping on the mattress in an unseen disturbance, he felt, from someplace far from him and someplace far within herself. He smiled at the comical leg then with more reflection frowned, thinking that the leg shook from an echo, a reverberation from experiences, though old, that were not blithely forgotten and may have been obscured but probably never would be erased.

He lay parallel to her. Without thinking, his arm stretched over, around her, tried to form a bowl, a hillock over her thumping self, a blunt response felt inadequate, and wished somewhere within himself, in a guttural, unworded way, that she would be rid of this twitching for the night or for all the years of her life to come. But his arm felt inadequate and he brought it back under his own chin.

Julia, within the blankets, had opened her eyes and like Michael experienced a sense of disorientation, even a pang of fright as strange weight pressed down on her, then felt a sense of relief, a tiny peep of relief, then the arm withdrew and she felt herself again. Her eyes closed and the blanket pile, as immobile as ever, remained unchanged.

He waited until morning, his mind dwelling on the details of this story of Julia's, as if they were leaf shapes flowing like a play of water on the ceiling, so were his thoughts until seeing through the window, light of day, he rose up and stood in the doorway.

In looking back, he could only see a single strand of her dark hair on the pillow. She slept as if she still were a little girl, tightly bound up in a cocoon of blankets.

She used two of the blankets and left a third undisturbed on the bed's foot, which in Michael's eyes boded well, thinking, "I suppose if she were not feeling well, then she'd use all three blankets and she'd be wound up in them like a mummy wrapping." He dressed and tied his shoes. In the town, the new sheriff substation had a single man on duty, and Michael explained what Julia had told him about her own life in a cabin that belonged to the seasonal migrant workers, and her sister, Elizabeth, whom Julia hadn't mentioned earlier.

While Julia slept a deputation of men and women gathered at the site of the old cabin, that long ago had fallen into disrepair, and the digging began.

"Do you remember what we talked about last night?"

She looked at him carefully, for a long time, before speaking, "I remember."

"The police detectives found the grave of your sister. Jonathan will take care of those matters, but he asked if you'd like to choose a place for her to be buried properly, and if you'd like to choose a gravestone. We can go to a place here in Napa, and they'll take care of the details."

"I thought of those things last night, and I wish she could be buried in the same graveyard with your grandfather. Then I can visit both of them at the same time. I'd like that. Madeleine you know is buried there too. All of our friends live there and I like that place best of all places outside this house."

Michael had sought out a mortuary business earlier, borrowed Bernard's car, and drove with Julia to the far side of the town, parking in a vast lot, empty now but used for services and he imagined it would be filled to overflowing for a large funeral. To his surprise, Julia seemed cheerful at running her hands over the various headstones, statuary, angels, children in poses of fancy or of somberness. Her hand rested on a small gray slab, the gray of a storm sky, "I wish she could have a stone like this with her name on it."

He nodded at the salesman, a boy of fourteen or so, who nodded too, and brought out a receipt book from his pocket, flipping open the cover with a practiced twist of his wrist, a motion that Julia admired.

On the car ride home, Julia pressed her hand, her fingers, against the glass, her fingers only with her palm cupped like a spider shape. And she walked her fingers up and down the glass as if it were a walking spider.

Michael felt comfortable in the babiche chair and often could be found reading a book with the chair arranged so the light from window fell over his shoulder onto the book. Only by raising his eyes from the book he watched as Julia came into the room with a handful of linen. "Look," she smiled, "I have always loved these but I've saved them, not to be used except for a special time."

She held over his book so he could better see the sheets of antique linen, well preserved, fragile and obsessed with the beauty of handmade things — delicate and imbued with a personal kind of value. Very few human things appealed to Julia, preferring tomatoes and garlics, but these sheets of linen, despite the luster of extravagant finery, had fascinated and captivated her.

"Where did this come from?"

"It's old. From an old Hardy bride's trousseau I believe. It seemed to me, when I was a little girl, the most beautiful thing."

Michael built a fire in the hearth, and moved the

babiche chair back from the flames. Even when he added a fire screen he thought a spark could set the wooden woven work ablaze. The fireplace in this room, long unused, was large enough to walk in. Julia said, "When I was a little girl I would sleep inside here, and I used to hide before Jonathan's Latin lessons. I could hide upside down like a bat in the chimney."

When the flames had burnt up the kindling and flickered in good health, he rubbed his hands on his pants and sat beside her on the bed, on the linen she had set out for herself. A moon lolled in the window, centered and full in part.

He pointed, "That's what my grandfather called, *the new moon in the old moon's arms*."

"He said the same to me. He used to hug me when I would start shaking for no reason. I would be standing at the sink in the kitchen, washing my dishes, and start to shake, and he'd put his arms around me and say, "Here's the old moon!" and I'd laugh if I could."

This memory made Julia smile, and she put a strand of newly washed hair into the corner of her mouth to chew. Michael undressed and when finished motioned that she put up her arms above her head, which she did, and he pulled her up her shirt, tugging sharply when the collar caught on her ears. And they lay down again together with their limbs all twisted up.

Michael brought up the edge of sheet to his eyes and took a deep intake of breath, "I've forgotten how different an air-dried sheet smelled."

"Nice eh?" Julia folded herself lengthwise, kissed his shoulder.

Bernard had dropped by for another visit, ostensibly he said for the muffins and jam but took the opportunity again to opportune Julia to spend time in Palo Alto and the OB-GYN department. To Michael, a more sympathetic listener, he added, "She needs better prenatal care than Napa can provide."

"I'm all for it," said Michael, "but try to persuade her. Look at her." And Bernard did without disguising his affection and irritation both.

She had wandered down the path, pulling the wagon with clothes from the line, saying, "I brought it in. I think it'll rain this afternoon." Her pregnancy was in its fourth month and despite her slight frame the bump in stomach didn't seem much more than if she had eaten a huge dinner and pushed her stomach out in an exaggerated way. But her cheeks were rosy and her mouth puckered in a mischievous smile as if she were bursting with a secret that she delighted in holding in and not telling. She often talked to herself, or to the bump within herself, and sometimes could be seen, with shaking shoulders as she began to laugh or giggle to herself with a private joke.

Sometimes Michael would be sitting at the kitchen window and Julia would trundle by, pushing a wheelbarrow, and seeing him, put down the wheelbarrow to shake a fist at him with an expression of mock outrage, and shaking done, pick up the wheelbarrow and disappear out of sight.

"You have become so petulant!" he mocked her. "Who knew you could be so demanding?"

"Isn't it nice?" She patted her belly and farted quietly. "If not for all the tests and shots in my behind, I'd be happy. Her eyes clouded momentarily, and though

Michael believed these moments signaled a flash of pain; Julia denied this vehemently, and her smiles, her giggling, her fits of fist shaking and frowning at him resumed.

As time wound itself onward, as if each new ounce of baby brought a corresponding increase in her self-confidence, Julia became positively outrageous with her demands, asking Michael to move furniture to suit her whims, to transplant the oft-fought-over patch of iris, liking nothing better than to petulantly see how he stifled his annoyance and bit his tongue. Once asking him, "What are you saying to yourself?"

"I'm praying for patience and forbearance."

"Praying to whom?"

"No one in particular. To all the gods."

"Have you found a god? Are you now a religious man?"

She responded to the expression on his face, "My requests are eminently reasonable and those few little tasks you do around the house and yard serve the public good."

"Public good…" Julia could barely hear his half-muttered reply.

"We could use another pair of hands around the house. I have plans for this place. Think of a baby as cheap labor."

Michael made a snorting noise through his nose, and she patted his arm in sympathy.

In fact, Julia would have liked to explain her behavior but feared his ironical response of old. She felt she was training him, in a sense, by asking him to call upon and develop those inner resources that seemed to appear so magically after Madeleine died. She felt that the responses of kindnesses that he brought to the house when he first reappeared at the house gate needed exercise as if with exercise the kindnesses and patiences would become ever more superabundant, and those resources as if pools of water, would swell to ever larger girths, the pools widening into oceans. In other words, the small tasks she asked him to perform would both confirm his willingness to work by her side, and to reconfirm that the ironical would diminish and the kindness would swell up in his head. He'd bloat from the kindness and his head would burst and he'd spray kindness over the whole Napa valley. That was her wish.

In feigning sleep Julia had thrown her arm out across Michael but in fact was carefully designed to hold him and test whether he had already tired of her nearness, so she felt contentment again that he didn't try to escape her grasp and he nestled under her arm.

She was flushed and elated at times when he played, and he played with her body with the attention of a musician, with concentration and sometimes even an off-handed casualness. Familiar and confident, diffident sometimes. She smiled often for having discovered this whole new realm of feeling. Of new sensation to explore at her leisurely and unhurried pace, but thoughts of the sex stirred up a hunger for him again and she flushed at her physical longings that surprised her, an affection that contrasted so strongly with her past fears and sense of propriety. She required his presence and felt a hunger for him at those times that even, given a choice between yam in hand or seeking Michael's touch, she would throw down the yam and set off in search of him and his touch.

Michael, too, would never have guessed how Julia would like sex, liked carnality — in its older meaning of something human and natural. Michael sometimes felt unprepared for her mischievous hints — that he should stop folding clothes and join her in the field of bluebells, or that he hold her when they pass in a hallway. That he place his hands *here*, *there*, or kiss her whenever it so pleased her.

"Look what I made." Julia had brought up a package wrapped in paper. "I practiced on the lathe in the basement for a long time, but finally I got things like I wanted." Out of the wrapping Michael brought out a miniature, child-scale wheelbarrow. The wheel was made of three sections held together with pegs and a metal band had been pounded into the rim with rough nails. The handles lathed and sandpapered smooth with tapered ends.

"Very nice. Very well constructed."

"How soon can a baby use this, what do you think?"

"I have no idea, but I'll bet you set him working even with a diaper."

"Do you think a boy? What if he's a girl?"

"Either way, I see a diapered baby moving dirt around, muttering to itself."

"Ha aha ha!" She looked more closely at a burr on one of the handles, something she would have to sand smooth again.

"Why don't you wear your glasses. You wouldn't squint so much."

"They're too heavy. When I put them on, my head drops forward. My neck hurts and all I can see are my own feet."

"You look nice in them."

"Do I?" She seemed genuinely surprised at his and

was instantly on her guard to see if he was being ironical. But relaxed her guard after examining his face, "That was the third compliment you ever gave me. It's been three in thirty years. Not that I'm counting."

"Three in thirty years!" She nodded her head in a sad way then instantly balled her hand in a fist and shook it at him when the ironical appeared and he added, "That many?"

"Oh, you."

Her eyes clouded again, the squint, this time not from looking at something, but from feeling something from within. Foreboding. Things couldn't remain happy like this for ever she felt. Humans were not made to be happy without a fall. The gods in China punished those who were happy, so a Chinese woman in a moment of happiness would take a moment to say, "Only bad joss here, gods, only miserable humans here, gods, none of us are happy."

When the spasm passed, she saw his concern and quoted something unexpected, saying, "*The mother in childbirth has anguish because her time has come, but when she has borne the child she no longer remembers her affliction because a human being has been born into the world.* That's from the book of John. I'm reading the Bible. I'm feeling Biblical these days. I keep reading about Sarah and Elizabeth and the other women in the Bible who were given healthy babies even though they were oldish women and lost their hopes."

"Are you oldish?"

In answer, Julia flared her nostrils, both at once.

"I have decided that I will die in this chair," Julia

informed Michael. She rubbed her hands over the finely sanded and finished texture of the repainted slats of a Shaker chair. "This is one of the places I stood in the lawn when I was a little girl and so I believe it is fitting and proper that when I start to die, I'll hurry over and sit in this chair in this spot."

"You're being too morbid for such a cheerful day."

"I have a thermos, and food, packed away here, and I'll sit here in my spare time, whenever I get any spare time, to increase odds that at the right moment when I start choking on a piece of cabbage that I die in this chair. You think I'm joking, but I've decided. Everything's set and prepared. If I start to choke on a piece of cabbage, carry me over to the chair."

"I see. Well pardon me but I think it's stupid. More likely than not you'll die while brushing you teeth or scratching an itch or napping in a sofa upstairs."

"Imagine away all the different places I might die. But I'll die in this chair, it's my death chair. Please don't disturb the chair at all or the picnic cooler. I'm happy and content right here in my chair."

In fact Julia sat in that chair often, waiting for her end, but impatience and the inactivity seized hold of her and dragged her back to the yards where ever more work, more tidying, sweeping, weeding, and sorting awaited. In the evening she cut out people shapes for a new diorama, read *The Glory of Roses*, fixed a cup of tea for herself, settled into her bed, patted her companion on his sleeping head, and said, "Well, I'll sit in that chair in case I die tomorrow but on the whole today was a fine day."

A flood of wishing.

Julia looked up in alarm at hearing a faint but determined knocking on the gate. She had been sitting on the porch in her death chair, accoutered as usual with cooler, cups and sandwich. She sat still, even keeping her eyes still, hoping the knocking would die away of its own accord, and felt further alarmed at hearing an unfamiliar male voice call out as if the head was raised upwards to call over the stone wall, "I know you're there!! Open up!!"

So Julia rose to peek through the postern door. Surprised that the stranger's face appeared right there in the small opening as if familiar with her routines. "Remember me? I'm Jasper!"

"Jasper!" Julia fumbled in her mind — she knew such few people that normally a name wouldn't be difficult but she had forgotten all. "I don't know…" then memories of the little boy who had once been beaten up on the asphalt road southwards came to mind, and she smiled a little shyly at the memory. "Oh but you're all grown up!" His head was larger, elongated in the way that childish heads grew. Thought that he was no longer a "grass-eating mulch cow" as they once called themselves. She opened the gate a trifle reluctantly.

He had brought a pie as present as if recalling that food would ease Julia's apprehensions and this did work as immediately she peered into the slits in the crust, trying to learn the contents. "A cherry pie? Did you bake this yourself."

"It's canned cherries. I remembered how you taught me to crimp the crust and roll out the dough, and I thought while I was visiting to resurrect those skills."

"Where do you live now?"

"I go to college…"

"College? How is that possible? How old are you…" She did the mental arithmetic on her fingers, folding some fingers over, suspecting her addition was wrong and started again, and no matter the different sums, groaned at the result, "Oh I'm an old lady!!" in genuine astonishment at her predicament. Jasper laughed, "You're not old!"

Michael appeared in the doorway, curious at the first visitor to the house since he arrived months ago. Since his defeat in the *great tractor race*, as Julia called it, he more or less assumed the permanent job of clothes washing and had returned from the utility room having started a load of clothes in the new washer machine. Julia made the introductions and they shook hands all around. Michael too inspected the pie and Jasper laughed at their open covetness. "Let's eat!"

"Hooray!"

Michael brought out plates, forks, cloth napkins, and Julia, in silent communication with Michael, hurried to the tool shed where beneath a flagstone, she stored her ice cream, brought out a wooden pot of homemade vanilla, which she doled out with generous scoops and she added a small, split vanilla bean to each serving. "Oh lovely, lovely pie and ice cream!" She savored each forkful with closed eyes. And only when the pot was empty and the whole pie eaten did they talk again.

"My family moved away, you remember, but my parents divorced, and when my mother returned to Napa to live this year so did I."

"What do you study?" asks Michael.

"Oh, Julia's had a big effect on that. When I was a little boy, she showed me veins of gold in rock, and we collected plant specimens, and talked about the animal world. I'm a geology major, but I'm really starting to specialize, to study ways that geology affects the flora and fauna of a region. For example the way the an abundance of iron or the presence of certain geological features affects speciation and adaptative features."

"Interesting."

Julia had run barefooted into the kitchen and run back at rapid pace, and showed them a cigar box in her hands, "Look. You forgot to take this when you left."

"My treasure box!"

He opened the box and showed them what he valued

above rubies and emeralds when he was last here, "A rock with green speckles. A beetle with iridescent shell that sparkled when you turned it in the light…"

"What's this?" asked Michael lifting a plastic vial with ordinary dirt.

"That's no regular soil specimen." Jasper looked at Julia with an appreciative glance. "That's a bit of earth from this house. I meant to take it with me when I left. I loved this house." Julia beamed with a happy face, she understood full well.

"I learned to read here. I felt safe here. I learned confidence here."

Julia nodded her head in wholehearted agreement. They spent the afternoon chatting and laughing and Michael left them to their reminiscences.

When Jasper left after dinner, Julia sought Michael out, and pressed her face against the sleeve of his shirt, "Time is passing so quickly. Do you know I could almost be Jasper's *mother*? Me, a mother, can you imagine that?"

Michael remained noncommittal.

"Time is passing. I'm growing old. All this time passing while I'm on the earth — oh, I feel bewildered, I feel happy."

"Which?"

"Bewildered and happy both. Do you love me? Is this what love is? I don't know what love is like."

"Of course I love you." Julia felt vaguely dissatisfied with the "Of course…" but accepted his statement until she added, "Do you love me more than chemistry."

"Definitely." Now he pretended to be deep in thought

and added, "But maybe not more than some kinds of number theory."

"What if we quarrel."

"Quarrel? When have we quarreled?"

"In a very practical way I'm thinking about what would happen. Would I have to leave this house if you asked?"

"You know very well that this is your house, not mine, and if anyone left it would definitely be me. But I don't intend to quarrel."

"Sometimes things happen that neither person intends, isn't that so?"

"That's so."

"When I was little I could not understand anything. I had no wishes. I could not feel affection for anything. Do you know how desolate I felt? I dream about those days still, and those days are like nightmares for me. Then I learned how to live with your grandfather. But each decade of my life I learned things that are a little more complex. Now this decade I am living with you like a real living woman. But it's like what Alice said to the Queen of Hearts at the croquet game. Do you remember?"

Michael shook his head.

"Alice said, *it's so confusing, all the things being alive.* I mean that I don't mind that my life is more complex but I don't understand very much of it. Normally I wouldn't worry. If I was confused I would ignore it. I would hide from it. But your grandfather told me about this. He said I should not be alone and I should share my life."

"Did he? He said the same to me…He knew about our dreams about the moon, remember?"

"That's why I try not to be frightened of the confusion because all the things are alive —"

"Madeleine had been very patient with me. But then she died. She died before I understood her. She was unappreciated in her own life."

In this way time with Julia passed not serenely, with flare-ups of irritation, but not monotonously, they prepared food, ate it, then washed the plates and began again to prepare food, several times per day. This preparing of food and eating seemed to be a major focus of the day. Between meals they never sat far apart. If Julia took a turn at gardening though she could reach the earth only by crawling on all fours, or squatting in an awkward way, sometimes being unable to get up again and motioned to Michael that he must help her up onto her own feet. Sometimes, amused, he nodded his head that he wouldn't help only because her attempts at righting herself were entertaining and worth the scowls and frowns that were inflicted upon him afterwards.

She could not bear to be alone and if she worked in a section of the yard she motioned that he must follow and thus he had become accustomed to be near her at all times. He would read, holding a book propped upon bench, and holding a bag of tomatoes in the other, needing both hands only to turn the page. Both she and he in this spate of good weather have become sun burnt.

On rainy days she sorted objects in the house into their interminable, innumerable bins and boxes and cupboards, sometimes putting things into a box and then out, so they remained exactly in the place they had begun. She seemed merely to enjoy the process of organizing and tidying, or else to reaffirm her knowledge of all possessions in the house. Sometimes he caught her saying, on opening a drawer, "Hello drawer. Hello soup spoon. Hello grater. Hello oyster knife."

They often bickered and argued, then it would be time to eat. And they would eat in peace, for it was Julia's rule, "Never eat in anger." Entire weeks had passed this way, and neither had left the bounds of the gate or the yard.

Michael paused in the doorway and watched with interest as Julia undressed. Though in her sixth month, her stomach still seemed only slightly rounded. When she stood before the armoire in her underwear, turning to examine herself in a mirror, in a critical self-scrutiny, he tiptoed into the room, "Stop right there, Buster," she said without taking her gaze from the mirror, "I don't like the way you're tip-toeing."

"I only wanted to pat your stomach."

"Hah!"

She waved her fist at him, her tiny fist, made of birdish bones that would crush themselves if they struck anything more solid than flesh and blood.

When he ignored this she hurriedly grabbed at her dungarees, draped over the armoire door, but he had put his arms around her and was indeed patting her stomach.

He kissed the top of her head, and she grunted roughly, "That's the only kissing you get."

"That's the only kissing I want. Pregnancy makes you so suspicious!"

She twisted away and waddled through the door and

yelped when Michael pursued. She waddled downstairs, faster in the hallway and slowly, carefully, with a firm hand on the banister, and out of fairness Michael too slowed to her pace on the stairs and sped when reaching the floor. She waddled through the kitchen, with hands in funny motion as if she were wading through waist-thick water, and shouting out warnings that he had better behave himself. Then out on the porch turned around, mouth downcast, because she discovered he wasn't chasing her any more. She looked into the kitchen.

Michael had been stopped by the smell of biscuits in the oven. He had opened the door and with pot holder taken out a single biscuit, which he was buttering.

"The biscuits need five more minutes. You can still chase me if you like."

Michael made a dismissive gesture with his hand and pretended to concentrate all his attention on the biscuit. Then laughed at her disappointment. "Eat a biscuit," he said in consolation.

Small details captured Michael's attention and amusement. For example, he was entertained to no end merely by watching Julia walk. As she gained weight, her gait changed, and walked with feet splayed outwards and arms angled downwards, pointed to her sides, as if she were walking simultaneously both to the right and left and couldn't decide which direction to choose, and walked straight forward only because her arms and legs were attached in the middle. He expected her to complain about minor aches and pains or the burden of what he considered unbearable changes of anatomy or metabolism but she never did. She seemed to be undergoing a metamorphosis of amazing beauty, but if she showed signs of appreciation, she did not show this in behavior or expression.

He told Julia his version of a favorite story, of Odysseus and Proteus, while they ate breakfast muffins — how to get to his home on Ithaca, Odysseus had to ask questions of Proteus who was a shape changer. Proteus couldn't be bothered and tried to escape the human questioner. In desperation Odysseus had to hold on as Proteus changed first into an otter and fish and horse then into fire and smoke and a spoken word. Yet Odysseus persisted. In a similar way Michael felt himself hanging onto Julia no matter how irritably she could singe him.

"Well, that's a mean story," protested Julia. "I'm not hurting you, am I?"

"No, Julia, you're not."

Julia propped herself up with several small embroidered pillows and had surrounded herself with her favorite things that she looked upon from time to time with evident satisfaction — a profusion of potted plants in various stages of bloom, some of the old blue-ringed dishes that as a small girl, or at least smaller girl, she had washed so very carefully in fear that one would have broken and all had survived to her adulthood intact, and in and out at times came Michael, who would forget what he came indoors for and would wander out again. Even in his absentness he'd look closely at her, with his soft brown eyes, and she surreptitiously kept a glance on him because she liked his glance so much, secretly.

Once she raised her arms in a gesture of affection and shouted, "You, things, are just right for me!" Michael had been in the hallway and she heard his low laughter. When he came into the room, she spoke, "Madeleine said something that stuck with me. She said that she never knew anyone, when she had at last got to know them well enough so they felt free to talk to the point when they would speak honestly and candidly to her, who was not at heart lonely or fearful. She said most people would deny this, but everyone became confessional and spilled out their loneliness to her at one time or another. She said that if you peeled away a person's appearance and public behavior, like these were layers of an onion, then there they were at the center, all naked and shaky. I thought about this a lot because I was the same way, I was lonely all my life but covered it with bluster. And I felt abnormal because I thought I was the only one.

"But now," and Julia seemed excited at saying this as if it were a revelation to her, "now I believe what she said was true and that everybody more or less is like this and that my life really had been normal all along."

"You're drooling."

She wiped her mouth with the back of her hand and wiped her hand clean on his shirt.

"But you've had a harder life than most people."

"But that's my point and why I feel so excited. Once I felt that I was lost and I wouldn't ever feel at peace. But when I understood what Madeleine said, now I feel that it's possible that one day I could be at peace."

To reread the inset in the book she had been glancing through, she squinted, bent closer to the page, then remembered that she had to wear glasses. She furtively looked to her right and left to be certain no one was watching, in a motion as if she were crossing a street, then bent her head to put on the glasses and read the insert. She took off the glasses again and hid them in a hard case under the pillow whenever she heard Michael's steps on the stairs.

Walking became painful to her, yet she declined to visit the hospital. When she complained about the cold, Michael would warm up a potato so she would lie in the bed with the warm potato in her hands, and when it cooled, she opened up the wrapping and ate the potato with a spoon and a pat of butter for its fat.

He brought into her room, *per* her directions, a wooden potty chair for a child, and a hand carved Windsor chair, with smooth well-turned legs, straight unadorned spindleback and bow of hard maple. She turned on her side and stared at these pieces of furniture for hours on end.

To surprise her, in rummaging through the attic, he brought down a miniature Queen Anne's bureau, which had been built long ago with oversized knobs for a child's hand. "I forgot that upstairs. Oh how nice!"

She took frequent delight in bending out of the bed to open and close the tiny drawer, and admired the careful workmanship that had been lavished on these pieces. "Wouldn't you like to try to make furniture? You might have good skill in these hands." She kneaded his hands in hers, as if by touch she could discern the pieces of furniture that lurked in the calluses and bone.

"How are the dog roses?"

"They're closing up. The cold weather."

"I wish I could see them."

Michael hoisted her into his arms as if she were a small kitten. Julia shrieked once, in surprise as he lifted and he patted her on the bottom to silence her protests. She had lost all dignity but no one was near to see how she was treated and abandoned her protest to simply enjoy her ride down the stairs if for nothing else than the novelty. He carried her gently most of the way but at the doorway pretended that he could not fit her within the jamb and tried first one way then another to carry her through the embrasure.

"Be careful! You'll hit my head," but miraculously he managed then they were outside for the first time in weeks. Julia, at first, felt contrite for asking Michael to be careful when in fact she trusted him implicitly and felt ashamed for her outburst. But Michael hadn't seemed to mind. In a few moments, she raised her head from where it rested beside his arm to sniff the air. She said nothing. She smiled.

The old bench on the knoll was overgrown with flowers, the marguerites strewn around the chair legs, and from the knoll she could see the dog roses. "Not on the bench, please, right in the middle of the knoll."

Julia sat reclined on her elbow, top of her head barely visible above the blooms and she motioned with her small hand, "Lie here with me." She had turned her face as a flower would to the rising sun and with closed eyes savored the beams of light that struck and warmed and caressed her face. Michael watched her silently.

"If I don't survive this baby business, I'd like to be buried beside your grandfather. I reserved two plots, one for you and one for me." She laughed at seeing the exasperation in his face, that she shouldn't be talking about dying. "I like to talk about dying. It has never seemed morbid to me and I don't know why people avoid the subject. I want one more thing." And laughed at seeing Michael's face change its expression again, "It's only that when we are both buried under the ground I want you to hold my hand sometimes and give it a good shake and touch."

Julia did not visit Bernard in his office the next day or the day after. She did not answer his knocks at the gate or reply to his summons by mail. Only when he appeared at her bedroom door did she appear surprised, and she blurt, "Well, hello." Rush was angry, "You would have made me climb that stone fence? If Michael hadn't heard my yelling, I would have brought a ladder and climbed that damn fence!" He shook his hand at her, pointing an accusatory finger, "What nonsense are you thinking? Sit still and don't fidget," and with stethoscope in hand, from the edge of the bed sitting in a dainty posture, he listened for the beat of the second heart.

"You won't be able to carry a baby to term. You know it just as well as I. Why don't you admit it now and save us all from catastrophe." He had an envelope full of proofs, medical images, ultrasounds, her childhood and adult abdominal x-rays. Julia put a finger in each of her ears and hummed a tune under her breath. She did not in her heart dispute the truth of what he said. She did not distrust him when he said, "You can see that these organs are pushed aside and the strain is likely to tear apart tissue. If the baby becomes even slightly bigger you'll hemorrhage. In fact I can't believe that you're sitting upright. The pain must be horrendous."

Julia took one finger out of her ear as if that were needed to reply, "I don't feel any pain."

Rush touched her gingerly on the waist, and she recoiled instantly, doubling up at the site of his gentle touch.

"I order you to go to the hospital."

Julia took the second finger out of her ear and looked at him directly, without evasion or guile, "I won't. I will bear this baby. I will bear any pain. I will not give up now or ever."

"You must go to the hospital. If not, you will simply die. There's no room for doubt. There's no ambiguity."

"No." She plugged up her ears again and bent her head down so not to look at him.

"What can I do? What can *you* do?" he asked as he saw Michael leaning against the door jamb.

"This is nothing new to me. I've said the same to her and got the same result."

That very evening before dinner Michael found Julia lying back in the bed on her side. The sheet, her favorite linen sheet had been darkened by blood. Oddly the room was spotless but the entire sheet had soaked up her hemorrhage. "Oh Julia," he said, and turned her head. Her eyes were shut and mouth tightened in a grimace, her face as waxy and lifeless as a bad painting, not seeming human any longer but something plastic or synthetic.

Julia woke in a hospital bed. When her eyes opened, Michael rose but Julia turned her head away to the wall. She would repeat this gesture whenever he entered the room or approached her bed.

Sometimes Michael sat in the room and they remained silent for hours at a time. Julia fingered the scar on her abdomen, sometimes through the bedclothes and sheets. When discharged from the hospital and Bernard had stopped his car outside the gate, Julia looked up at the house and wall through the tinted window of the car, and began to whimper. Tears ran down her face, down the clenched muscles of her jaw as if she were unable to control, to staunch the flow of tears. Michael assisted her and tried to walk her through the gate, but as he propped her against the wall while he unlocked the green door, she gripped a railing and refused to enter the grounds of the house, making a wild, animal-like wail.

Michael propped her back up against the wall and scratched his head, wiping sweat from his brow. Bernard contorted his face in an expression of incredulity, and stood beside Michael, saying after a thoughtful pause, "Now who would have predicted this?"

Michael tried once more but Julia began wailing again and wouldn't let go of the rail, making a guttural growl seeming unearthly, an ululation that pierced them and shocked. He propped her up against the gate, and returned to Bernard's side and put both hands in his pants pockets, "I suppose we could visit Jonathan. Would you give us a ride that far?"

"Absolutely." They drove Bernard's car to Stinson with Julia crumpled alone on the back seat, and Jonathan gave them a place to stay, opening his door and closing it again behind Julia, saying nothing but appearing shocked at Julia's appearance.

While lying on her bed on the first evening in

Jonathan's house, Julia remained inert and limp. During the night, Julia wet the sheets. And when Michael discovered this in the morning, silently exchanged the wet sheets for clean.

Seeing Michael caring for her, uncomplaining, seemed to affect Julia though and she meditatively watched him go about his nursing duties, with widened eyes as if comparing the Michael of the here and now, compared to the young scurrilous Michael of her old memory, and thereafter she rose and went to the bathroom herself when needed.

Weeks passed. Julia had begun walking again and spent several long days slowly inspecting the woods and the shoreline near the house. She spent mornings, afternoons and evenings outdoors and sat in a chair on the shady porch when the afternoon warmed. When free Michael would follow her at a prudent distance and saw that she walked for hours beside the beach, sometimes until in the distance she could see the red gabled span of the Golden Gate Bridge, an apparition that to him seemed as wondrous and beautiful a sight as a scene described in the travels of Ibn Battuta, his favorite traveler of old, something disbelievingly described by a traveler from the early Ottoman Empire in illustrated, fancy manuscript. Or else she walked north past lighthouses and straight green pines, not to touch because of sap on trunks and sharp needles, and shingle beaches with flat grey stones each with sharp fluted edges on the stones — beaches which had not been named, for she came upon these crescents of sand only at walking across the low tide. Once she found her return blocked by large furious waves at high tide which had filled the shingled crescent and she had to stand on a small ledge while waves smashed against her feet. The stones were sharp enough to cut her feet. Yet she did not shiver or look about her as if for escape. Michael sat on the cliff above her head, in a tumult of fear himself, that she could be swept out to sea but after a span of anxious hours, the tide subsided and Julia calmly, resolutely, resumed her walk.

Jonathan suggested, beneath a cone, a crescent of light in his study so only the beak of his nose was visible, "Why don't you travel with Julia? Do you think it's a good time to see the world? Wouldn't it be a distraction?" Michael raised his head to better ponder this, then nodded his head in agreement, "If she agrees." To his surprise she acquiesced without speaking, posed for a passport photo in the study, scrutinized her picture in the passport and quietly packed a small suitcase. Julia walked on beaches in the Mediterranean, Aegean — on Greek and Turkish islands — as silently as she had beside Jonathan's house and they rode wooden boats through choppy seas in the Dodecanese, Julia standing in the prow cutting the spray with her streaming wet hair, and walked through the Grand Bazaar in Istanbul and the Khan al'Kahili in Cairo. Julia sat in a café below the Parthenon and ate feta cheese and tomato salads, wincing at the acidity which surprised her but finished the salad. Julia ate, slept, walked, but didn't speak a single word, merely followed Michael's suggestions and accepted his arrangements.

The singing.

In December of that year, two years after her miscarriage, Julia and Michael returned to their house in Napa. Michael saw that the paint on the gate had flaked off and noticed, for the first time in years, the etched bas-relief of the constellation that his grandfather had spoken of long ago. The yard and garden were overgrown and had seemingly returned to a pre-Julia state. In the interim a flash flood swept over the main part of the yard. The town itself had been sandbagged and preserved but a grape crop was lost. The flood's effect on Julia's garden had been devastating. Many trees, many shrubs were lost, broken. The vegetables and flowers were in disarray and lost any semblance of order. Within the house was laid a fine, barely perceptible carpet of dust, the windows streaked with evidence of past rains. Mice scurried over the tabletops, unaccustomed to fear, unaccustomed to visitors in their own domain.

Jonathan entered and whistled at the state of disrepair, "I'd dropped by about once per month but you know how busy the O'Dell court case had become. The life of a busy lawyer. Your grandfather warned me how one day I'd complain about success." Michael nodded, smiling. According to Jonathan's update, he had been proved the biological father of Louise but Roserie O'Dell refused to relinquish custody and threatened to flee the country. Due to Jonathan's prescience and the evidence of a detective, Roserie's application for a passport was noted and suspended.

"You haven't heard the news since my last letter probably didn't reach you. Roserie O'Dell died last week in her house right across town. I just heard this from the sheriff. Louise is in temporary foster care tonight. On Monday we expect the judge to award full, complete custody to you."

Michael raised his eyebrows.

"Isn't it ironic how things work out?" said Jonathan.

Michael spoke, "I'm not sure about the timing. I don't know, I don't know how Julia will take this. It might be that seeing a small child will set her back again. Or, it might help. But this is all so sudden."

"Ahh. If we can only live and die on a convenient schedule."

Michael spoke to Julia but, as expected, received no answer. She didn't appear to react except a slight nod in acknowledgement of hearing the news, and after debating this point with Jonathan, went to the foster home in Napa to pick up Louise. They walked hand-in-hand into the house but were barred by Julia's locked bedroom door.

"You'll meet again at dinner time." But at dinnertime Julia remained hidden. Louise seemed smaller to him than when they met last, with a child's nonchalance for the recent changes in her life. She played with Julia's old plastic pipe, that once blew soap bubbles. "Look at this," he created a mixture of liquid soap from the sink with tap water, and blew a pipeful of bubbles. Louise smiled and took the pipe from him to investigate for herself. Michael poured wine for himself and sat down at the table for dinner with an empty plate for Julia. After a moment's reflection, just as the grandfather did for Julia long ago at this same table, he poured Louise an inch worth of wine in her glass tumbler, and poured iced water from a carafe to fill the rest of the glass.

Louise crept into the hallway upstairs, and explored cautiously at Michael's encouragement, tiptoeing near Julia's closed door in response to Michael's gesture for quietness. He saw that her feet left tiny imprints in the dust blown through the open window at the far end of the hall. They had not had time to tidy the upstairs, so Michael fetched a set of towels for himself and Louise, and they silently scrubbed the hallway parquet clean of dust. Downstairs again Louise sat for a few quiet moments at the table then slid off the chair when Michael did not look at her or answer her fidgety expressions.

Being thirsty she looked for a glass in the kitchen and thoughtfully regarded the pile of dishes in the large sink. She wanted a clean glass. None on the counter, so she arranged a step stool under the sink and rinsed her used glass tumbler clean with water, rubbed her fingers under the water along the rim of the glass.

Michael, alone in the dining room, drank the last of the wine straight from the bottle, looked appraisingly at the chaos in the room, groaned to himself and began the cleaning process, finished the clearing of dishes, the sweeping of floors. In the kitchen he saw Louise huddled at Julia's small sink, back bent, and experienced a strong sense of *deja vu*, shuddering as if he were a ghost outside of time and only recently returned to the exact scene when Julia were once again new to the house and furtively scrubbing dishes, fearful at being discovered, fearful of being sent away out of the house, out into the out-of-doors.

In the morning Michael and Louise ate their breakfast alone. He made pancakes in the shape of the letters of her name which were arranged on a baking sheet. While Michael brought the dishes into the kitchen, he showed Louise how to wash and arrange the dishes. Unknown to them, while in the dining room Julia had reappeared, tiptoeing with an exaggerated posture of secrecy, and watched with a mild astonishment, head slightly crooked to one side, how Louise stood in her old place at the sink and washed dishes as she had once been accustomed. Julia stole into the pantry and slipped back upstairs with a bunch of bananas under one arm, a jar of peanut butter and box of crackers, knife and spoon, a pair of scissors and a few pine cones she had set aside for a new diorama.

In this way, with similar food and playthings, Julia had occupied herself while Michael and Louise thought that she was fasting and meditating, suffering, but in the afternoon Michael noticed that the bananas were missing, and he smiled to himself.

On the morning of Julia's third day of seclusion, Michael shouted at the locked door and receiving no answer, propped a ladder outside her window, clambered up and peered inside. The room was empty.

Louise stood barefooted below, and Michael asked her to put on her shoes. They walked out past the gate, along the lane on the outskirts of the town edge to the cemetery. Louise ran forward, knowing the location of her mother's grave. And rapidly her little figure returned, out of breath, ran to him and pointed back accusingly. "Someone…Someone!" Michael felt alarm and held her still. Angrily looked outward at the hostile world, "What happened? Are you hurt?"

"Someone wiped my nose!" Louise pointed outward to a secluded portion of the cemetery that Michael knew well, and let Louise lead him first to her mother's grave site and, as he expected, towards a small figure in man's raincoat and Gloustershire rain hat, tending to the edging of grass beside the familiar headstone of his grandfather.

"Go ask that person if she or he would like breakfast," directed Michael, pointing to the figure.

Louise ran away and could be seen peering up into the stranger's face and she ran back quickly.

"That lady-man had a moustache made of paper! It was funny!"

"What about breakfast?"

"The moustache lady said that she would like breakfast, please," huffed Louise, still out-of-breath.

"Should we wait?" Louise scurried forwards and back.

"That lady-man said she would show up later."

"Okay, then you can squeeze the oranges for juice and I'll make pancakes."

"I know the letters to spell. I will spell J-U-L-I-A!"

"That's exactly right," said Michael.

At the breakfast table, Julia walked into the dining room with the coat under her arm. Michael took the coat to hang up beside his own and Louise's coat, searched the pockets of the raincoat and found her paper moustache, which she had attached to her upper lip with a loop of masking tape. "Good disguise," he said and gave the moustache to Louise to wear, and for the rest of the breakfast Louise ate with the moustache obscuring her lower face. She must lift the moustache like a flap when she put a piece of pancake into her mouth.

"How are you feeling?"

"Hungry," said Julia at last. This was the first word she had spoken to him in two years but Michael didn't comment on this, only offered his plate and Julia speared two pancakes with a graceful motion of the fork.

Julia stood barefooted in the desolation and detritus that once had been her garden. Heavy rains and the flood let an unsecured hillside fall upon the far side of her vegetables. The stream had overflown its banks and left an ankle-deep layer of mud over the low-lying bluebell field. She turned and unconsciously grasped a long antique key which had been secured around her neck with a shoelace. She had all through her life at the house rarely taken off the key, even for bathing, but having become accustomed to its weight, she looked at the key strangely as if unfamiliar with its meaning. Recognizing it she placed it back under the sweater.

Grasses grew wild and she studied the scene, uncertain whether she liked the wild effect or not. In a corner, in the direction of the carriage path almost like a small unnoticed figure in a landscape painting, she saw Michael kneeling, barely visible on a far hillside, working on a foundation for a brick wall to better secure the hillside. She turned to her left and walked a few steps. This had been the site of her very first garden, where she planted her packet of radishes and the contents of the envelope labeled, "A child's flower garden." She dropped to knees and began to pull out weeds, separating weeds from descendants of the first radishes that once filled her whole body with joy.

Michael walked downhill and joined her in the radish patch. They worked side by side pulling weeds, and putting the weeds in a communal pile. Birds sat in the trees above their heads and sang out songs for them in the language of flying creatures. Julia paused in her weed pulling to scrutinize his work but found no fault. Michael was pulling out the weeds properly, she saw, by the roots.

During another pause later in the afternoon, she spoke to him without raising her head, "When I was suffering so much, after I lost our baby you had taken me to Jonathan's house and one day I was walking along the beach. At one time the tide came up and crashed along the shingles and trapped me high up on a rock. This was very dangerous and I stood up against a wall and the water started to pull at my feet. Then I saw that you were watching me from above, though you thought you were hidden. So I stayed on the ledge and waited for the tide to pass because I knew I was safe."

Michael said nothing but pulled his share of weeds in a steady, silent rhythm.

Julia continued, "Who would have known, when I was such a little girl, hating the world, that I could grow up to feel so much love and trust. Who could know?" She spoke with a touch of outrage and astonishment in her voice, with her head raised as if she spoke to the birds above their heads, and they the birds continued their singing as if yes indeed they understood but in the singing alone they expressed the understanding.

Julia paused at a window at hearing a ferocious crunching noise, wood snapping unnaturally, and rushed outdoors barefooted. Michael followed and stayed on the porch. Louise stood in the courtyard with her foot stuck, comically, in the seat of Julia's death chair. Apparently she tried to stand on the seat and her foot broke through the wood. Julia stood beside her in a emotional frenzy, scolding her, angrily jabbing her finger. Louise put her down her head and began to cry, thinking that Julia was angry at the loss of the chair, but in a few moments raised her eyes to seek a cue from Michael. And Michael motioned to her that all was well and that she didn't need to worry.

At seeing the little girl surprised but safe, and Louise begin to shake shoulders in the beginning of a crying fit, Julia calmed a bit then bent to extricate Louise's leg out of the broken slats of the chair.

And gruffly, "Did you hurt your leg?"

Louise stuttered a *no*.

"Chairs can be fixed. Even this chair, which was very important to me, once a long time ago. But it isn't important to me any longer." And she folded the chair away into the scrap wood pile, beside the wall in the tool shed and she thought about it no longer and quickly forgot about its purpose.

Julia clenched her jaw, tilted her head backwards, better to yell at Louise pattering up and down the stairs, "Stop that running. You'll trip and fall down." From downstairs came a loud thump, a crash, a pounding of body on wood, a plaintive moaning, then a mixture of muted human voices with the cadences of a quiet conversation among equals, a shout of outrage and laughter, and ending with a stream of sounds, of happy, undistinguished protest and shouting, and laughing. Laughter like a singing song.

Michael entered the room again a little wearily. Still the racquet from below continued, yelling, banging on the walls. Julia added at the top of her lungs, "Stop yelling and making so much noise." This had a good effect because the noise ceased, until pattering on the stairs and Louise popped her head into the door, "But you're yelling too," she pointed out with self-righteous logic. Michael and Julia looked at each other, and both shrugged their shoulders in the same gesture at the same time.

"Are you ready to walk into town? You'd better put on your galoshes. The better for stomping in puddles."

Louise gave a short wail, popped her head out of sight and pattered down the stairwell.

"Do you need anything while we're outside in the world?"

"Nothing I can think of at the moment. I'm sure I'll think of something once you're gone."

Michael stood at a window beside the sill when Julia and Louise appeared below him, walking along the path to the gate, watching as they paused at the street edge beside the wrought iron street-lamp, both turning their heads carefully in one direction and then the other checking for imagined dangers. And he saw that, before stepping off the curb, Louise sought Julia's hand and Michael could hear as a feeling almost like contentment burned him, he saw Julia bend to Louise and say, "Don't be afraid." He could hear their conversation if he stood still and didn't breathe.

Louise added, "I like to hold your hand."

Julia smiled, "I like to hold your hand too. Whenever you like just run up to me and hold my hand. We'll be crazy for hand holding all day long."

Louise smiled, feeling very grateful and contented and with these hands clasped tightly, they set off together onto their errand into the town and of the two only Louise felt afraid and glad for the comfort of Julia's firm and reassuring grip.

David Torigoe lives in the Pacific Northwest, where he reads books and writes novels as a hobby. He travels extensively and loves to see people as they live in the world.